CW00816425

LONG I

A SAM POPE NOVEL

ROBERT ENRIGHT

In loving memory of Bernie Prosser.
A true hero.

CHAPTER ONE

The car horn blared angrily into the night, its continuous roar echoing off the tall, white buildings that framed the streets of Rome. A few concerned members of the public stood in shock; others quickly reached for their phones to call for help. Some, perversely, snapped pictures.

Sam Pope slowly lifted himself from the steering wheel, blood streaming from a gash above his right eye thanks to his collision with the solid leather. The airbag had deployed, saving him from a worse fate. With a shaking hand, he reached for the buckle of his seat belt, his knuckles slashed by the deluge of glass that had rained down on him like confetti at a wedding.

His mind raced to Lucy.

How beautiful she'd looked walking down the aisle towards him.

How happy they'd been, sat in the hospital, watching a screen that showed them their impending future as parents.

Her devastation as she knelt on the side of a London road, watching as the medics drew a sheet over the dead body of their son.

Jamie.

Outside on the street, an audible scream of panic cut through the ringing in Sam's ears and he snapped back to the situation. He turned for the door and a searing pain shot up his spine and hit his brain like a test of strength. He gritted his teeth and shoved open the door, glass sprinkling the pavement. Smoke gently rose from the indented bonnet; the metal wrapped around the lamppost he'd careered into.

He'd been run off the road and now the person behind the wheel of the truck that had caused the accident was approaching.

To finish the job.

Fighting the pain echoing through his body, Sam collapsed out of the broken door, his blood-soaked shirt ripping on a sharp, shattered welcome mat. His right eye had swollen almost shut, the blood smear across his face caused more shrill cries of terror. The bullet wound in his shoulder was oozing blood down his chest, each pump sending an agonizing throb to his brain. He looked up at the sky with his good eye, the thick clouds that hung over the Italian capital had covered the city in a freezing shower of rain most of the evening. Now, only the biting wind carried winter on it. He looked to his left; the whiplash trying its best to stop him. A few people scurried away in fear, dashing past the bright window displays that were decked out in the usual Christmas decorations. A lazily tinselled tree along with a cheap nativity set. A tacky, illuminated snowman.

Christmas cheer.

Sam winced at the irony, then strained his head to the right.

The figure, decked completely in black, was approaching, walking slowly from the semi-truck that had smashed into the side of his own car, obliterating his escape plan and rattling his brain like a maraca.

Sam pressed his hands down, the glass puncturing the skin, and he groaned as he pushed himself up. A sharp pain from his leg caused him to lose his balance and he stumbled into the shattered shell of his car. His entire thigh was maroon, the blood from his bullet wound had soaked through the denim of his jeans. It had been a little over three weeks since his thigh had been ripped open at the Port of Tilbury where he'd taken down the Kovalenko trafficking empire.

All to save a young girl from a fate worse than death.

Although that moment had led him on a path that had taken his fight overseas, he knew it had started long before then. Before he took down the 'High Rises', the protected buildings run by Frank Jackson, one of the most notorious criminals in London. Long before he was battering rapists like Chris Morton for cheating the justice system.

Even before his son had been killed by a drunk driver.

Sam Pope had been one of the most decorated soldiers the United Kingdom had ever had, with his career as a sniper tantamount to legendary. With tours in Afghanistan and Iraq, his impeccable record saw him recruited to an elite task force, shrouded in secrecy. It should have been the crowning moment of a glittering career before he put away the rifle for good and enjoyed his life with his family.

Instead, he was shipped home in a coma with two bullet holes in his chest and two words haunting his mind.

Project Hailstorm.

But now he knew the truth.

That's what this had all been about and as he shuffled down the panic-stricken streets of Rome, stalked by a man intending to kill him, he knew his search for what truly happened could be coming to an end.

In the distance, the wailing of a siren pierced the air, the police racing in vain to his rescue.

Sam was built to survive, but with his head ringing and his vision blurry, he knew what was coming.

The bullet exploded from the gun and sliced through the cold air, burrowing through his back and bursting out of his abdomen.

Sam hit the ground instantly, the burning sensation of the bullet wound growing through his body. The street was deserted now, the public long since fled from a trained gun man. Sam could feel his good eye watering and as he limply pushed himself up to his knees, he spat blood into the puddle forming around him. He'd seen enough bullet wounds in his time to know what was happening.

He'd been behind the trigger for most of them.

He'd been shot to wound.

Whoever his executioner was, the man was trained and didn't want this to be quick.

Sam feebly pressed his hand to his stomach, the warm blood flowing freely through his fingertips.

Behind him, the car horn still roared its single note into the night.

Somewhere in the distance, the sirens gave false hope.

Footsteps approached him.

Sam tried to move but he couldn't, his mindset of fighting for survival was betrayed by his body. The blood loss was already beginning to take its toll and his head began to spin. Vomit threatened to race up his throat and join the large puddle of blood that he knelt in. With his last remaining effort, he pushed it down and straightened his back, his spine cracking slightly. The pain was unnoticeable now.

Sam Pope was going to die.

But he was going to die with his head held high.

Behind him, boots crunched on the glass that littered the road and Sam took a few deep breaths.

Visions of his life began to flash through his mind,

from his childhood following his father from military posting to military posting. The visions of his mother, drinking to hide her sadness.

Visions he'd locked away long ago.

His pride at receiving his first sniper rifle.

The horror of watching his spotter, Mac, decimated by the rocket of an Apache helicopter, leaving Sam to fight his way back to civilization. The cold evenings in the desert, playing cards with Theo, talking sports with Corporal Murry, or being bamboozled by Etheridge's thirst for data.

He'd been honored to serve with them.

They were good men.

Good friends.

Images of his sniper scope flashed through his mind like a flicker book, remembering every face he'd sent to the afterlife.

The footsteps drew to a stop. Sam could hear the man's strained breathing, a wheezing that filtered into the wind, intimating a deformation.

Sam coughed, blood spraying outwards as he tried to steady his final few breaths. The warm puddle of blood had encircled him, marking the spot where he would finally be put to rest.

The vision of Lucy appeared in his mind once more, his eyes slowly opening on a hospital bed to see her tear-streaked face crack with relief. She'd stuck by him when he'd turned down an honourary discharge to join the elite task force and stayed glued to his bedside when they sent him back riddled with bullets.

Sam took another energy sapping breath, the air struggling to reach his lungs and he could feel his hand falling away from the bullet wound in his side. He let it flop to the side in acceptance, allowing his life to pour slowly from his stomach. A light speckle of rain fell on his wrist, and with his final few moments, he lifted his blood-spattered head upwards, locking his one open eye on the heavens above.

He thought of Jamie.

Sitting with him in the nook they'd built in his bedroom, where his son baffled him with his love of books. Lying next to him at bedtime, listening as his son read *The Hungry Caterpillar* to him for the umpteenth time.

Watching as he investigated everything in the playground, overturning every stone and smiling at every insect he came across.

While Sam had loved every minute of being a soldier, even when bullets were raining down on his location and he flirted with death, he'd never loved anything more than he'd loved his son. He'd loved Lucy unequivocally, and part of him always would.

But Jamie was his world.

As Sam stared up at the thick, dark clouds that had gathered over his demise, he felt the cold rain crash against his battered face. A tear joined them as he thought of the body of his dead son. The victim of a drunk driver, recklessly ending the life of a child on his way to meet his dad.

The death which had spurned Sam to take to the streets, to go where the justice system couldn't and set him on a path of redemption that had seen him leave a trail of bodies and broken criminal empires in his wake.

A path that had led him to this moment.

On his knees on the cold streets of Rome, battered and beaten, with blood pumping from his stomach and his life ebbing away.

Behind him, he heard the safety catch of the pistol and took one final breath. He forced his broken body to straighten, adamant he would die with a sense of pride.

He thought about the good people he knew, the likes of DI Adrian Pearce and DI Amara Singh back in London, who had ruined their careers to help him on his mission.

Paul Etheridge, who had served with him in Iraq and had helped him locate the missing girl; a mission which sent him headfirst into a war with a notorious Ukrainian crime family.

Theo Walker, his best friend, who had laid down his life to help him protect an innocent woman.

All of them were worthy of being with him in his final moments.

He said a silent goodbye to Lucy, knowing she'd been right to leave him, to start a family elsewhere and find some sort of happiness after their tragic loss.

He didn't blame her. He'd loved her for it.

He thought of Jamie, and how he would be with him imminently.

Behind him, the sirens wailed as the police cars turned onto the street, too far to help. An engine of a car roared loudly.

The attacker finally spoke through the cacophony of noise.

'I've waited a long time for this.'

Sam's eye opened in shock, the voice reaching into his mind and grasping at a horrifying memory from his past. Before he could turn and confront the vengeful ghost of his past, the screeching tires of an oncoming vehicle almost threatened to drown out the sound of his attacker pulling the trigger.

Everything went black.

CHAPTER TWO

ONE WEEK EARLIER...

'They'll kill me.'

Carl Burrows wept pathetically, his portly body squeezing its way through the tight rope that bound him to the wobbly, uncomfortable chair. His eyes, hidden under the green contacts used as part of his failed identity change, were red through tears.

The man had fallen a long way from the top.

For years, he'd worked diligently alongside several high-ranking politicians in London, earning a sterling reputation as a man who could put anyone in the mayoral seat. Stern, well-educated and with a cold, cut-throat mentality, he'd been as respected as he'd been feared. Little did the opposition, or the men he repre-sented, know that he was on the Kovalenko payroll, facili-tating the lucrative sex trafficking operation the Ukrainian crime family had brought to London. While he'd never stolen a girl from the streets, violated them to instil fear, or stuck the needle in their arm to keep them dependent on their terrifying lives, he was the one who opened the gates.

He made sure the right palms had been greased and the right heads turned the other way.

Carl Burrows – respected political advisor and feared campaign manager – was nothing more than a criminal.

Sam Pope stood, his arms folded, staring at him from the other side of the grotty bedsit. A broken bed with a stained mattress lined one wall, while a tiny sink and oven threatened to poke through the limescale in the far corner. An empty shell of a cupboard hung from the wall, the doorless hinges coated in rust. Sam's suitcase rested on the pathetic bed, shrouded in the shadow created by the lone, halogen light that tried its best to bring a semblance of light to the room.

Sam had been in worse, his time spent recovering from an explosion to a derelict village in southern Sudan had been a particular eye opener. But ever since he'd embarked on his war on organized crime, material items or luxurious abodes had become irrelevant.

To him, this was more than adequate.

To Burrows, it was a nightmare.

Sam leant back against the chipped wall of the room, his muscular arms folded over each other. His right forearm bore the scar of a knife slash, his shoulder ached from being stabbed. His leg, freshly patched up by an old medic buddy of Etheridge's, burned in agony from the fresh bullet wound and was in need of proper treatment.

But that could wait. It had to wait.

Not while there were still more girls lost to the horrors of sex slavery. While Sam had eradicated the London side of the Kovalenko business, he knew there were far worse things happening in the Ukrainian capital.

Sergei Kovalenko was one of the most dangerous men in Kiev but due to his contributions to the economy through laundered channels, he was revered by many. The police stayed away; the government turned a blind eye. As long as he kept the right pockets full, he did as he wanted.

Kovalenko wanted revenge.

Sam had asked Etheridge to pull everything he could on Burrows the second the connection was made between the rotund weasel and the Kovalenkos. Etheridge had delivered and then some. Not only had he been able to trace Burrows to his hideout in Birmingham, he'd also been able to hack into all communications between Burrows and Sergei himself.

The plea for help.

The promise of asylum.

The demand for everything Burrows had on Sam Pope.

Well, if Kovalenko wanted him, Sam wasn't in the mood to disappoint. Slowly, he pushed himself off the wall and walked towards his quivering captive, doing his best to disguise his limp. Burrows cowered as much as he could, his T-shirt soaked with sweat.

Sam gently leant down, grimacing as he reached eye level. Burrows squirmed on his seat and Sam fought back a smile.

'I'll kill you,' Sam responded calmly. 'If you don't tell me everything I need to know about his nightclub, I'm going to take you apart piece by piece.'

The colour immediately drained from Burrows's face and he swallowed. Having spent nearly forty years in politics, he was accustomed to empty threats. But knowing that Sam Pope had abducted and tortured a gang leader with home-made acid only a few weeks prior, he felt nothing but terror.

His groin turned warm and wet as he urinated, his body giving into the very real threat before it. What had looked like an easy way out of his situation, one lined with money and women, had quickly turned sour. Upon being picked up at the airport by one of Sergei's men, Burrows had sunk into his seat and accepted his fate as a wanted man. But they would never have caught him. Sure, he would have to live the rest of his life under the new identity of Gregory Baker, but it was a small price to pay for his freedom.

To have gotten away with it.

Thirty minutes into their journey from Kiev airport, a car had collided into the back of the 4x4 carrying him, and Burrows had been jolted awake. His driver, a burly man with a thick unibrow, had slammed on his breaks and leapt from the vehicle with murderous intentions. The side street was empty, and Burrows had sighed deeply at the likely beating the careless driver would have taken.

It was only when his own driver's head was smashed through the passenger window and a gun placed in Burrows' face did the realization hit him.

Sam Pope demanded he leave the vehicle, ushering him into the boot of the other car before knocking him unconscious with a swift blow to the head.

When Burrows awoke, he was tied to the chair in the centre of the freezing cold flat, with nothing but Sam Pope and the threat of pain for company.

Sam slapped Burrows across his wrinkled, flabby face.

'Answer me,' Sam demanded, straightening up and taking a few steps to the large sports bag that rested on the rickety bed.

'It's big,' Burrows eventually stammered. 'The club holds probably a hundred, maybe two hundred people. There are rooms upstairs where customers take the women. That's all I know, I swear.'

Sam tutted, shaking his head as he unzipped the black bag, pulling it open. He turned back to Burrows and slowly reached into the bag. With their eyes locked, Sam pulled a Glock 20 from the bag, theatrically discharging the clip and checking it was loaded. Burrows gasped with fear.

Sam turned to him, menace emanating from his glare.

'You're going to have to give me more than that.'

'That's all I know, I swear,' Burrows pleaded, straining against the ropes. His eyes were watering, and his cheek was already red from Sam's strike. Sam shook his head and slapped the clip back into place.

'How many guards? Exits? Guns?'

'I don't know,' Burrows begged. 'I can't remember.'

Sam lifted the gun and pointed it straight at the man's sweat covered forehead. Burrows froze, stiffening like a statue.

'Remember. Now.'

Burrows took a deep breath and his head dropped. Sweat and tears dripped, joining the puddle of urine on the cracked, laminate floor.

'Sergei revamped the place about a year ago. It went from being a run-of-the-mill night club, filled with drunk fuelled idiots, to an elite members club. Nowadays, you had to have money or power to get in. Preferably both. But by making the guest list exclusive, he upped security.'

Sam relaxed his arm, tucking the handgun into the waist band of his jeans and pulling the black T-shirt over it.

'How many?'

'I don't know. He usually has a few on the door. Mean bastards. Then another four or five inside, patrolling the main rooms.'

'Armed?' Sam asked, as he casually pulled a bullet-proof vest from the bag and slid his arms in.

'As far as I know. Most of them are ex-Berkut who needed a new career after the Crimea crisis and Sergei pays them well. The kind of people who will kill now and not bother with any questions later. Hell, even the bartenders could be armed.'

Sam nodded firmly as he clasped the vest together, locking it over his imposing frame. He held back a smile, enjoying the avalanche of information pouring from Burrows. The man had cracked, knowing his survival was unlikely. When faced with one's mortality, the majority forfeit loyalty for a faint hope of mercy. It was what separated Sam from most men.

He was a soldier.

He lived and died for a cause.

Burrows sniffed back a few more tears, his breath catching in the cold air and gliding from him in white clouds. Despite the freezing conditions of Kiev, the man was soaked through with sweat. He slowly lifted his head, his eyes widening in horror as Sam lifted a L85IW assault rifle from the bag, his hands caressing the body with worrying familiarity. It had been the same rifle he'd taken the High Rise with over six months ago, along with the raid of the Kovalenko's operation in Tilbury.

He knew every detail of the weapon.

The ferocity of the kick back.

How quickly the bullets filtered through the barrel.

That gut-wrenching moment when it had jammed during a hellacious gun fight in Kirkuk, under the unrelenting Iraqi sun.

Everything.

Burrows pulled him away from his reunion.

'How the hell did you get that stuff through customs?'

It was a good question and Sam knew he owed Paul Etheridge a beer or two if he made it home. Etheridge had served with him on a few tours, with Sam even saving his life on a mission in the hills of Sudan. The man was a genius, was willing to fight for the cause but he wasn't a soldier. After he was honourably discharged following a horrendous break to his leg, Etheridge started contracting for the government, his knowledge of coding and databases had increased their security from cyber threats tenfold. It was all alien to Sam.

His skills led to him being able to hack most online security infrastructures, so he developed specialist software to keep people out. He'd made millions selling this to a select few governments and now lived a life of luxury in a big house with an unhappy trophy wife.

But he still fought for a good cause.

And he was more than willing to help Sam.

Not only had he issued Sam a whole new identity and tracked Burrows for him, he'd manipulated the cargo manifests for Sam's bag to arrive in Ukraine undetected.

In theory, the two of them were just doing what was needed to bring an end to a vile criminal organization.

In reality, they were smuggling guns into a country that had seen its fair share of war.

After Sam had incapacitated a SWAT team in Etheridge's house a few weeks ago, they knew the police would soon be sniffing around Etheridge and digging into his history. Sam thought of his friend now, hoping the wolves he'd led to Etheridge's door hadn't eaten him alive. He turned back to Burrows, a glint of excitement in his eye.

'You're not the only person who knows powerful people.' Sam draped the strap of the gun over his head and let the rifle swing back and rest against his spine. 'What about Sergei's private security?'

'Two men. Vlad and Artem. Where he goes, they go.'

'Nasty bastards?'

Burrows fixed Sam with a look that told him his answer. To finish this, he was going to have to go to war. And unlike Tilbury, there would be no planning. No preparation. The driver Sam had introduced to the passenger window would no doubt have reported back, putting an already irate Sergei on red alert. His nightclub would be locked down. Extra fire power would be called in.

All orders will be to kill him, and most likely Burrows, on sight.

The odds were against him, but Sam didn't believe in no-win situations, nor would he walkaway. He thought back to the night he confronted Jamie's killer, the agony of facing the man who had taken away his boy.

Miles Hillock.

Sam had wanted nothing more than to end the man's life, but after giving him a severe beating, Sam had spared Miles. A clarity had washed over him like a wave, telling him to put his skills to use stopping other innocent people feeling the same pain he did.

Since then, he'd killed dozens of criminals to save hundreds of lives.

The police had painted him as a dangerous vigilante, with their task force no doubt upping the ante to bring him in. He would deal with that if he made it back.

It was a long road home from here.

Sam walked to the window and watched the derelict streets around the old, decrepit building, waiting until darkness fell over the city, ushering with it a chilling wind that cut through to his bones.

It was time.

Sam marched across the room, removing his rifle, slipping on his leather jacket, and re-arming. He swung a booted foot out and rattled the chair, startling the dozing Burrows with a panic.

'W-w-what?' Burrows flashed a worried glance.

'It's time,' Sam replied coldly, flicking his pen knife open and going to work on the ropes. 'You try anything, I'll put this in your throat.'

Burrows obediently nodded, slowly rising from the

soaked chair and stretching his back, his spine cracking with glee. Sam slipped the knife back into his jeans and headed for the door.

'Please let me go,' Burrows begged.

'Let's move.'

Accepting his fate, Burrows pathetically trudged towards the door. From sitting in Number 10 Downing Street to marching to an inevitable death in a seedy, Ukrainian night club. The irony was, it was he who had most likely sanctioned the same thing for a number of those young girls, snatched from their families and thrown into a horrible oblivion.

Karma had certainly come knocking for him.

The message delivered by Sam Pope.

As he stepped out into the dark, ill-smelling corridor, he turned back to his captor.

'What's your plan? Do you expect to reason with this man?'

'No,' Sam said sternly, filling the doorway and the lone light behind casting him in shadow.

'Then what?'

'I'm going to burn it all to the ground.'

Sam slammed the door shut and the entire hallway went black before the brightness of the moon crept in through the thin window, they marched to the street.

One man accepting his fate.

The other ready for war.

CHAPTER THREE

Sam pulled his car up in front of the night club and cast a murderous eye over it. He'd driven through the rougher parts of Kiev until he'd arrived at the more affluent streets, each one lined with nice houses and expensive eateries. The gentrification of the city, shimmering under the light drizzle of freezing rain gave it a beautiful shine.

It was a shame a place so beautiful could hold such evil within.

'That the place?' Sam barked. Burrows, sat in the passenger seat beside him, sighed deeply.

'That's the one.'

Sam glared at the man before returning his focus to the building, appreciating the gothic aesthetic. Large windows burrowed into the side of the brickwork, each one shielded by a metal barrier and hidden by thick, red curtains. A large, bright sign crudely hung in the middle, the word *Ешелон* proudly displayed. Burrows had told him the word translated as 'Echelon', with Sergei Kovalenko optimistically rebranding the seedy night club into something grander.

Sam rolled down the window, the ice-cold wind

squeezing through the opening and coiling round them both like a snake. Sam felt the chill through the layers of his jacket, T-shirt, and bulletproof vest.

He didn't care about Burrows.

Both of them knew Sergei was unlikely to let him live.

And that Sam was unlikely to save him.

Through the light downpour, Sam could hear the loud music within the gentlemen's club, the thumping base was undoubtedly accompanying one of Sergei's women as she paraded on stage. Burrows had told him how it all played out. The women were ushered out one at a time, each one forced to dance for the leering eyes of the rich. They performed until a bid came in, enticing the raised hands by removing their clothes and debasing themselves under the spotlight.

When one of the customers saw what he liked, he was able to purchase that woman for hour-long sessions in the private rooms upstairs, where the only rule was, *he paid in full.*

It turned Sam's stomach and his knuckles whitened as he gripped the steering wheel.

A black car slowly approached the door, stopping out front and putting the two security guards on alert. As the door opened, both men reached to the inside of their dark suits, only to relent when three middle-aged businessmen stepped out, clearly inebriated.

Drunk and rich.

The perfect customers.

The men were patted down and then ushered inside, and Sam watched as the two intimidating doormen shook their heads in disgust. Sam felt the same and knowing the recent arrivals were there to do 'business', he'd seen enough.

'Let's go."

Sam stepped out of the car and Burrows dejectedly

followed suit. The night nipped at them with frosted teeth and Sam walked slightly behind Burrows as he meandered to the door. One of the doormen approached, his large frame blocking the door, but his crooked smile was welcoming.

'The politician.' He chuckled. 'Welcome back. You here for Alegra? She tells me she misses your small cock.'

The man's English was broken, but the message was clear, and Sam felt his blood boil in the freezing temperature.

Burrows didn't just help send these girls to their fate.

He actively joined in.

The other doormen stepped up, towering over Sam by several inches. He stank of coffee and his lips snarled. A small scar ran across his cheek and his dark eyes locked onto his.

'Who this?'

'A friend of mine,' Burrows said meekly. 'I'm bringing him to see Sergei.'

'He police?' The man responded. 'He stand like policeman.'

'I have news about what happened to Andrei and Oleg,' Sam said calmly, refusing to break the stare. 'Now you can leave me out in the cold and go and tell Sergei that the only chance of finding the man who killed his family fucked off. Or you can let us in.'

The gruff doorman took a step closer, sizing Sam up, who clenched his fists, ready for combat. Before anything escalated, the more welcoming of the two stepped between them.

'Denys, relax.' He patted his colleague on the back. 'The politician is good friend of Sergei. Has been for many years. Come, but we must search.'

'Really guys?' Burrows questioned. He looked up at the security camera above the door. 'Sergei is watching right now and when he sees you treating me and my guest this way…'

'Okay, okay.' The man relented, holding his hands up. The other doorman, Denys, kept his eyes firmly locked on Sam. 'Go in. Have fun, eh?'

Burrows marched straight through the door and into the warmth and Sam smiled at both men as he passed.

'Oh, I plan to.'

Sam stepped into the hallway, welcoming the warmth that hummed from the long radiators. The lighting was dim, the red carpet just about visible, and the grey walls were permutated with the odd, light fittings designed to look like a candle. There was a small sink, with towels and wet wipes just before the grand door into the club itself.

'Classy,' Sam uttered, his skin crawling at the perverse nature of the entire place. Burrows reached for the large, metal handle to the door but paused. He took a few deep breaths, his eyes watering. On the other side of the door, the bass of the music thumped through causing him to shake.

'Please, Sam. I'm begging you.' Burrows wiped his nose with his shirt sleeve. 'Let me leave. You can do what you came to do, and I promise you, I'll disappear.'

Sam folded his arms and adjusted his back, the rifle pressed between his jacket and vest was digging into his spine, but he'd snuck it in. He eyed Burrows with disgust.

'How many girls have disappeared because of you? Huh? How many parents have never seen their daughters all so you could watch your bank account grow? No, you're going to be held accountable for the pain you've caused.'

'I don't want to die,' Burrows wept.

'I'm not going to kill you,' Sam stated coldly. 'But I'm not going to stop whatever you have coming to you. Now open the damn door.'

Burrows composed himself and yanked the door open

and both men collided with a mixture of dance music, cigar smoke, and sweat. Sam shoved Burrows in and followed behind, his eyes quickly scouting the room. Two suited men stood at the far end, their hands clasped and their eyes scanning the punters. At the bar, two scantily clad women served drinks while a young guy cleaned glasses. Two more suited men stood in front of a door marked 'private', which Burrows turned and headed towards. On the stage, a young woman, no older than twenty, writhed on the floor. Completely naked, her soulless eye conveyed nothing but the yearning for drugs as the grotesque men leered over her supple body. A large man in his mid-fifties raised his hands, and a well-dressed man rushed over to take his money. A few of the other customers gently applauded the man, who jokingly bowed before awaiting his prize.

Sam shook his head, watching as the young woman lazily got to her feet and approached the man who immediately placed his hands on her back and ushered her towards the guarded stairs. He knew he couldn't save her from the drugs they had her hooked on, but he could save her from what he could only imagine would be a horrendous encounter.

They approached the guarded door and the two men nodded to Burrows, who shrunk shamefully into himself. Sam marched through with him, noting there were six men including the doormen. Another two guaranteed with Sergei and then the man himself.

The head of the snake.

Burrows trudged up the staircase, followed by Sam, each step another resignation to the fate he'd built for himself. They stopped on the landing, met by another henchman in a dark suit. Sergei certainly wanted his men to look the part. The man eyed Sam suspiciously, but nodded and opened the door for them.

Ten men, Sam noted.

They stepped into the office. Clouds of cigar smoke circled the ceiling like a storm cloud and Sam surveyed the room. The floor was covered with the same cheap carpet as the entrance way, with rows of bookshelves propped against each wall for the vague illusion of culture. Large paintings were dotted between them and to the left was a small, private bar, being tended to by another scantily clad woman in just a thong.

Sam could see the needle marks on her arm and her vacant stare passed through him like a ghost. He shuddered, the anger tempting him to reach for the pistol in the back of his jeans.

Stood by the bar was Vlad, one of Sergei's enforcers, his war weathered hand around a half full pint of beer. His tattoo-covered arms were visible under the rolled-up shirt sleeves and he glared at both men like a dog eyeing its dinner. Burrows kept his head down as he approached the desk, walking past Artem, who rose from a comfortable looking sofa to the side of the room, folding his large arms across his chest and resting them on the slight paunch that over hung his trousers. His head was shaved, with a tattoo of a skull being swarmed by spiders covering half his scalp.

Sam laid his eyes on Sergei.

The man was in his late fifties but was as fit as he'd been two decades earlier. Dressed in an expensive grey suit with a maroon shirt, he eyed up his new guest with suspicion, running a ring covered hand through his slick, silver hair.

'Welcome back.' Sergei smirked at Burrows. His English was fluent, if not a little stunted. 'What name did we give you? Greg…'

'Baker,' Burrows stammered; his brow covered in sweat. 'Gregory Baker.'

'Ah, yes. Gregory Baker. It suits you, eh?' He extended

a hand to Burrows, who took it sheepishly. Sergei wiped the clamminess away, his suspicion growing. Burrows took a seat and he turned to Sam. 'And you, what is your name?'

Sam said nothing. Sergei ran his tongue on the inside of his lip and then smiled.

'Few words. I admire that.' Sergei chuckled, smiling at Artem who raised an eyebrow. Sergei strode back behind his desk. 'Tell me, Gregory, why does your friend seem to hate me?'

Burrows looked surprised at being asked the question, as Sergei kept his eyes fixed on Sam. Behind him, Sam heard Vlad moving behind him and the very clear sound of him locking the door.

'He has information about what happened to your nephews.' Burrows struggled to speak, the fear pouring out of him. Sergei flashed a glance at him.

'My boys. They were like sons to me. My brother, he was not a good man.'

'And you are?' Sam interjected. Sergei smiled again and reached into the draw of his desk. His hand returned holding a finely crafted, serrated blade. Burrows adjusted himself in his seat, uncomfortably.

'I make those boys into men,' Sergei began, slowly walking around the desk towards a now crying Burrows. 'They came to me when Andrei killed his father. He showed me he had guts. I like guts. He also had brains; he was smart. He told me your English girls get a much better price. So, I sent him to your country, and he made me a lot of money.'

Sam gritted his teeth, refusing to rise to the bait. Sergei made his way to the front of the desk and sat on the edge of it, directly in front of Burrows. In Sam's periphery, he could see Vlad and Artem moving into position. Sergei leant forward.

'You, "Greg", have no guts. You weep and cry for your sins even though they've made you rich.' Sergei suddenly lunged forward and pressed the blade against Burrows's throat. 'Now, if you have brains, you tell me who the fuck this man is.'

Before Burrows could respond, Sam spoke as clearly as he ever had.

'My name is Sam Pope.' Sergei flashed him a venomous look. 'I put both your boys in the ground.'

'Kill him,' Sergei barked, before slashing the blade crudely across Burrows's throat, blood spraying forward and splattering the oak desk. As Burrows collapsed forward, grasping at his open throat, Vlad lunged for Sam. Instinctively, Sam turned on his heel, and caught Vlad's arm by the wrist. He twisted it, wrenching the shoulder from its socket and Vlad dropped to his knee with a roar of pain. With his other hand, Sam flicked open his knife and rammed it into the side of his neck, twisted and then pulled back. With one fluid motion, he straightened his arm and flung the knife towards the fast approaching Artem. The blade spun in the air, travelling the few feet between them before bedding into the large man's left pectoral.

Sam dropped Vlad to the floor, his life gushing out of the hole in his neck, and charged at Artem, who had dropped to one knee. Sam expertly placed his hand on Artem's greasy forehead and then slammed it has hard as he could into his quickly raising knee.

The crunch of bone told him instantly that he'd broken the man's neck and he let Artem's prone body drop the floor, the hand still twitching.

It had taken him ten seconds to kill both men.

Sergei stood shocked, his back pressed against the wall and Sam straightened his jacket and then walked towards Burrows. His skin was deathly pale, and the blood had covered his entire body. The final few breaths were filtering through the gaping hole in his throat and Sam tried, but couldn't muster any pity for him.

The man had made his bloodstained bed and now he would lie in it for eternity.

Sam reached down and picked up the blade Sergei had used, stepping away from the hopeful reach of Burrows, the last fragment of life spilling out into the pool of blood around his now motionless body.

Sam approached Sergei, who frantically looked for a way out. The desk was blocking the potential two storey drop from the window. His murderous guest stood between him and the door. With all options exhausted, he cracked a smile.

'Very impressive, Mr Pope,' he said nervously. 'I could use a guy like you. I'll make you a rich man.'

Sam took a few more steps forward and then lunged, his hand wrapping around Sergei's throat and pinning him to the wall. Face to face with the man responsible for one of the most profitable sex trafficking operations in Europe, Sam felt his other hand tighten around the blade.

'You have ruined the lives of so many girls. Of their families.'

'Why are you doing this?' Sergei croaked, as Sam pressed down on his throat. 'These girls mean nothing to you.'

Sam paused, remembering how helpless he was to save his own son. How helpless he would be to save the girls who were too far gone. Sam looked Sergei dead in the eye.

'It's the right thing to do.'

To Sam's surprise, Sergei began to laugh. After a few chuckles, Sergei smiled a cruel, twisted smile.

'I like you, Sam. You have guts.'

'You like guts, right?' Sam asked. Before Sergei could respond, Sam plunged the knife deep into the side of

Sergei's abdomen, the warm blood oozing out and over Sam's hand. Sergei's eyes widened with a mixture of pain and fear and in one swift movement, Sam dragged the blade through the flesh, ripping open the man's stomach. 'There you go.'

Sergei dropped to his knees, his hands trembling as he tried hopelessly to hold his innards inside his body. He fell forward, splashing onto a pile of his own intestines and blood. Sam dropped the knife next to him and walked towards the door, listening as Sergei's life came to an end.

He'd decapitated the snake.

Sam stopped at the bar on the way out and peered over, finding the half-naked woman crouched behind, her hands over her head and trembling with fear.

'You're okay,' he said, but she couldn't hear through her sobs. He knew she was terrified. 'Call the police and tell them to get as soon as possible. Tell them there was a shooting.'

The woman looked up at him, her eyes bloodshot. It didn't surprise Sam to discover she was English.

'But there was no shooting?'

Sam reached for the unfinished pint on the bar and took a large swig before looking back at her.

'There will be.'

The colour drained from her face with fear, and Sam turned towards the door, knowing his way out was going to be just as eventful.

Starting with the man guarding the door.

As he pushed himself away from the bar, Sam lifted the glass ashtray and carried it with him. He stood to the side of the door, then gently wrapped his knuckles on it.

The door swung open instantly and the man stepped in, startling at the blood bath that welcomed him. Before he could call for help, Sam slammed the glass ashtray into the side of his head, the glass embedding into the side of his skull.

The man went limp.

Before he could hit the floor, Sam reached under the man's arms and held him up, the extreme strength needed to move a dead weight body causing his muscles to strain. The pain in his leg intensified and he felt the stitches of his bullet wound rip. Sam gritted his teeth and began to drag the lifeless body down the stairs. Judging by the amount of blood oozing from the side of the man's skull, Sam knew the man was either dead or close to it.

Sam struggled to the bottom of the stairs and then, with all his might, he heaved the body into the door that opened up onto the club. The body slammed into the doors, bursting them open and the sleaze of the gentleman's club rushed to meet him.

The sight of their dead friend caused the two henchmen guarding the door to lose focus, their shock and anger colliding in a fatal few seconds. Sam drew the Glock from his jeans and sent a bullet in each of their directions.

Both burrowed their way through skull and brain and the men joined their comrade in the afterlife.

The music cut out, replaced by the terrified screams of the dancers and customers, the gunshots spreading panic like a virus. Sam stepped out into the nightclub, his vision slightly skewed by the cocktail of darkness, flashing lights, and smoke. Dozens of people were scrambling in terror, but Sam knew two of them would be armed and heading for him.

He raised his gun and fired a shot into the ceiling.

Survival instinct took over and everyone fell to the ground for cover. Except the two other henchmen who were marching his way, their hands buried in their blazers, their fingers wrapping around their guns.

Sam emptied two more rounds.

Both men hit the ground, their brains and skull painting the wall behind them.

Before Sam could turn, he heard another ringing gunshot and felt the impact of the bullet collide with his spine. It drove him forward, his hips hitting the top of a private booth and he collapsed over onto the supple leather chair.

The vest had stopped the bullet, but Sam still felt like he'd been hit with a sledgehammer. As he struggled to recapture his breath, he slid under the table, unclasping the strap of his assault rifle and slid it from under his jacket.

Thankfully, the bullet had missed it completely, but his spine wasn't so grateful. He heard the footsteps approaching, before the booming familiar voice of the doorman echoed through the club.

'You're a crazy man.' There was a hint of enjoyment in his voice. 'Crazy but dead.'

Sam pressed his feet against the wall and steadied the stock of the gun to his shoulder. It was an awkward angle, but he had to make it work. His mind shot back through its archives to the shots he'd made during his career, shooting a flying cannister of petrol to save his troop from a certain death.

It was awkward, but doable.

The doorman's shoe crunched on the broken light fixture caused by Sam's warning shot, giving away his position. With his instincts toned to zoom in on any noise, Sam gritted his teeth, ignoring the rising pain in his leg and the ache in his back and he pushed himself back from the wall. The propulsion sent him sliding back onto the floor and before the doorman could correct his aim, Sam squeezed the trigger.

A flurry of bullets ripped through the attacker, blood spraying out in delicate bursts. The man collapsed dead to the floor, accompanied by more screams of terror. In an instant, a large boot collided with Sam's rifle, knocking it into the darkness. Sam tried to scramble up but within seconds, Denys was on top of him, pinning Sam to the ground with his vast weight. Sam swung a few hard fists into the man's midsection, but it was like hitting a brick wall.

Denys wrapped his fingers around Sam's throat and pressed as hard as he could, his dark eyes twinkling with pleasure.

Bang.

The gunshot was deafening, and the side of Denys's head blew out, sending his limp body in the same direction. Gasping for breath, Sam struggled to his feet, rubbing his neck before hobbling towards the holder of the gun.

The barmaid from upstairs stood both arms outstretched, her fingers still uneasily resting on the trigger. Her eyes were wide with shock, something that the army had trained out of Sam.

With slow, painful steps, Sam approached her, his hands outstretched in a show of obedience and he gently reached out for the gun. Resting his hand on top of it, he slowly pushed it downward before the young girl relented and let him take it. She stepped towards him, burying her head in his chest, the sheer horror of her life, culminating in her killing a man burst forward and she wept.

After a few moments, the customers and other women began to rise to their feet, realizing the iron fist that ran the club had been severed. With great discomfort, Sam eased himself out of his jacket and draped it around the young woman's shoulders. She gratefully accepted it, pulling it closed and zipping it up to the collar. Sam tucked the pistol in the back of his jeans and then hobbled a few feet to his rifle. His back roared with pain as he bent down to retrieve it.

As he stood, he noticed all eyes were on him. His arms

were covered with the blood of the most dangerous criminal in the country and the room was littered with bodies.

They had no clue who he was or why he'd come.

But the look in their eyes was a mixture of fear and gratitude.

In the distance, the sound of sirens carried across the night sky giving Sam his cue to leave. He looked around at the girls, the magnitude of his actions not yet hitting them. He gave them a forced smile.

'Wait here for the police,' he ordered. 'They'll get you home.'

Sam turned and began to limp towards the exit, his jeans covered in his own blood. As he passed the bar maid, she reached out and placed her hand on his arm.

He turned to her; her eyes wet with tears.

'Thank you,' she whispered.

Sam nodded, then with a grunt of pain, he hobbled to the door and out into the bitter night. As the freezing grip of Kiev closed in on him, he headed to his car, ready to drive to anywhere but there.

CHAPTER FOUR

'Alma?'

The barista yelled the name out with the usual uncertainty, his eyes scanning around the busy Starbucks. The mid-morning rush was in full swing, the regular caffeine addicts rushing in before the mayhem that was lunchtime. Just after eleven, and DI Amara Singh was stood by the collection counter, gazing out of the window and onto the wet, freezing streets of London. Her nose still wore the bruising from the clubbing blow she'd received in the gun fight at the Port of Tilbury, where she'd recklessly entered the war zone against her superior's orders.

Coupling that and the claims that she helped Sam Pope escape, meant she was at the bottom of a pit with very little rope.

It certainly wasn't a good look for the person who sat at the top of the task force designed to catch him.

Well, she had been.

Staring ruefully out of the window at the busy city she'd spent the last decade of her life protecting, Singh knew she was in trouble the day after Sam Pope had saved her life and the lives of four teenage girls. Assistant Commissioner Ashton, who had personally vouched for her, read her the riot act. Not only had she failed to control the Sam Pope situation, there was a strong suspicion that she had in fact aided him.

While Singh denied helping Sam escape, she couldn't deny that she'd worked with him to retrieve the missing girls. She even went as far as to call him a hero, saying he'd risked life, limb, and his liberty to find four girls that the police didn't even have on their radar. While she knew they did the best they could, the political nature of the Metropolitan Police Force meant sometimes you had to pick your battles. Which is what Amara Singh had done when she'd turned a drunk Aaron Hill away from the station, ignoring his pleas for help and focusing on catching the most wanted man in the UK and making her career.

The desperate father had found his way to Sam Pope himself, and Sam had put her and the Met to shame with how far he was willing to go to get Jasmine Hill, and the other missing girls, back.

The very thought caused her to grimace.

Sam was a criminal. Singh had accepted she was going to be abducted, abused, and killed by Andrei Kovalenko when he had her cornered and ready to bundle into the shipping container. Had it not been for the intervening bullets sent from Sam Pope's sniper rifle, she would most likely be dead.

Or begging to be.

She knew Sam had saved her life and that he'd done the right thing. But she'd dedicated almost half of her thirty-two years to the law, believing vehemently in what it stood for and the line that upheld it. The line was getting thinner by the day, but she still knew in her heart, that despite being a good man, Sam Pope was a criminal.

So, comparing his efforts, where the law and the preservation of life held no weight, with those of her upstanding colleagues made her feel dirty.

Amara Singh had faced a lot as an Indian woman on the police force, especially at a time where any praise or promotion could just be seen as filling the diversity quota. She'd had to work triple to prove that she not only deserved her spot, but that she was ready for more. Her dedication to the job had meant no lasting relationship, which had upset her traditional Hindu parents. They wanted her to marry and start a family, like her sister, but over time, her constant achievement and rapid rise through the ranks had seen a different pride emerge from them.

Amara Singh didn't fail.

That was what she'd told herself her entire career. But now, staring out into the dreary, winter afternoon, with a beaten face, aching body, and recent demotion, she didn't feel like much of a winner.

'Alma?'

The voice echoed again; this time tinged with annoyance. Amara quickly scanned both ways until she realized she was the only customer. A split second later, it dawned on her that she was once again a victim of the very questionable listening skills of the Starbucks barista. She offered a half-hearted smiled before reaching for her flat white, heading towards the row of stools that lined the far window of the shop. Opposite the coffee house, the iconic triangular sign of the Met Police spun slowly, the New Scotland Yard building stood behind. The police HQ cast a gloomy shadow over the London Southbank, the beginning of December bringing with it an icy chill. Singh held her piping hot coffee in her delicate hands, two of her fingers taped together from where she broke them fighting two Ukrainian henchmen.

It had only been a week, but it felt a lifetime ago.

In those seven days, Ashton had relieved her from her command as head of the task force, taking over the responsibility until a more suitable candidate became available. Singh would have questioned the decision, but she knew that Ashton's close friend, Mark Harris, the former leading candidate to be the Mayor of London, had just had his life shattered by calls of corruption and greed.

Harris had been stitched up by his confident, Carl Burrows, who had since disappeared.

So had Sam Pope.

Singh had a sneaky suspicion that those two facts were not coincidental.

With a deep sigh, she dropped onto the stool and took a sip of her coffee, willing herself to pull herself up and get back to it. Her career had been forged by her unquenchable thirst to learn and her need to succeed. This was her first major blip, but it wouldn't stop her.

That wasn't the issue.

The issue was her wavering belief in the fine line between right and wrong.

The line that Sam Pope walked.

A line that, for a brief moment in that port, when the gunfire had ended and the trauma had finished, she'd wondered about walking too.

'This seat taken?'

Singh's attention was snapped back into the room and she looked up, startled by the warm grin of Adrian Pearce. His beaming white smile a contrast with his dark skin, a grey beard framing his welcoming grin. Pearce had been a Detective Inspector for the Department of Professional Standards, forging a long and fruitful career as a man tackling internal corruption. Although it had made him few friends, he'd been known as a man of relentless tenacity and ill-wavering integrity. In the six months since he'd started investigating Sam Pope, he'd seen his career dwindle, the higher ups not appreciating the vigilante's success in exposing the links between the Met and the organized crime they were fighting.

They especially didn't like his rumoured corroboration with Pope, although they could never prove it.

Singh had been suspicious of Pearce too, even clashing with him a few weeks back when she had Sam in her cross hairs. But since the fall of the Kovalenko empire and her brush with death, she'd found they had more in common than she thought.

She returned the smile, her sharp cheekbones the main highlight of her striking face.

'Of course, not.' She gestured for him to sit. 'I don't seem to have a lot of people wanting to sit next to me.'

'Ah, I know that feeling.' Pearce chuckled, easing himself into the chair, his fifty-year-old body creaking slightly. 'How you holding up?'

He pointed towards the bruising on her face and the bandages around her hand.

'I'm fine. Few weeks and I'll be right as rain.'

'You know, I remember a long time ago, I was on Armed Response when I came this close to death.' He gestured with his thumb and finger. 'Some mean bastard had us pinned down, a mate of mine took a bullet to the shin. I thought for sure that was it. I wouldn't be making it home. All I could think about was what I'd never said to Denise when I had the chance.'

'Denise?' Singh sat up, annoyed that she knew so little about Pearce. 'Your wife?'

'Ex.' Pearce shrugged, taking a sip of his coffee.

'I'm sorry.'

'Don't be. She isn't,' Pearce said grimly. 'Anyway, I

remember someone else took the guy out and we made it home. For the first few days I was fine. Pumped up on adrenaline and feeling like I was invincible, you know? But after a week or so, when the world returned to normal, I started shaking and for the first time in my life, I questioned my own mortality. Knowing I could die trying to do the right thing really shook me.'

Pearce looked warmly at Singh, who stared at her cup with a solemn look etched across her face.

'I was on my knees, beaten, and with a gun pointed at my head,' she began quietly, her hand shaking slightly. 'I accepted I was going to die, and you know what? I was okay with that. I would have died trying to save that young girl's life. But now, I feel sick knowing how close I actually came to the edge and…'

Singh shook her head and sighed deeply.

'Now you don't know if what Sam Pope is doing is wrong.'

Singh sat up, glaring at Pearce before quickly shooting her eyes around the coffee house, ensuring there were no colleagues nearby.

'No, I'm clear that what Sam Pope does is wrong. Despite why he is doing it and who he's doing it to, there is a clear line that he has crossed.' She shook her head. 'But if he hadn't have crossed it, I'd be dead and so would them girls.'

'It's a thinker, isn't it?' Pearce said, taking a sip of his latte.

'It's a pain in the arse, is what it is,' Singh said, drawing a smile from her senior colleague. 'Anyway, it won't be long now until I'm shipped off to a cupboard, too.'

'It's not all bad,' Pearce replied. Ever since he and Sam Pope had exposed Inspector Howell for orchestrating a bombing during the London Marathon, Pearce had been ushered to a small office and given cold cases to work.

They couldn't fire him, but they were damn sure trying to make him quit. But Pearce didn't believe in the notion and he sensed the same in Singh. 'I mean, I still managed to derail that Mark Harris's mayoral campaign. That was fun.'

'God, that man was a dick,' Singh said bluntly, causing Pearce to nearly spit out his coffee.

'That he was.' Pearce's expression dropped. 'Again, none of that was possible without Sam.'

Singh looked guiltily towards the Metropolitan Police logo on the building opposite and composed herself. Knowing she'd spent her life dedicated to what the badge stood for, it burned in her stomach that she felt this way about Sam.

That maybe, just maybe, he wasn't the bad guy.

A criminal, yes.

But a bad guy?

She took the final sip of her coffee and turned to Pearce whose wizened face offered something she hadn't felt since she'd been shunted from the Sam Pope task force.

Friendship.

'I was given a job to do. To bring Sam Pope in. Now, I don't know if this country is better off with him out there, doing whatever he is doing for whatever reason he has. But what I do know, is there has to be something we can do. Because the path he's on, there is only one way it ends.'

Pearce nodded sadly.

'I know.'

'So, while I may not be in there, hunting him down and trying to bring him in, I'm going to do my best to make sure it doesn't end that way. Whatever I can do to save him, I'm going to do it.' Singh was surprised at the fury bubbling within her. 'He saved my life. The least I can do is try to return the favour.'

Singh reached out and rubbed Pearce on the shoulder

37

before pushing herself up from the stool. Her body ached from the brutal fight she'd been involved in, but her new sense of purpose shut the discomfort down. Pearce swiveled on the chair.

'You remember a few weeks ago, when you barged into my cupboard and gave me all that shit?'

Singh stopped, turning with an apologetic shrug.

'I didn't know you then.'

'Oh, believe me, I've been called a lot worse. Do you remember what I said? The advice I was given?' Singh looked at him blankly. 'I told you to leave Sam Pope alone. You didn't listen.'

'I know.'

'I'm pretty sure, if I relayed that advice again now, it would go the same way, right?' Singh nodded. 'Then just be careful.'

'Thanks, Adrian.'

Pearce gave a small wave and Singh marched back through the freezing rain and into head office. As she walked through the corridors and past her colleagues' desks, she felt the eyes of the force on her. Whereas before, they were longing looks of envy or respect, they now oozed suspicion. The story of the Port had become office news, with theories of her alliance to Sam rife though the building. One rumour was she was sleeping with him, a notion she found hysterical but surprisingly, not all that unappealing.

She made her way to her desk, the photo on her locked computer screen of the Canadian woodlands bathing in the glow of the sun mocking the current weather.

Singh glanced up over her desk, her eyes scanning the other people in the room, watching as they all went about their business, working diligently on helping the public. In an office upstairs, Ashton was barking orders to the Sam Pope task force, the pressure ramping up on finding the man who was singlehandedly waging war on crime.

And winning.

Singh cracked her knuckles and logged in, praying her access to the Sam Pope files was still active. While rumours of her trysts with Pope were running rampant, official orders and the necessary paperwork to remove her access wasn't.

She entered her credentials.

Success.

With a muted shriek of delight, she started back at the beginning, irritated at the heavily redacted files pertaining to Sam's military career. It told the tale of a war hero, his expertise and accomplishments were increasingly impressive and she realized that despite living and breathing him for past few weeks, she'd been so focused on what he was doing that she'd never taken the time to find out who he was.

His military career had come to an abrupt end and he was honourably discharged after miraculously surviving two gunshots to the chest.

The report was almost non-existent, the scanned copy showing nothing but thick, black pen covering any useful information.

With a sigh, she moved the mouse to the 'x' in the corner, only to stop with a jolt. The faintest ink could be seen at the bottom of the page, the handwriting almost unreadable. Singh zoomed in.

It said three words.

Wallace – Project Hailstorm.

Singh scribbled it down on the pad of Post-it Notes she kept by her keyboard, exited out of the document and did one further glance around the office. With her heart thudding with excitement, she typed 'Project Hailstorm' into the search bar of the encrypted folders.

No results found.

Singh clenched her fist in anger, her search futile. Little did she know, that upon hitting search, a flag was sent to a database far away and she'd unwittingly placed herself on a very exclusive, very dangerous list.

CHAPTER FIVE

Having been in a number of life-threatening situations, high pressure combat scenarios and most recently, been in several fights to the death, Sam was surprised by the nerves he had as he stood at the passport control at Kiev airport. It didn't help that his face had acquired a few cuts from his recent endeavours, and a small bruise had formed just under his left eye. Behind the glass booth, a skeptical looking Ukrainian official stared intently at the passport, his eyes flashing up now and then, scrutinizing the beaten man before him.

'I was mugged,' Sam said, immediately cursing his lack of composure. Staring down the scope of a rifle with the intent to kill was easy. Passport control, not so much.

A few more agonizing moments passed before the man slowly closed the passport and slid it back under the glass partition. Sam noticed his pristine uniform which the man clearly wore with pride and felt a twinge of respect.

'I am sorry for your experience in our country, Mr Cooper.' The man smiled, stating the fake name that Etheridge had provided on his flawless documents. 'Have a safe journey back and please visit us again.'

Sam pressed his beaten hands on the leather booklet and slid his passport from the counter and tucked it into the inside of his jacket pocket. Wearing a casual shirt, jeans, and boots, Sam wanted to look like just another passenger making his way home. He doubted any of the other passengers had left a trail of bodies in their wake.

'Thanks.' He nodded to the control officer and continued on, his shoulders relaxing now he'd cleared security and the passport check. Security at Kiev airport had massively increased since the Crimea Crisis and Sam was glad to be in the final stages of his journey home. Although it had been less than twenty-four hours since he'd eliminated Sergei Kovalenko, it felt like a lifetime ago. Limping through the pain that screamed from his wounded leg, he found an empty seat in the waiting area, offering a view of the dark, dull skyline and the few aeroplanes going through their stages of take-off.

The rain clattered against the window and Sam sympathized with the crew members, wrapped up in as many high-vis layers as possible, battling the freezing elements as they refuelled a plane. Having spent days motionless, wrapped in shrubbery and cooking under the hot, Sudan sun, Sam knew about working through tough conditions.

He groaned, his back was aching and every swallow caused his throat to burn, the souvenir Denys had left when he'd tried to strangle him. Ironically, as Sam had tried to save the girls forced to perform whatever the Kovalenko's customers wanted, it was one of them who had saved him. She would have nightmares about pulling the trigger. Ending a person's life was never easy, even with the training and experience Sam had. But it would be a far cry from the horrors of her life had he not intervened.

It was why he'd done it.

It was the right thing to do.

Sam knew the pain in his chest wasn't from the war

42

he'd just raged, but the guilt. The same, numbing guilt that accompanied every kill since he'd embarked on his mission of justice.

He'd broken his promise to his son.

'I'm sorry, Jamie,' he uttered, shaking his head with a bitter realization that he would undoubtedly break it again. But having been helpless to save his boy, he knew he'd been built and trained by the army to do good in the world. That ended with two bullets to the chest and a foggy memory. Now, after the injustice that followed his son's death had led him to breaking point, Sam had decided to turn his grief onto those who did nothing but damage.

To fight back for those who couldn't.

When the time came where he would be reunited with his son, and Sam was well aware that day could come soon, he knew he would have some explaining to do.

With a serious ache dancing up his spine, he reached into his carry-on bag and pulled out his book, determined to keep his other promise to his son. Jamie had been a bookworm, his thirst for the written word had surprised and enchanted him in equal measure. Sam had never been the studious type, so seeing his little boy take to reading so quickly was almost magical. Lucy encouraged it and Sam had spent many evenings quietly watching as his family huddled together, sharing the wonders of Roald Dahl together.

His perfect life.

Knowing he would never relive it, he flicked open the first page of *Moby Dick* and tried his best to get lost in the story. He'd promised Jamie he would read more.

It was one promise he would keep.

A few moments after his introduction to Ishmael, Sam heard some commotion from the passport control where he'd ventured, and he fought through the discomfort to twist his neck to investigate.

The Ukrainian control officers were yelling loudly, as a squad of eight, heavily armed men in black polo shirts and bulletproof vests walked through, their eyes fixed on Sam. With his weapons being safely transported back through customs through Etheridge's genius, Sam knew he was in no position to fight.

He had no weapon.

His body was battered.

Time to face the music.

The other passengers shuffled away quickly, the panic of a terrorist attack rising like a crescendo through the crowd. Armed security guards were ascending in the group's direction and Sam knew that resistance wouldn't only be futile, but potentially life threatening to the innocent people nearby.

Carefully, he placed his book back into his bag and pushed himself from the stool, raising his hands in a show of surrender. The eight strong crew, consisting of men and women with various military tattoos and cropped hair, spread out, blocking any potential getaway. Behind them, he heard an American voice sternly telling the airport security that he had jurisdiction given to him by their government to retrieve a valuable asset.

It was a voice Sam recognized but couldn't place.

The recognition was soon confirmed when the man stepped through the barrier and strode towards him, decked out in the same, expensive attire as his crew only he didn't have an assault rifle strapped to his chest. On his waist, which strained against the gut his mid-fifties had created, was a Beretta M9. On his chest was a bulletproof vest, with the words 'Blackridge' written in slick, futuristic letters.

The light bounced off his balding head.

On his chubby face was a shit-eating grin.

Trevor Sims.

Sam tried, but clearly failed to mask the confusion on his face. Arrogantly chewing gum, Trevor strode towards him, looked him up and down and smirked again.

'Christ, Sam. You look like shit.' He scoffed and then quickly waved his hand.

Sam turned in the direction and was met head on with a clubbing blow from one of the squadron's rifles.

Everything went black.

―――――

With his coat pulled up over his head, Aaron Hill ran from the driver's side of his car and up the front path to his front door. The weather had taken a horrible turn for the worst, the early December bringing with it a little festive cheer, but a freezing, death like quality. Wedged under his arm was a brown paper bag, the waft of KFC dancing through the rain and ushering him into the house quickly.

It was a treat for his daughter.

Jasmine.

It had been a little over a week since she'd been returned to him, having spent a number of days locked in a shipping container, ready to be deported into a world of unspeakable horrors. Having been snatched by a street gang and sold to a terrifying sex trafficking business, Aaron sometimes had to stop and take a moment to realise what he went through to get her back.

He'd gone to the police, but they'd dismissed him due to the fact he'd doused his fears in alcohol. That drunken haze had sent him spiraling into the under belly of West London, purchasing a gun and laying siege to the last place her phone had been located. It was a drug den, filled with street thugs who were ready to put a bullet in his head.

That was when fate intervened.

Well, Sam Pope did.

Aaron had heard about Sam Pope on the news, the man responsible for a brutal slaying of an organized crime gang earlier that year. After the sad passing of his wife, Aaron had lost all faith in the world. His grief had collided with his daughter's and had pushed her to make bad choices. One of them had led her to that party, which could have led her to a life he dared not think about.

A world where people could take a young girl and sell her to the highest bidder was not one he believed in.

But Sam Pope had changed that.

Burning a relentless, ruthless hole through the criminal underworld to find her, Sam had shown Aaron how far some people are willing to go to do the right thing. Despite giving information to the police, Aaron could never repay Sam for risking everything for his daughter and seen as how he'd disappeared, he hadn't had the chance to thank him.

In the follow-up interviews with the police, the young detective, Singh, had told him they hadn't caught Sam or found his body, so they assumed him to be alive. Aaron had thanked her, her own bravery in the pursuit of his daughter had seen her applauded by her colleagues but shelved by her superiors. He didn't know a thing about the internal politics of the Metropolitan Police but in his mind, she deserved a goddamn medal.

It had felt like a lifetime ago, and as he stepped through the door to his house, all he wanted to do was see his daughter. Jasmine had wanted to return to school as quickly as possible, pushing the horrors of her capture aside and throwing herself towards a brighter future. Knowing it could have been something horrific had ignited her passion for studies and she'd already told him she wanted to pursue a career in law and help other families who'd had their children stolen.

He'd never felt so proud.

As a treat, he'd brought her her favourite take away and they'd promised they would watch the latest Marvel movie together.

Just the two of them.

'Jasmine. Honey,' Aaron called out as he slid his drenched coat from his slightly chubby frame, his thinning blonde hair pressed to the scalp, accentuating his losing battle with Father Time. 'Delivery!'

He chuckled at his own, poor attempt at a 'dad' joke, before draping his jacket over the bannister. There was no response.

'Jasmine?' he called again, louder in case she was in her room. A noise from the kitchen caught his attention and he sighed, annoyed that he was still fearing the worst. He walked down the hall, past the living room where he'd shared a cup of tea with Sam and pushed open the kitchen door.

Jasmine sat at the table, stiff with fear and with tears in her eyes.

Next to her was a man, head to toe in black, with a balaclava covering his face.

'Who the fuck are you?' Aaron barked angrily, stomping forward with intent. The man raised his gloved hand from the table, his leather clad fingers wrapped around Sig Sauer 226 handgun. He aimed it directly at Jasmine's temple, who shuddered with fear.

'Please, sit down,' the man calmly asked, gesturing to the seat in front of Aaron with his other hand. Aaron immediately obliged.

'Jasmine, it's going to be okay. Just stay calm,' Aaron spoke softly, reaching across the table. Jasmine glanced at the intruder who nodded, and she took her father's hand. Aaron offered her a smile, battling his own fear with every fibre of his being. He turned to the man. 'Please put the gun down.'

The man waited for a few moments, burning a hole through Aaron with his piercing blue eyes before slowly lowering the gun and placing it on the table. He rested his hand atop of it, ready for anything. He wore a black, leather trench coat which hung over the sides of the wooden chair, along with a black jumper, jeans, and boots.

Whoever he was, he didn't want anyone to know.

Behind the balaclava mask, Aaron could see what looked like scarring around his left eye and the left side of his mouth. With his other hand, the man reached into his jacket and pulled out a sheet of paper. He slammed it on the table, causing Jasmine to jump. Slowly, the intruder slid it across the table to Aaron, who snatched it up immediately.

It was an article from the *London Echo*, accompanied by a picture of Aaron, as well Sam Pope's army profile picture. Portraying Sam as a hero, the interview Aaron had given was to counteract the official line by the Met that Sam had left another trail of bodies and then disappeared.

It had led to DI Singh knocking on his door, rapping him on the knuckles but then telling him she knew Sam had saved his daughter's life.

It was meant to paint Sam Pope in a better light.

Now it had seemed to have brought the devil to his door.

'Where can I find Sam Pope?'

'I don't know,' Aaron replied immediately, sensing the level of danger rising in the room.

'According to this article, and many others, he did an awful lot to save her.' The man pointed at Jasmine, his words carried a Manchurian accent and an thinly veiled threat. 'You're telling me he did that outta the goodness of his heart?'

Aaron nodded.

'He's a good man.'

The man slammed his fist against the table with blind rage.

'He is *not* a good man!' he exclaimed, reaching for the gun and raising it to Jasmine's face again. The young girl wept quietly, her panicked eyes flickering to her dad for help.

She'd been through enough already.

'For the love of God, stop pointing that gun at my daughter.'

'You have five seconds to tell me where I can find him.'

'I don't know.'

'Five.'

Jasmine burst into tears, the fear wrestling hold of her consciousness.

'Four.'

'Please, I don't know!'

'Three.'

'I don't know, I swear!'

'Two.'

'There is a guy… a smart guy, used to be in the army with him.' The man in black stopped counting, but kept his muscular arm up, the gun a mere inch from Jasmine's forehead.

'What's his name?' The question fired out like a final warning. Jasmine's face was glimmering with tears. She squeezed her father's hand.

'Paul… something,' Aaron stammered, his mind racing, trying to find a memory among the sheer terror of losing his daughter again. 'Ever… Evering. No, Etheridge.'

The man retracted the gun. Jasmine was still breathing heavily, the idea of a bullet to her temple still firmly in control and causing her to shake with shock. Calmly, the man stood, his imposing frame was only exacerbated by his height. He slid the gun into the holster hung from his belt and he drew his coat across.

'Thank you.' His words were calm, as if holding a child at gun point was as normal as offering someone a cup of tea. 'Enjoy your evening.'

The man strode out of the kitchen, through the hall-way, and out into the rain, leaving the door wide open and the freezing night to rush in. Jasmine collapsed from her chair, falling into Aaron's arms as he dropped to catch her. After everything that had happened, all the terror of her abduction, this would only cause more damage. Whoever that man was, he meant nothing but harm.

To his daughter.

To Paul Etheridge.

To Sam Pope.

Aaron closed his eyes, feeling a warm tear peak over his eyelid and slide down his cheek, knowing he may have just put a good, honest man in danger. But he had to protect his daughter.

As the freezing wind shook the front door on its hinge, he held Jasmine as she wept, knowing her life would never be normal and that there was nothing he wouldn't do to protect her.

CHAPTER SIX

'*Check.*'

Theo Walker tapped the table with impatience, his eyes staring at the three cards laid out in the centre of the room. Sam smiled, knowing his hand was strong and he also checked. To his left, Paul Etheridge sat, his brown hair scruffily peeking beneath his camouflage cap. All three of them were decked out in their combat trousers, with Sam and Theo opting for rather flattering khaki vests. Etheridge, on the slighter side, wore a camouflage T-shirt, his glasses hanging around his neck from a plastic chord.

Both he and Sam were sun kissed, their patrol of the south side of Camp Bastion, just north of Helmand Province, Afghanistan. Theo, with his dark skin, had mocked them incessantly as they slathered sun cream on. The three of them had been in the same platoon for a few years, with Sam and Theo especially building a strong friendship, with them visiting each other during the end of their tour. Sam had introduced Theo to Lucy and was seriously considering him as a god parent to their unborn child.

Theo had graciously turned it down, saying his life as a Military Medic had sapped all faith and belief in God from him. Sam understood. Crouching in the mud, under heavy fire, holding a friend's heart together with your bare hands was enough to eradicate any one's fate.

Sam had often questioned his own faith against his role, whether it was truly God's will that he ended life after life with the deadly squeeze of a trigger.

Still, Sam had never been big on religion, but Lucy had already decided on the school she wanted their child to go to and apparently, not believing in a higher power voided your membership.

As Theo readjusted his cards, Sam shot an inquisitive glance at Etheridge. The man may have been a genius, but his poker face was abysmal. The two jacks on the table had made for an interesting flop and considering Sam had the other two in his hand, he now knew that Etheridge was cursing himself for raising. The man could disarm a bomb in seconds, had written enough bespoke coding to override a number of security facilities, but when it came to cards, there was no hiding it.

Paul Etheridge was shit.

Sam turned the fourth card over, a six of diamonds which he placed carefully down, his eyes locked on Etheridge. He wanted him to keep betting, the fifteen-pound pile would soon double.

'Theo?' Sam asked, not taking his eyes off Etheridge.

'Nah, I fold.' Theo slapped his cards down onto the table. 'This game is a load of horse shit, anyway!'

Sam chuckled then turned back to Etheridge. With a nervous hand, he rearranged his cards, lamely attempting to maintain some semblance of power.

He had nothing.

Sam knew it. Theo knew it. He knew it.

'Check,' Etheridge said nervously.

'All in.' Sam dropped the remaining thirty-five pounds of his stake onto the pile of cash in the middle of the table. Theo let out a whistle of admiration, knowing full well Sam had Etheridge in the same position he'd found many enemy soldiers.

In the centre of his crosshairs and ready to pull the trigger.

'Tick, tock,' Sam said and just as Etheridge was about to respond, a large crash erupted from outside, quickly followed by a barrage of raised voices. Instinctively, all three men shot up, rushing to *the doorway of their tent. Sam was the first through, emerging to an escalating scene between the US Forces and his own sergeant, Carl Marsden.*

Mid-fifties and built like he was made of granite, Marsden was as respected as he was feared, but despite his intimidating service record and ice cool demeanor, he was as passive as a puppy and Sam knew it. To see him stood, fists clenched, ready to take on the three American soldiers must have taken some provocation.

That was when he saw Trevor Sims scrambling from the floor, his lip busted open.

Sam didn't even question his superior.

Sims was universally disliked. The man was a politician, not a soldier, worming his way into power and brown nosing every authority figure until his own nose became a part of them. He'd inexplicably been put in charge of a specialist unit, ensuring he only picked the glory missions.

The man was a parasite and everything Sam despised about the US Army. The man was pro-privatising the military, charging the world top dollar for protection.

In Sam's mind, it went against the whole 'freedom' bullshit the man constantly spewed in his southern accent.

'You're gonna regret that, Marsden. You black piece of shit,' Sims angrily jeered, his added racism doing little to rile up Marsden, but sending Theo into a blind rage.

'What the fuck did you just say?' Theo stepped forward, ready to continue the fight his ancestors had begun years ago. Calmly, Marsden placed an arm across Theo, pulling him away and pushing him to Sam. Despite his proud African heritage, Marsden offered Sims a smile.

'Do yourself a favour, Sims. Take your frat boys here and fuck off. Before I really lose my patience.'

Sims sneered at Marsden, who maintained his cool. Sims was a few inches shorter, his gut pressed against his light blue, sweat-stained shirt. The difference not only between them physically, but in terms of stature, was stratospheric. As the silence hung in the heat between them, Sam pushed Theo back into the muggy tent to calm down and Sims turned on his heel and stomped off back across Camp Bastion towards the gate that housed the US troops. Etheridge shook his head, sweat dripping down from under his cap and he followed Theo into their quarters, ready to lose some money. Sam stood, arms crossed, waiting for his commanding officer to brief him. Marsden calmly watched the antagonistic Sims march away and then he turned to Sam, a smile, framed by a grey beard, cracking across his face.

'I'll tell you what, son,' Marsden said. 'I've seen some shit in my life, but none of it stinks as much as that man there. Believe me, no matter what he says or tries to do, do not trust him.'

Marsden reached up and patted Sam on the arm reassuringly, before pulling a cigar from his shirt pocket. With a wry wriggle of his eyebrows, Marsden headed off towards the command HQ, flicking a match and leaving a large plume of cigar smoke in his wake. Sam watched for a few moments, smiled, then re-entered the tent, ready to take his friend to the cleaners.

———

The memory slowly dissolved from Sam's conscious, replaced by the sharp pain the earlier strike to his head. The man responsible for the knock-out blow was named Buck, and he was as arrogant as he was physically imposing. The clear 'alpha' among the squad that had captured him, Buck had made his disdain for Sam quite clear.

Sam couldn't care less.

What he did care about, was being locked in a white interrogation room in a Ukrainian airport, being fed bullshit by the repugnant Trevor Sims.

'Thoughts?' Sims asked, closing the manila folder in front of him and reaching for his cigar.

'Well first off, my head is killing me,' Sam started, a chuckle echoing from behind him where Buck guarded the door. 'And the constant stream of crap you're feeding me isn't helping.'

Sims rolled his eyes and sat back in his chair, a cloud of cigar smoke following him like a grey, floating sheep. Sims had aged in the eight or so years since Sam had dealt with him, his hair almost completely gone and the metabolism clearly fading with age.

'You don't like me, do you, Sam?'

'No,' Sam said coldly. 'I don't.'

'That's fine. I'm not in the business of being liked or giving a flying fuck what people think. I'm in the business of national *and* international security. I put Blackridge together to be able to operate without the bureaucracy of the military. We don't have to worry about hurting the feelings of whatever snowflake country thinks we can save the world by holding hands and sharing a fucking avocado on toast.'

Sam started laughing and was met with a glare from an obviously agitated Sims.

'Bullshit,' Sam said calmly. 'You couldn't give a damn about the safety of anyone. You're mercenaries. You pick and choose based on nothing other than money.'

Sims sat forward, his mouth turned up in a snarl, revealing his stained teeth.

'How about you, Sam? Huh? What do you class yourself as? A hero? A man of the people? Just because you go around fighting criminals doesn't make you Batman. It makes you a criminal. You're not a soldier. You don't serve anyone. You're a vigilante and a criminal.'

'Maybe,' Sam responded, leaning forward and meeting Sims's glare. 'But at least I'm not whoring myself out and pretending I'm anything more than a gun happy prick in a polo shirt.'

Sims sat back, folding one leg over the other and took

another, long puff of his cigar. The smell hung in the air, threatening to choke them all.

'Careful, Sam. You're beginning to try my patience.'

'What do you want from me?' Sam shrugged. 'Like you said, I'm not a soldier. Also, added to the fact that I don't believe a word you just said.'

'It's in the file.' Sims gestured with an open palm to the folder in front of them.

'If what you're saying is true, then let me talk to him. There must be some mistake.'

'That's not what's on the table,' Sims stated coldly. 'As of right now, Carl Marsden, your former commander is in possession of top-secret information that could cause a lot of damage to a number of countries and organisations. He has been treated as not only a traitor, but a potential terrorist.'

'A terrorist?' Sam exclaimed. 'Really? That man served his country for years with distinction. There is no way he would be involved in what you've been told.'

'Then why is he running?' Sims asked bluntly. 'Why has he abandoned his family, why has he made contact with various countries looking for asylum, and why was the last thing removed from his computer an unhackable file with the same tracking IP as the information that went missing?'

Sam sat back in his chair and took a moment. It had been less than a day since he laid siege to *Echelon* and put Kovalenko down. Now he was sat in custody, his freedom in extreme jeopardy, being blackmailed to hunt down a man who he held in high esteem.

The evidence against his friend was stacking up. Marsden was in possession of a file that could be catastrophic for several military operations. Sam speculated it was an undercover list, documenting the names and aliases of several agents.

Not only would that put them in immediate danger, it would work wonders to destroy the shaky trust most countries existed on these days. The only thing worse than being humiliated was being lied to too.

But Sam was still struggling to believe that Marsden was capable of such an act of treason. The man was the army, through and through. He'd been on more tours than the Rolling Stones and had nurtured the careers of some of the UK's finest soldiers.

The man was not a terrorist.

The man was on the run, but for what?

'What do you want from me?' Sam asked again, this time with a hint of defeat in his voice which brought a twinkle to Sims's eye.

'I want you to join my team and guide them to him. We know his whereabouts; we just can't get inside his head. I remember him being a stubborn prick, but you know he thinks. How he acts. Plus, you know his tricks.'

'Tricks?'

'The man led countless covert missions with a number of different squadrons,' Sims said with begrudging admiration. 'The chances are, he's covering his tracks.'

'And if I don't?' Sam said defiantly.

'Then I'll drag you back to Ol' Blighty myself,' Sims joked, mocking the English accent. 'I'll hand you over to your government and let you rot in a cell for the rest of your life.'

Sam shrugged.

'Prison doesn't scare me. I know I'll have to face up to my crimes one day and I'll gladly do that before I turn on someone who has more integrity in his little finger than you or any of your half-wit crew have in their entire body.'

Behind him, Sam heard Buck shuffle uncomfortably, clearly angered by his comment. Sims's snarl turned into a menacing smile, his chin wobbling as he leant forward.

'Imagine how awful it would be, if your ex-wife got caught in the crossfire of your war on crime?' Sims shook his head slowly. 'It would be tragic.'

'Don't say her name.'

'Lucy, wasn't it?' Sims said cockily, puffing on his cigar. 'Join the fucking mission, Sam, and I'll make sure nothing happens to her.'

'And if I don't?'

'Well, I can't make any promises.' Sims took a proud puff of his cigar. Sam gritted his teeth, the idea of working with this man against one of the people dearest to him was heartbreaking. But the idea of being responsible for any more of Lucy's pain held a heavier price tag and Sam drilled a fist into the table in frustration. Behind him, Buck chuckled, eager to antagonise Sam. Sims leant forward, the smug look on his face making Sam's blood boil.

'Well?'

'Fine,' Sam strained to say. 'I'll do it. But you leave her out of it.'

'Consider it done.' Sims stood, extending a meaty hand towards Sam, who slowly stood as well. 'Put it there.'

Sam looked at the man's clammy palm and then swung over it, his fist colliding with Sims's jaw and knocking him backwards. The cigar spun into the air, dropping onto the table which shook as Sims collapsed backwards. Behind him, Sam heard Buck lunge forward and he stepped to the side, shifting his weight and latching onto Buck's arm. Similar to how he eliminated one of Kovalenko's guards, Sam wrenched the arm and drove Buck face down into the unforgiving wood of the table. The spray of blood told him that Buck's nose had broken.

The panicked wrenching on the door handle behind told him he was out of time.

With Buck pinned down to the table, Sam wrenched his arm further, causing him to submit completely. With his other hand, Sam reached for the holster strapped to Buck's hip and pulled out the handgun, slid his finger expertly over the trigger and aimed it squarely at Sims. The colour drained from his face as he clambered to his feet, and he stared at Sam with a mixture of awe and horror.

Behind Sam, two more men burst in, their tattoo covered arms aiming their weapons squarely at the back of his head.

'Jesus,' Sims called out. 'Everyone … lower your weapons. What the fuck, Sam? Are you trying to get yourself killed?'

'I want to make something perfectly clear.' Sam's words were eerily calm. 'If you ever threaten someone I care about again, I'll put a bullet through your skull. Do you understand?'

Sims nodded.

'Everyone, lower your weapons.' Begrudgingly, his men followed his orders and Sims felt his jaw start to ache from the hammer-like blow he'd received. He looked at Sam nervously, the gun still pointed squarely at his head. 'How about it, Sam?'

Sam looked at him for a further few seconds, his bruised and beaten face motionless. Eventually, he lowered the gun and released his hold on Buck, who staggered backwards. Desperate not to lose face, he tried to lunge for Sam, knowing full well his comrades would hold him back. It didn't matter, really. Sam knew that at any given moment Buck would try to even the score. In fact, there was nothing about the whole mission he trusted. Sims was a slimy, corrupt desk man who had a personal agenda against the man he'd been tasked with catching.

All Sam knew was that something was happening.

Whatever it was, Marsden was involved and needed Sam's help.

Sam turned back to Sims, who had relit his cigar.

'Where is he? Marsden?'

Two large puffs of smoke shot forward, encapsulating Sims's round head. As his face began to disappear behind the smoke, his mouth contorted into a cruel smile.

'Berlin.'

CHAPTER SEVEN

'Jamie, be careful.'

Sam called out lovingly from the park bench, watching with pride as his son climbed the rope ladder that hung from the side of the metal climbing frame. The sun was beating down on another glorious summer's day and Sam took a long, deep breath. The last time he'd been under such heat he was out in the desert, his arms wrapped around his Accuracy International Arctic Warfare bolt action sniper rifle. He opened his eyes, peering through the visors of his Ray-Ban sunglasses and all that was resting in his arms was Jamie's rucksack. It contained his juice bottle, a toy fire truck, and another one of his books. Sam wasn't sure which one, he was struggling with his son's love of reading, but Lucy was adamant they encouraged it.

But for a five-year-old, Jamie was reading at a very high level and his teachers were already talking about making special plans for him. The kid was smart, and Sam felt a warmth inside his chest, his heart aching with pride for his boy.

Sam had promised him he would read more too, and he picked up the book sat next to him on the bench.

'Hey, Dad. Look!' Jamie called out from the top of the frame, waving wildly in excitement. He'd made it up and now was facing the exciting descent down the metal slide.

For such a glorious day, Sam realised they were alone. The park was empty, and the only noise was the excited yell that accompanied his son down the slide. Sam looked out across the fields, expecting numerous groups of kids or families to be huddled together, a spontaneous game of football being played out in the sun. Elderly couples enjoying a stroll with their dog, while young, fitness enthusiasts dipped in between the mayhem as they continued their run.

Nothing.

Just the clear, empty fields baking under the glorious sun. Sam shuffled uncomfortably on the bench, a feeling of guilt spreading through him. Confused, he pulled his phone from his jean pocket and flicked his thumb to Lucy's number. Keeping an eye on his son, who was once again carefully ascending the rope ladder, he waited for the first few dials.

'Hello?'

'Hello, lovely,' Sam said with a smile. 'When are you getting here?'

'What?' The response was cold and curt, and Sam raised his eyebrows.

'We're at the park. You should see Jamie climb, he's like a little monkey.'

'Jesus, Sam.' He could hear her voice crack with tears. 'What the hell is wrong with you?'

'Babe?'

'I told you not to call me. It's not fair.'

Before Sam could respond, the line went dead and he slowly pulled it from his ear. Sam felt like he'd been hit in the gut, the love of his life snapping at him with such vitriol he wondered what he could have done to deserve it?

Like a wood worm burrowing through the back of his skull, he had a nagging suspicion they'd had the same conversation before.

But when?

Why?

As he watched Jamie disappear down the slide again, a plume of cigarette smoke wafted around him.

'Women, eh?' The voice was instantly recognisable. The south London accent was brimming with a mixture of manners and menace and Sam turned his head to the left to see Frank Jackson sat next to him. Despite there being no sound or movement throughout the entire playground, Sam hadn't seen the man approach, nor felt him sit down.

He didn't question it though. The gangster, once responsible for running one of the most lucrative 'High Rises' in London, was sat in one of his impeccable suits. Known as 'The Gent' for his devotion to good manners, a trait he'd learnt from his put-upon mother, who in the face of extreme poverty, never lost her sense of dignity. Living up to his reputation, Jackson offered Sam a cigarette and he politely waved it away. Jackson took another puff before gesturing to Jamie, who was climbing the ladder again.

Sam noticed his movements were the same, like a video stuck on a loop.

Just a lovely day in the park.

'That your boy?' Jackson asked.

'Yup. Jamie.'

'Looks like a nice kid.' Jackson smiled. 'Nothing better in this world than looking after those you care about.'

'Exactly,' Sam said, feeling an uneasy glare from Jackson.

'Is that why you do it?' Jackson asked, taking another puff.

'Do what?' Sam asked, turning with irritation.

'Break your promise to your son,' Jackson said calmly.

Sam opened his mouth to respond but Jackson cut him off. 'You promised your boy that you wouldn't kill again, but look at you, Sam? You're a natural born killer. Hell, you probably killed more people than I have.'

'I'm not a murderer,' Sam tried to reason, with himself more than Jackson. 'I killed those people for a reason.'

'Like him?'

Jackson pointed to Sam's right, and as he followed, a body of an Iraqi soldier was laid out, his arms lying unnaturally, his back resting against a jagged rock that wasn't there moments before. The centre of the man's forehead was blown through, the stone of the rock visible through the bloody gap between his open, lifeless eyes.

'Or him?'

With another point of Jackson's cigarette, Sam's vision was sent to the climbing frame his son was stood on, once again proudly waving to his dad for the umpteenth time that day. On the platform where he stood, Jamie was heading to the slide. In the other direction were the monkey bars, where the large body of Oleg Kovalenko swung, a metal chain wrapped around his meaty neck and the rusty hook ripping through the flesh of his neck and into his mouth. Blood dripped rapidly to the wood chip below, turning the brown cuts red. Sam had fought the man to the death to save a group of young girls from a life of sex slavery.

The brutality was necessary.

'And me?'

Sam turned to Jackson, who was now sprawled on the bench, his white shirt littered with several bullet holes, each of them staining the shirt red. Jackson's eyes were closed, the cigarette hanging loosely from his mouth.

It was a vision Sam had seen before, when he'd emptied a clip into the gangster's chest after storming the High Rise.

It wasn't murder.

It was justice.

'Hey, Dad. Look!'

Sam looked up again, as Jamie once again began to climb the ropes, the familiarity of his movements felt like echoes from a previous moment. Sam was sure of it and as he stood, he walked across the woodchip, which was now strewn with the bodies of all the men he'd killed. Soldiers, criminals, anyone who had been unfortunate enough to be in his crosshairs.

The path back to his son had been painted with blood and he felt that guilt again.

The guilt that he was still killing. Breaking that promise to the thing he cared for most in the world.

Despite doing bad things for the right reason, Sam knew he walked the wrong side of the line and when the day came for him to face his crimes, his punishment would be swift. It would be deserved, and it would keep him away from his boy.

Jamie.

Suddenly, Jamie screamed with terror and Sam heard him collapse from the frame. Jumping to action, Sam hurdled the dead bodies that blocked his pathway and as he rounded the slide, he dropped to his knees. Moments later, he vomited.

Jamie was lying, his body broken, his arm trapped beneath him. A trickle of blood cascaded from his ear.

Sam felt the tears running down his face, his throat burning. Beyond Jamie, he could see Lucy crying hysterically into the shoulder of a policeman, beating his arm with a blind rage at losing her son.

Jamie was dead and Sam knew that this moment had been a long time ago. That this pain had existed since the moment he laid eyes on his son's motionless body.

The need to put things right.

For some reason, as he watched his life disintegrate before his eyes, he thought of Carl Marsden, a man who Sam trusted implicitly. Marsden had risked his life for Sam, gone to bat for him on several occasions and had reached out to him when all was lost. As the body of Jamie disappeared, so did the rest of the bodies, the long list of men who Sam had sent to the afterlife.

All of them gone.

Sam knelt among the bloody woodchip, the park empty, the sun beating down.

He was surrounded by death. It was in him. While he couldn't run from it, he knew it would claim him one day. But for now, he needed to find Marsden and try to save him.

Somehow.

Before Sam could get up, a dark, charred hand reached out and grabbed his wrist. The fingers were clammy with blood. Sam turned and came face to face with the dismantled, burnt remains of Theo Walker, who had given his own life to protect Amy Devereux from a grenade. He'd ensured she was locked away, while his bullet riddled body had absorbed most of the blast. His face was singed almost to the bone and one of his eyes was gone, a charred, hollow gap in its place. His left arm was missing, blood pouring from the wound and a large portion of his stomach was blown apart, exposing his decimated internal organs.

Shaking, Sam tried to reach out to his friend.

Theo swallowed, trying to speak through his fried throat.

'You can't… save… everyone.'

With that, Sam shot upright in his bed, the darkness of the room blurring his vision. With quick, sharp breaths, he tried to regain his composure, retrace his steps to arrive at his current panic.

He was on a train, the motion accompanied by the noise relocated him and he remembered his conversation with Sims and his Blackridge team. They were headed to Berlin, with Sims booking him and three members of his crew onto an overnight train from Kiev to the German capital. The train would take just over twenty-five hours and Sam had slept before his head had hit the pillow.

With the prospect of sleep as appealing as a sandpaper suppository, Sam slowly swung his legs over the side of the bed and pressed his feet to the cold, tiled floor of his cabin. He reached for a T-shirt, sliding it over his bruised, battle-worn body and then stuffed his feet into his boots. If he wasn't going to sleep, then finding out whether the direct line between Germany and Ukraine had a bar or not, seemed like the next best thing.

———

Amara Singh sat upright with a jolt, the loud thudding from her front door startling her awake. Her eyes were blurry, the sheets of paper laid before her on the table were melting into each other, the words indecipherable. She took a few deep breaths, pushing the hair stuck to her fore-head and tucking it behind her ear. The room slowly started to familiarize, the furniture finding its edges and the writing on the page sharpening.

The files were all on Sam Pope.

Singh had found herself tumbling down a rabbit hole of information as she dug deeper into the past of the man she'd been obsessed with catching. Now, she was hunting the truth. Sam saving her life in that shipping yard had shaken her through to her core, all the way to her belief in the justice system.

She had to know what put him on this path.

What made him this way?

Next to the papers, which were fanned out across her breakfast bar, was a mug of stone-cold coffee. Singh sighed, knowing she should get some sleep but the wave of excitement, the thrill of detecting rushed through her, shaking her awake harder than any dose of caffeine would.

She was a great detective.

And Amara Singh didn't fail.

Singh raised an eyebrow and looked across the living room to the front door of her flat. She glanced back up at the clock, the time was a little past one in the morning.

She was off duty.

Who the hell was calling for her at this time?

She stretched out her neck, the muscles sore from the awkward sleeping spot and lifted herself from her seat. Her back ached, cursing her for sleeping hunched over her files as opposed to the comfort of her bed. Singh straightened her spine, feeling a gentle click and then straightened out her work shirt. Tentatively, she made her way from the table across the living room, past the pristine leather sofa, opposite the flat screen TV. Both of them were as good as new and barely featured in her life. They'd been bought with every intention of snuggling down on the sofa and binge-watching Netflix.

Sadly, with the avalanche of work that came with being a detective, the time for that never arrived. If she wanted thrills, she would chase her own.

Singh slowly reached for the chain of the door and pressed her other hand to the handle. She gently lifted herself on her tiptoes and peered through the eyehole, getting a concaved view of the hall.

A large figure stood in the dark shadows, its back straight, its feet together.

A powerful stance.

'Who is it?' she called out, hoping her nerves didn't stowaway on her words.

'Detective Singh, please open the door. I need to speak to you.'

'Not without some identification,' she barked, relinquishing her grip and want to open the door.

'It's about Sam Pope.'

Singh felt her stomach turn and despite every part of her telling her to walk away, she allowed her curiosity to take the wheel. She reached out and released the chain and then quickly pulled the door open. Emerging from the shadows was a stocky, bald man, standing just under six foot. His world-weary face was wrinkled with time and his dark, black eyes carried wisdom and menace with equal measure. He wore a smart suit with an open collar, the blazer fitting snugly around his burly arms, the shirt sagging slightly under a protruding gut. His shoes gleamed under the light from Singh's living room and he extended a large, leathery hand.

'Detective Amara Singh?' he asked. She nodded.

'And you are?'

'General Ervin Wallace.' He offered a large smile to go with his handshake. Singh cautiously reached out her hand and slid it into his grip. The fingers squeezed her hand like a vice, and she racked her brain for a link to that name.

The man was a General, but had his name appeared in any of the files?

'I know and please accept my humble apologies for calling on you so late.' Wallace smiled, the friendly tone unsettling. 'May I come in?'

'What for?' Singh said sternly, attaching her small, powerful frame to the doorway.

'It would be best to speak inside.' He gestured again, a little firmer in tone.

'You said it's about Sam Pope. Not a matter of national security.'

'Ms Singh, when it comes to Sam Pope, it's *always* a matter of national security.'

The two of them shared an intense stare for just a moment before Singh's curiosity erupted like a volcano and she stepped back, ushering the senior military man inside and not knowing the danger she'd just willingly placed herself in.

CHAPTER EIGHT

Amara Singh flicked the switch of her coffee machine and then slid her lean frame into the thick, woolly hoody she'd retrieved from her bedroom. The winter cold had been creeping into her flat over the last few weeks and she shuddered as she reached for two mugs.

Was it the cold that caused her to chill?

Singh had always had a good intuition; it was one of the reasons she'd risen so quickly up the ranks within the Met. Those who pointed out her gender or ethnicity as the reason were those who lacked the intelligence or intestinal fortitude to climb themselves. That said, she was beginning to question how smart she was being right now.

In her living room, an unknown military official was waiting to discuss Sam Pope, the man she'd been tasked with catching and whom she owed her life to. If Assistant Commissioner Ashton were to find out about her snooping, she was sure she wouldn't only lose her position on the task force permanently, but possibly her cherished place within the Met.

'Sugar?' she called out.

'Two, please.' Came the gruff reply, the man's voice

carried with it a weight that commanded respect. Singh obliged, dropping two spoons full into the mug and then filling it with the now boiled coffee. Her entire body ached, craving sleep, but she knew it was unlikely.

A General wouldn't arrive at her house in the middle of the night if it wasn't important.

Singh made her way back to the living room, where General Wallace was stood by the fireplace, his arms behind his straight back and casting his eyes over the framed photos on Singh's mantel piece. Cherished snapshots of her life, the key moments that filled her with pride and love. Wallace turned from the photo of her passing out parade and offered her a warm smile. He gratefully accepted the mug and took a sip. Singh followed suit and then offered Wallace a seat.

'Thanks, but I'll stand,' he stated firmly. 'Detective Singh, exactly how much do you know about Sam Pope?'

Singh took another sip and then placed her mug down on the white coffee table. She gave up almost a foot in height to Wallace and his experience at commanding a room was evident.

'Sir, I know he is a danger to himself, to society and after what he did just over a week ago to my AR team, a threat to the Metropolitan Police.'

'Good answer.' Wallace said with a smile. 'Did you know that I personally commanded Pope for two tours?'

Like someone clicking their fingers in her brain, Singh linked the name Wallace to Sam. She looked up, feeling Wallace analysing her every movement.

'I did, yes.'

'Where did you find that information?' Wallace's tone carried a slightly tougher edge.

'Sir?'

'Where did you come across my name?' Wallace demanded, taking a step closer.

'I was doing some research on Sam.'

'Sam?' Wallace raised an eyebrow.

'Pope.' Singh corrected, cursing herself. 'When I was placed in charge of the task force to catch him, I pulled as much information as I could find. That was where I found your name, sir.'

Singh offered a firm nod, trying to hammer home the lie she'd just told. Wallace took another sip of his tea and then placed the mug down on the table too, he then turned on his heel and slowly walked back to the mantel piece, lifting the photo of Singh stood in her police tunic, her parents proudly stood either side of her in the Hendon sunshine.

'This must have been a very special day,' Wallace said, not looking up from the photo. 'I remember the pride my parents had every time I received a medal or made a new rank. Bless them. They've been dead a long time now, but you never lose that sense of satisfaction, do you? That feeling of knowing your parents are proud of you.'

Singh smiled and shrugged, looking towards the door. Wallace nodded and placed the photo back on the mantle-piece. Without turning, his voice boomed out, a tinge of authority wrapped around his words.

'Tell me, Detective, were your parents proud when you were unceremoniously kicked off the task force?' Singh startled and Wallace turned, his eyes locking onto her like a homing missile. 'Or have you not told them?'

Singh tried to gather her thoughts, desperately trying to fan away the red mist the comment was designed to create.

'That is none of your business, General,' Singh said.

'Oh, it is my business. Anything to do with that man, is *my* business. Do you know where he is now?'

'No, sir,' Singh said, trying to compose herself. 'There have been no sightings of Sam Pope since he left the Port of Tilbury over a week ago. Also, there have been no sightings of Carl Burrows, the chief aide to the former candidate—'

'Mark Harris, yes, I'm aware.' Wallace cut in dismissively. 'See, last night, reports came in that Sergei Kovalenko was brutally murdered in his own nightclub in Kiev, along with seven of his staff. The body of Carl Burrows was also found at the scene and all eyewitnesses claim that one man did it. Any guesses?'

Singh sighed, her anger bubbling below the surface but refusing to rise to Wallace's condescending tone. He continued.

'This is now a matter of international relations. Eastern Europe isn't going to be thrilled to know a British vigilante is spilling blood in their streets.' Wallace shook his head. 'I read through all the reports after Pope took down the Kovalenko's UK base of operations and it seems a number of people are questioning what part you played in it.'

'I saved the lives of four young girls, sir.'

'Hmmm… perhaps. There are also strong claims of collusion between Pope and yourself.'

'As I said in my report, he saved my life to help save the lives of the girls. I made the snap decision that finding four abducted kids was more important than stopping Pope.'

'See, the reports also state that you were ordered by your commanding officer to stay behind. Yet, you turned up at the very place Pope was and have now admitted you helped him.'

Singh felt her cheeks flush and her fists clench. The man was good, she had to give him that. With careful, measured steps, Wallace approached her, the size of his frame encasing her in shadow. Singh refused to flinch.

She never flinched.

Wallace stopped a foot away from her and leant in, his warm breath tickling her ear.

'There are no reports linking me to Sam Pope on any file in possession of the task force.' Singh felt her body tighten. 'Forget the words *Project Hailstorm*. Erase them from your mind. If not, I'll tie you to Sam in enough ways that they'll throw you in the deepest, darkest hole I can find. Do you understand me?'

Singh nodded, pulling her lips into a tight line, refusing to respond. Her knuckles were whitening, and she could feel her nails puncturing the flesh of her palms. Wallace patted her on the shoulder with his meaty hand and then strode across the room towards the front door. Yanking it open, the hallway light bathed him in a dark shadow. He turned one last time, his dark eyes burning a hole through Singh, which chilled her to her marrow.

'Stop digging, Singh. Before you get too far that I don't let you out.'

With a slam of the door, he was gone. Singh let out a deep breath and stumbled nervously across to her kitchen, pulling the fridge open. She took a bottle of beer from the shelf and then, with a shaking hand, popped the lid with the novelty bottle opener her sister had gotten her for her birthday.

Shaking, she took a swig of beer.

Singh knew she was in deep. The army were watching and now, unless she stepped carefully, she could lose it all. She took another large swig, knowing full well that the detective in her was about to lead her to a very bad decision.

―――――

Sam pressed the button to activate the automatic door and then stepped through into the next carriage. The overnight train from Kiev to Berlin was twenty-two carriages long, with eight of those designated sleeping zones. He had carefully made his way through five of them and now stepped into the first-class seating zone. The comfortable, leather seats were placed opposite their own individual tables and a few well-dressed gentlemen adorned several of the chairs. One of them was engrossed in the tablet in front of him, his noise cancelling headphones encasing him in the magic of his film.

Sam wandered to the end of the carriage and slowly lowered himself onto one of the seats, his leg aching. Sims had insisted Sam see a medical professional about the injuries sustained in the UK and Ukraine and although he ached like hell, Sam was grateful for the treatment.

At least he didn't have to worry about the bullet hole in his leg in anymore.

Sam turned his attention to the window, glancing out at the dark vista, not knowing where they were. He imagined, given the amount of time they'd been on the train, that they were racing through Poland, but he couldn't be sure. It had been a long time since he'd been to Germany and he was sad it wasn't on better terms.

The idea of sightseeing and then enjoying the fine, local ale was an empty hope from a life he would never have. All he had now was the aching pain through his body, the fear for his mentor's safety, and the very likely threat of prison at the end of it.

It was the road he'd chosen.

And one he walked fearlessly.

'You should be in bed.'

A voice cut through his thought process and Sam lifted his tired gaze upwards, to the smug sneer of Buck. Sims's right-hand man towered over him; his huge arms folded with his Marine tattoo sneaking out from under the sleeve of his polo shirt. His nose was purple, two plasters crisscrossed over the broken cartilage and dark bruising was appearing under his eyes.

Sam offered him a wry smile.

'Sorry, Daddy. I needed a glass of water.'

'Very fucking funny,' Buck spat; his New York accent was lighter than most.

'How's the nose?' Sam gestured at his own. 'And the arm?'

Buck leant down, so his broken face was level with Sam's. If it was an act of intimidation, it failed as Sam calmly returned the glare with a sigh.

'You know what, when this is over and we kill your friend, I'm going to beat the living fuck out of you.'

'Is that so?' Sam said, bored.

'You bet your ass.'

'I look forward to it.' Sam turned his gaze back to the window, when Buck reached out and grabbed his chin, yanking his head back. Sam immediately reached out, grabbed Buck's wrist, his finger trained to find and squeeze the pressure point. As Buck jolted in pain, Sam pushed himself to his feet, still holding the arm but before he could do any further damage, he heard the familiar click of a gun safety being unlatched.

'Sam, for Christ's sake, let him go.' Sims stood, the Sig Sauer he held was pointed directly at him. Sam begrudgingly obliged. Behind Sims, two further members of his crew stood. Another meathead, covered in tattoos and clear steroid induced veins and a young, slim mixed-raced girl with short, dark hair and piercing brown eyes.

'Sir,' Buck began. 'Let me kick his—'

'Shut the fuck up,' Sims barked angrily. 'Twice now, this man has made you his bitch so why don't you stick your tail between your legs and fuck off back to your room?'

Buck turned back to Sam with murderous intent. Sam offered a smile and a small wave.

'Yes, sir,' Buck finally said and stepped past him, heading back towards the cabin.

'Sweet dreams,' Sam yelled after him, provoking Buck to turn back, his eyes wide with anger. The other muscular soldier stepped in, ushering Buck towards the door and saving his comrade from further embarrassment. Sam sat back down in his seat and returned to gazing out of the window. Sims holstered his handgun and placed his hands on his hips, shaking his head like a teacher.

'It's not wise to piss off my soldiers, Sam.'

'Like I said, they're not soldiers,' Sam responded quickly, his eyes still searching the dark outside.

'Try to get some sleep. My sources tell me we won't have much of a window tomorrow.' Sims turned to head back down the carriage.

'Sims,' Sam called out, grabbing his attention. 'Just let me talk to him, okay?'

Sims smirked.

'Goodnight, Sam.'

As Sims marched back down the corridor, he glared at the two other passengers who had been distracted by the confrontation and similarly scared by the gun. Sims knew the scowl he shot them would keep them quiet for the remainder of the trip. He walked past the young, female member of his crew and nodded, before stomping through the door and back towards his quarters.

The young woman, dressed in black khakis and the Blackridge polo shirt they all wore, approached Sam.

'Can't sleep.'

Sam shook his head, offering little in way of response.

'My name is Stone. Alex Stone.' She extended her hand, but Sam didn't move. After a few moments, she sheepishly retracted it. 'I don't know about you but spending time with these assholes is tough work.' Sam turned and met her smile with a raised eyebrow. 'I could use a drink. Coming?'

A smile broke across Sam's stubbled, slightly cut jaw.

'Are you going to try to kill me?'

Alex shrugged playfully, her New York accent was deep and unmistakable.

'I wasn't planning on it.'

'Good enough.'

Sam lifted himself out of the chair and followed Alex to the door, realising in that one moment, he wanted nothing more than a cold beer.

The train shot through the dark, continuing its journey to Berlin.

CHAPTER NINE

'I don't think you have much choice.'

Trevor Sims leant back in his chair, folding his arms and placing them across his slight gut. His shirt was stained with sweat and his greasy head was shimmering. The lighting in the room didn't help, the long, halogen bulbs hummed loudly as they pumped the room with heat. In front of him on the table, was a file filled to the brim with damning evidence.

Alex Stone said nothing.

The room was dank and empty apart from the metal table she was cuffed to and the two chairs either side which were occupied. On the wall was a large mirror, obviously a two way, but who was watching she didn't know.

She didn't care.

She was about to lose her family.

It had been a tough road to this point, and she wasn't blameless in the direction it had gone. Over time, she'd made some bad decisions, but usually for the greater good. Despite breaking the law, she was never a criminal.

Alex Stone had never done anything for personal gain.

She had too much to lose, which meant there was easily a way to leverage her. The type of scenario that a man like Trevor Sims thrived on. Slowly, he placed a thick cigar between his lips and with the flick of his wrist, a match sparked into life. They were in the seventy-eight precinct NYPD station in Brooklyn, only five blocks down from where Alex lived with her siblings.

She was just returning home. Nothing out of the ordinary.

The men who accompanied the officers to her location, the seven-eleven where she was picking up some milk, had been decked out in polo shirts and sunglasses.

They weren't police.

Government, maybe?

All she knew was the unit was called Blackridge and the man sat before her, puffing clouds of thick, dark smoke into the room and over-casting them both, was the man in charge. Whoever he was, he clearly held some sway to not only use the police like his personal lap dogs, but he could violate the smoking law in their very building.

Alex sat on her hands, her toned, brown arms were covered in a few random tattoos of skulls and butterflies, permanent reminders of her previous life.

She'd gone straight.

But clearly, not straight enough.

After a few more awkward moments of silence, only broken by the theatrical puffs of the cigar, Sims sat up straight again, resting his hands on the table. Alex's hands also rested on the table, unwillingly. The chain of her hand cuffs had been latched under a metal bar, pinning them in place.

Sims smiled and then reached for the file once again.

'Let's go through this again, shall we, Ms Stone?' He flashed her a smile. 'You're twenty-six years old, correct?'

She nodded.

'Correct?' Sims's voice echoed with authority.

'Yes, sir.'

'It says here, you attended four months of police training when you were twenty-one. You attended community college to get the neces-sary credits, which is very impressive. Remind me, why did you need to attend the community college?'

Alex shuffled uncomfortably on her seat, knowing full well the question was rhetorical. Outside, she could hear the hustle and bustle of the NYPD police station.

'It says here that you were expelled from your school for fighting. Looking through your file, I see that this is probably linked to your home life. Pill popping mom, three kids, no dad. Must have been hard.'

Alex felt her fist clench but took a few deep breaths. Take five and keep calm.

'Anyway, you turned it all around, even helped your mom get off the pills and then what? Thought you would give back to the community? Become a respected officer of the law? Thing is, what we didn't cover is between the ages of fifteen to nineteen, you participated in…' Sims theatrically checked the file. '…over ninety illegal street races. Is that correct?'

Again, Alex said nothing.

'So, not only did you break the law, you lied about it, am I right? You used your father's name, Willis, instead of Stone. Surely, you must have known they would soon connect the dots. I mean, it wasn't straight away but shit always comes out in the wash, darlin'.'

'What do you want from me?'

Sims smiled. It was a question he loved hearing, especially when he'd backed them into a corner with no other option but to ask it.

'I need you to drive for me.'

'Excuse me?' Alex tried to raise her hands in confusion, but the chain caught tight and the metal dug painfully into her wrists.

'Look, I know your mom is back on the pills. Which is why you're back behind the wheel.' Sims caught the flash of panic in Alex's eye and latched on like a cobra pouncing on its kill. 'Trust me, they know out there. They have enough evidence here to put you away. Not only that, but that means Nattie and Joel will be put away too.'

Suddenly, a wave of emotion crashed into Alex and she felt the tears rush forward. Sims smirked, enjoying the moment of someone breaking to him.

Time to go for the kill.

Alex, I know you've been working shifts at that diner to make it look like you have a job, but I know it's just a front. You're racing illegally again and this time, there is no slap on the wrist and get back to your buddies. No, this time, you'll probably be sent to Rikers, where a girl as lovely as yourself will get passed around like a bong at Woodstock.'

Alex felt herself shaking, the fury of having her beloved younger siblings threatened angered her more than the idea of being sent to prison. After a few moments, she regained her composure and exhaled.

'You need a driver?' she asked, returning to the fact of the matter. Sims took a victorious puff on his cigar.

'Yup. I need someone who can drive to join my team. And when I say drive, I don't mean the way they teach you here in the academy. I need someone who drives like there's no other way out. Do I make myself clear?'

Shaking her head, Alex thought of her younger brother and sister. Nattie was halfway through high school. A straight 'A' student with a love for science, Alex knew her sister could go on to do great things. Joel was a freshman but was already one of the top football players in the school and was destined for a sports scholarship.

Both of them had bright futures, ready to be shrouded in her own dark past.

If she went down, they would be taken into care. Their mother was a non-factor and her drug addiction would mean they would be taken by the state.

Maybe even split up.

Knowing the statistics of kids going into care, Alex had been doing whatever she could to give them the best life possible.

She would do whatever it took.

'If I drive for you, I want guarantees that my brother and sister will be taken care of. The state stays away.'

'I'll do enough to keep the wolves from the door. They can stay where they are and in their school.' Sims leant forward, his face twisting into a smarmy, evil scowl. 'But if you fuck me over or step

out of line, I'll make damn sure you never see them again. Are we clear?'

Alex nodded, furious with the situation and at being blackmailed. Whoever this Sims was, whoever he worked for, they were high up. To wield that much power was terrifying, especially when it allowed them to manipulate a petty street racer into a potentially dangerous job.

But Alex had promised she would do whatever it took, and it was a promise she intended to keep.

———

'That was just over a year ago,' Alex said, taking a sip of the unbranded beer in the label less bottle they'd procured from the bar. Sam shook his head, amazed that his opinion of Sims could fall even lower.

'Jesus. I'm sorry.'

'Don't be. I just feel kinda bad that I saw him do the same thing to you and didn't try to stop it.'

Sam took a swig of his beer and shook his head.

'Don't be silly. I'm big enough and ugly enough to fight my own battles. Besides, Sims and I sort of go back. He knows how to push people's buttons to get them to do his bidding. It's why he runs his own task force and it's why he's so high up on the list of the biggest arseholes.'

Alex chuckled.

'Arse?' She laughed again. Sam smiled, finding himself enjoying a friendly conversation for a change. The last few weeks had been intense, whether he was ripping through the underbelly of London looking for abducted girls or engaging in warfare with Ukrainian mobsters. Even Singh, who he found himself thinking about, was after him.

It was nice to just have a pleasant conversation, regardless of the manipulative circumstances it was under.

'You know, I know that feeling,' Sam began, pausing to have a quick swig of his beer before continuing. 'That feeling that no matter what you do, you can't save those closest to you. It eats at you. Up here. It chews away at your mind until you need to do something to let it all out.'

'Is that why you do what you do?' Alex asked.

'What I do?'

The train shook slightly, the carriage taking a bend through a field at breakneck speed and reminded both of them where they were.

'Sims said you used to be the most lethal sniper he'd ever seen. That you were a killing machine.' Alex noticed Sam look uncomfortable. 'He then said something sent you loopy and you became a criminal.'

'The man has a way with words.'

Sam finished off his beer and with a firm shake of his head, slammed the bottle down on the table.

'For what it's worth, I don't think you're loopy.'

Sam offered Alex a forced smile. Her light brown skin shimmered in the dull lighting of the carriage. She was very attractive; Sam couldn't deny it. But what was drawing him to her was their similarity. They were both beaten and broken by their previous lives, which they were now paying for.

They were both doing what they thought was right.

Doing the only thing they knew how to.

'No offence, Alex. You don't know me.' Sam hated feeling ashamed of the things he'd once been so proud of. He ran a hand through his short hair. 'I've done a lot of bad things in my life. Whether they were orders or not, these hands have a lot of blood on them. I might not be a soldier anymore and what I do is against the law, but I'm not a criminal.'

Alex reached out and rested her hand on Sam's arm. He flinched slightly; it had been an awfully long time since he felt any sort of intimacy from a woman.

He thought of Lucy. How happy they'd been before

everything disintegrated into painful fragments of a previous life.

He thought of Singh, how their paths had crossed in two very different directions.

Now his mind was on Alex.

Slowly, he turned, his green eyes catching hers and he took a deep breath. The nerves were not about the possibility of them sleeping together. They were for what he was about to confess.

'Nearly four years ago, my son, Jamie, was killed by a drunk driver.' Sam saw the horror on Alex's face, but he continued, refusing to let the pain overpower him. 'Due to some technicality, the driver got off after a year. A year. Anyway, I fell off when Jamie died. I closed up and eventually my wife walked away. I had a voicemail on my phone, my son telling me he wanted me to come home. That he loved me.' Sam could feel a tear forming in the corner of his eye. He continued, 'I kept it on my phone this whole time I was grieving, refusing to let go. Until I'd found something to replace that pain. A purpose.'

'So, what did you do?'

'I was so angry, so consumed with revenge that I found the guy who took him from me.'

Alex stared at Sam, tears streaming down her face. Her voice broke as she spoke.

'Did you kill him?'

'I tried to.' Sam's voice shook and he wiped a tear away with the sleeve of his shirt. 'But I couldn't. I had him right there, but I walked away. Because I knew the only way to stop my pain was to make sure other people didn't go through it too. That I would find justice when the system couldn't. It's been a long road since that night, and I have no idea where it's heading or for how long. But Marsden, he is one of the few people I have left who I care about and if he's in trouble, then I need to help him.'

Alex leant in closer, her face a few inches from Sam's ear. Her breath tickled his neck and he felt his body tighten.

She smelt terrific.

'Is that why you agreed to come? To save him?'

Sam turned to her, their faces a few inches apart. Her perfect skin was glistening from the tears. He reached out and wiped it dry.

'I'm going to find out what the hell is going on.' Sam lowered his hand and his fingers found hers. They intertwined and then locked in, his murderous hands engulfing her skilled ones. 'When all of this is done, I will help you, Alex. I'll help you get out of this and get your family back.'

She chortled slightly, shaking her head as she leaned in closer to him, her forehead resting against his.

'Why? You don't even know me.'

Sam felt her move in a little closer, their lips almost touching.

'It's the right thing to do.'

Sam pressed his lips against hers, the electricity between them shaking him like a bolt of lightning. She wrapped her hands around his neck, pulling him closer to her with a furious passion. After a few moments, they released and with a few other patrons watching on with a wry smile, Alex Stone stood up from her chair, took Sam by the hand and purposefully led him back towards the overnight carriages.

CHAPTER TEN

Just after two o'clock the following afternoon, the train slowly pulled into Berlin Central Station. The capital of Germany welcomed them with the bitter cold that was spreading through Europe, with every country doing its level best to remind everyone it was only a few weeks until Christmas.

The station, a magnificent, glass structure in the centre of the city, was a cavalcade of traffic, with commuters from all walks of life rushing through the giant station in varying stages of panic. It was a gigantic creation spread across two wide, long floors, each one packed with eateries and shops. Large escalators connected the two floors, allowing passengers to manoeuvre to one of the seven large platforms. Sixteen separate tracks wormed through the station like veins, each one running punctually in different directions.

An underground section housed two further platforms, allowing people to ride the underground train as well as using the connecting subways to manoeuvre through the station without hitting the heavy foot traffic on the main concourse. Above the second floor was a third tier, with entrances towards the car park, but also to allow the security guards to patrol, casting their eyes down from their vantage point to ensure the safety of their commuters.

As the train came to a stop, Sam stood in the corridor of the train, surrounded by the black polo shirts and shifty glances of the Blackridge crew. To his right, Alex Stone leant against a wall, her headphones in and her thoughts with her family. After they'd made their way back to their cabin, they'd undressed in a matter of moments, two trapped and lonely people finding solace in another.

They'd made love twice through the night, before Sam left, telling her he would keep his promise to help her. She made a crude comment about how he already had, but then told him to be careful.

There was no future for them, they both knew it. Their lives were too strained, too wrapped up in their own mess to clear up another.

Sims meandered out from his cabin, his thinning hair still wet from the shower and Sam noticed he'd cut himself shaving. It was the little details Sam had been trained to remember, knowing anything could be turned into his advantage. He knew that of the three Blackridge members who joined them, two were left-handed. Buck and the other crew member, called Ray, were both left-handed, their holsters strapped to their left hip. He noticed that Alex had a metal chain running from her belt to her back pocket.

That Sims kept his cigar cutter in his back-right pocket.

It was something Sam had been conditioned to do, to memorise and assess. He subconsciously counted his steps when moving from one point to another, allowing himself to calculate how quickly he could retreat or move to similar distances before he arrived.

It made him highly efficient, only adding to his terrifying prowess with a sniper rifle.

'I trust everyone slept well,' Sims said dryly, flashing a

look towards Sam and Buck, a reference to their confrontation the night before. Sam shot a quick look to Alex, who returned a wry smile.

'Yes, sir,' Buck said enthusiastically. 'Ready to catch this cockroach.'

Sam ignored the clear attempt to wind him up and cracked his knuckles. He was wearing the same clothes as the day before, refusing to wear a Blackridge polo shirt. Sims had told him his bag had been intercepted at Kiev airport, but Sam was sure he wouldn't see it again.

It was a shame. He'd grown attached to his assault rifle.

The train came to a complete stop and the seated passengers in the carriage rose to their feet, wrestling with the overhead storage bins and vying for their spot in the queue to debark.

The door dinged and Sims pressed a gloved finger to the button, releasing the lock on the door and careful not to leave a trace. The doors slowly slid open and Sims stepped out into the bitter chill, pulling his scarf tight and zipping up his coat. Sam went to step off the train next, cutting in front of Buck, who instantly rose to the provocation. Angrily reaching out and grabbing Sam by the lapel of his leather jacket, he pulled him from the door and slammed him against the wall. Ray took a step, assuring Buck of his back up and Sam held both his hands up in surrender. The other passengers on the train watched with concern.

'Jesus,' Sam said. 'Sorry.'

'Don't fucking push me,' Buck spat, his bruised eyes narrowing with fury. He shoved Sam one final time before storming off the train, pleased to have asserted his dominance. Ray sneered at Sam and then followed like a shadow. Alex didn't say anything, but raised her eyebrow at Sam.

Sam held up his hand, his fingers wrapped around Buck's mobile phone.

She smiled and then stepped off the train, followed closely by Sam himself. As they made their way down the platform, Sam grimaced as the cold wind bit at him, his jacket and shirt nowhere near enough to fight off the freezing temperature of Germany. Sims had made no effort to make him more comfortable and the further Sam went down this rabbit hole, the harder he knew it would be to get out.

There was no way Sims would let him walk away.

The prestige he would receive for handing Sam over to the authorities would be too much for Sims to turn down. Sam knew that, but it didn't matter. One day, he would undoubtedly have to face the law for the crimes he'd committed and people he'd put in the ground. But all he cared about was finding Marsden and discovering what the hell was going on.

As they passed through the ticket barrier, two more military types approached, both decked out in black parker jackets and woollen hats. The 'BR' logo of Blackridge adorning them all.

At least they were consistently on brand.

The duo was also American, a man and a woman, both looking jacked up and ready for action. Combining that first impression with the gung-ho Buck and his lackey, Sam was wondering if it was a pre-requisite for joining to be a gun happy, adrenaline junkie.

'Welcome to Berlin, sir.' The guy welcomed Sims, his thick beard greying round the edges. All of them but Sam were armed, their handguns concealed within their thick coats. 'The German police want a word.'

Sims nodded and followed the man across to a group of German police officers. Sam had no doubt that Sims had jurisdiction. How, he would never know. But Sims was a slimy character, and would no doubt owe favours to some nefarious, yet powerful people.

The international world of espionage and terror was a mystery and one Sam didn't want to be in for too long. The crew were all watching the conversation between Sims and the local authorities, no doubt in awe at their boss's command for respect. As they did, Sam tried to unlock Buck's phone, the screen flashing on but demanding a passcode.

Shit.

Sam pocketed the device and then rubbed his hands together, blowing into them to fight the bitterness that patrolled the platform. Sims patted one of the men on the arm and then turned back to his crew. His face was twisted in a smug grin and Sam rolled his eyes.

'All good,' Sims said proudly. 'They said they appreciate the severity of the situation and are willing to help anyway they can. I've told them we'll need extra spotters on the top tier where myself, Sam, and Buck will be. Evans, bring everyone up to speed.'

Evans, the bearded man who greeted them stepped forward, clearly in charge of the second squadron.

'We've located Marsden to be staying in *Friedrichstraße*, just south of Mitte. He arrived three days ago and from what we have surveilled, he has procured travel documents and is looking to move out soon.' Evans clicked his fingers and one of his crew handed him a tablet. With a few flicks of his finger he activated the screen and turned it to the group.

'Now, one of my men has spoken to the man who provided the documents to Marsden, who has said he's leaving today by train.'

'How did you get him to talk?' Alex asked. The whole group raised their eyebrows. Evans and Sims both smiled before Sims answered.

'My guys are very… how should we say… persuasive.'

Sam knew what they meant. Whoever the poor guy was who had helped Marsden had been tortured and most likely killed. Either that, or they would hide him away where no one would hear his complaints. Evans continued, shooting a disapproving glare at Alex who put her headphones back on.

'Now Marsden is on the run and will be travelling light. From what we know, he is not armed, but due to his training, we should treat him as hostile and dangerous.' Sam shook his head, attracting attention. 'You got a problem with that?'

Sam looked up to see Evans staring at him. Buck, stood beside him with his arms folded, looked on eagerly.

'No, you seem to have done all your homework.'

'Fuck you,' Evans spat. 'Ignoring Hugh fucking Grant over there, does anyone have any questions?'

'Just one,' the other female member spoke up. 'How do we identify him?'

'I've circulated his photo to the Federal Police, who will be walking the concourses and platforms for us. We'll take up our position on the main gates on this level. Sir, yourself, Buck, and dick-head over there are on the top tier.'

Evans shoved a thumb in Sam's direction, getting a few chortles from the rest of the team. Sam smiled, knowing all of them would turn on him in a heartbeat.

'One last thing,' Evans said. 'During our surveillance, Marsden has been in a red and grey ski coat. He hasn't been alerted to our presence, so we expect him to still have it. Eyes open people.'

Sims stepped forward, asserting his dominance over the group of mercenaries who held him in such esteem. Despite Sam's objections to their cause, he was impressed with the devotion Sims had garnered.

'You heard the man, folks. Let's bring this bastard down.'

Sims handed everyone an earpiece, and Sam slid his into his left ear. The teams split, with Evans leading himself, Alex, Ray, and the other lady towards the main concourse, while Sims marched towards the escalators, ready to ascend to the next floor up and then take a private stairwell up to the top tier. Buck followed closely, but Sam scurried up next to the man in charge.

'Sims, I think it would be best if I was down here. If we find him, I may be able to speak with him and see what's actually going on.'

'We've been over this, Sam,' Sims said without breaking his stride. 'You're not here to have a conversation, you're here to instruct me on how Marsden will approach his departure.'

'If he is in any danger, or you do anything to put him in danger, I'll…'

Buck stepped between Sims and Sam; his battered eyes wide with fury.

'You'll what?' Buck demanded, chest puffed out, clearly ready to try to wrestle back his pride.

'Really?' Sam shrugged. 'Don't make a tit of yourself again.'

Buck stepped forward but Sims put an arm across his chest, dragging him back. Irate, Sims stepped up to Sam.

'You better start fucking listening, Sam. You're not out on one of your little missions, taking on drug dealers or fucking pimps. Like it or not, Marsden is currently being hunted for terrorism. Now put aside your loyalty and look at the bigger fucking picture. If he needs help, then we'll help him, but right now, our intel says he stole pertinent information and is now running from both our governments.'

'There has to be a reason,' Sam said defiantly.

'And I will find it. But right now, I need you to shut up, fall in line, and for the love of God, stop humiliating my fucking men.'

Buck's shoulders slumped slightly as he followed his leader onto the escalator. Sam accepted the back-handed compliment but took a moment to scan the platform and the entrance to the concourse. It was a blissfully hopeful attempt to locate Marsden, which he knew was futile. As he stepped onto the escalator and began his ascent, he felt the noose tightening around his mentor's neck, as well as the rope uncomfortably rubbing against his own throat.

As they made their way to the top tier, Sam was beginning to hope that Marsden had rethought his plans.

The police were patrolling.

Blackridge were spread out, ready to pounce.

As they reached the top walkway, Sam stood, looking out over the entire station, the German public no wiser to the mission that was being played out around them. Up high, the cold rose, lashing against the thin layers of Sam's clothing and chilling him to the core. To his left, Buck and Sims stood vigilante.

Two hours passed.

Just as an irritated Sims was about to call for a regroup, the excited voice of Evans crackled through every earpiece.

'I have eyes on Marsden.'

CHAPTER ELEVEN

It had been six days since Sam had been shipped back from Afghanistan. Usually, it was to the fanfare of the Army, a number of high-ranking officials waiting to shake his hand and place another medal to his chest.

A pat on the back by his commander.

A kiss from his patient, adoring wife.

This time, he'd come back on a stretcher, his life in the balance and his career in the army finished. Six days, and Sam hadn't moved.

Nurses came and went.

Doctors cast their eyes over him.

Lucy sat vigil by his side, refusing to leave her husband. Marsden assumed she'd arranged for her parents to look after their infant son. Jamie.

It broke Marsden's heart the first time he'd walked into the room.

While he'd been tasked with recruiting the elite team, he himself was not part of the mission. After a long, decorated career, Marsden was now able to command a safer role, one which prepared the best of the best for the next level. The covert work that the government didn't want to know about.

Project Hailstorm.

The entire mission had been shrouded in secrecy since day one, with General Ervin Wallace tasking Marsden with pulling together an elite extraction team that would be capable of infiltrating and disbanding multiple terrorist cells. A team capable of over throwing governments, liberating oppressed cities and fighting the wars that would never be won.

That's what he'd believed.

Now, as he walked into the hospital room for the sixth, straight day, all he felt was guilt. Guilt that he'd promised Sam Pope a glittering end to his formidable career, but instead had sent him into the bowels of hell.

From the vague reports, the mission went as smoothly as intended, with the Alpha Team infiltrating an Al-Qaeda hideout based on intelligence of a potential chemical weapon. After eradicating the enemy, Sam had been found in a room near the back of the run-down building, two bullet holes in his chest and grasping onto life by his fingertips.

He should have died, then and there.

In the dark in the middle of nowhere.

But he didn't. He fought, and Corporal Murray had carried him to safety, ignoring the apparent orders to leave him behind as collateral damage.

Sam Pope deserved better than that.

From the British Military Service.

From Marsden.

As he entered the room, he noted Lucy curled up on a nearby chair, her coat draped over her like a quilt. Her usual, radiant smile had dissipated long ago, her skin a ghostly pale and her cheek bones more prominent than usual. She needed a hearty meal and a good night's sleep. But Marsden knew she wouldn't. He'd never met Lucy before, but had heard loving stories from Sam under the star-spangled skies of the desert. They were clearly in love, and Sam's resolve to return to her from every mission had seen him beat the odds when a lesser man would have been killed.

Marsden could understand why.

Not only was Lucy a stunningly beautiful woman, but she doted on Sam. Her horror at seeing him strapped to a table, his chest a bullet-riddled mess, had almost brought her to her knees, but she'd refused, she was strong like her husband and she demanded he fight it and come back to her and their son.

She was a good woman.

A wonderful wife.

He just hoped they would be together again.

To her right was a small side table, where her handbag, mobile phone, and an empty glass of water sat. Next to that, was Sam's motionless body. With heavy, guilt-ridden steps, Marsden approached the metal bar that ran around the side of the mattress, careful not to make a sound. Although he hadn't pulled the hangman's switch, he felt like he'd led Sam to the trapdoor.

Sam's eyes were closed, they had been since he'd been discovered, and his shirtless body was covered in bloodstained bandages. The man had been through six hours of life saving surgery, the two gunshots wreaking havoc through his lungs, ripping through them with murderous intent. A few millimeters to the left and the superior vena cava would have been severed, stopping the blood flow to his head and causing serious brain damage, if not killed him.

With the blood loss, damage to his lungs, and lack of oxygen he experienced, there was still a chance Sam would have further complications beyond the mental scarring of being left to die in the dark.

'Awful,' the voice boomed behind him. 'Just awful.'

Marsden felt a chill dance down his spine, turning on his heel to be greeted by a solemn looking General Ervin Wallace. Wearing smart shirt and trousers, Wallace's well-polished shoes clicked loudly against the tiled floor of UCHL in Euston, one of the leading medical training hospitals in the world. Marsden took a deep breath, feeling himself instantly fire up, sweat threatening to pool through his light blue shirt.

The hangman had just walked in.

Wallace shot a glance at Sam's sleeping wife and dismissed her with a raised eyebrow. He approached the bed, standing next to Marsden, his wide, powerful frame in complete contrast to Marsden's slim, lean *physique*. The two of them had served their country proudly for over two-and-a-half decades, with a begrudging respect formed between them. Since Wallace had gone 'off the books', Marsden had seen a darker side to the man.

It was as if Wallace preferred fighting the war beneath the war.

Wallace looked over Sam and shook his head with a deep sigh. Marsden felt his temper threaten once again.

'Hello, Ervin,' Marsden offered, almost through gritted teeth.

'It's a terrible shame,' Wallace continued. 'Such a good man.'

'He is a good man.'

Marsden angrily turned to Wallace, their dark eyes locking and daring the other to blink.

'What the fuck happened out there?' Marsden's anger surprised them both and Wallace frowned.

'We did our goddamn jobs. We stopped the bad guys and we kept the innocent people safe.'

'Why were there orders to leave Sam, huh? Who gave that order? You?' Marsden could feel his rage taking control, and his raised voice had alerted Lucy who slowly blinked herself awake. Wallace noticed too, smiling as she would act as a deterrent.

'Look, Carl. You and I both know what this life is like. Sam has lived and breathed being a soldier for over a decade and we all know there are no guarantees in this war.' Wallace stepped in closely. 'And believe me, Carl, this is a war. Terrorism isn't curable. It needs to be killed.'

Marsden offered Lucy a comforting smile, trying to placate her confusion. The last thing she needed was to come face to face with the man who had led her husband into the slaughterhouse. Gently, Marsden leant in and lowered his voice.

'Whatever Project Hailstorm is setting out to achieve, it's not worth the lives of our men.'

'Oh, I agree,' Wallace said firmly. 'But the war rages on, Carl. And I intend to fight it.'

With the command of a high-ranking official, Wallace turned on his heel and headed back to the door, offering a warm smile to Lucy on his way out. As the clicking of his shoes disappeared down the corri-dor, Marsden turned back to Sam, his heart aching at the condition of his friend. Slowly, Lucy's frail frame appeared next to him. She yawned, still trying to launch herself into the new day.

'Hey,' she said sleepily. 'Who was that?'

Marsden shot a concerned look over his shoulder towards the door, ensuring Wallace had completely gone.

'No one,' he replied, cursing himself for lying. Both of them stood and watched, as Sam, lay motionless, not knowing when or if he would return to them.

———

New Scotland Yard was a beehive of activity the following morning, with the news of Sam Pope's assault on the Ukrainian gangster, Sergei Kovalenko and his establish-ment sending Ashton and the Sam Pope task force into overdrive. The press had also cottoned on, with images of the night club hitting all the news outlets, along with inter-views with the girls Sam had liberated.

They were calling him a hero.

As she burst into the office, she felt a number of suspi-cious eyes latch onto her, the rumours of collusion would surely heighten. Sam had killed another seven people. Among the dead was a British politician, Carl Burrows, whose throat had been slit.

The murderer was pinned as Sam, but Singh didn't believe it.

He killed criminals. Not dodgy politicians.

As she walked through the office, she could see Ashton in the incident room, stood in front of a group of eager detectives, gesticulating wildly at the Sam Pope board. A fresh push had seen his place of residence found, with a large map of London, colour coded with stickers now front and centre of the room. Singh tried to peer through the blinds, keen to see the latest piece of evidence.

'They busted his house,' Pearce's voice startled her, and he held up a hand in apology. In his other, a warm cup of coffee, which Singh was immediately envious of. After her late-night visit from Sam's past, she hadn't been able to sleep, and her body craved a caffeine boost. It was if Pearce could read her mind. 'Coffee? It's fresh.'

'Thanks.' Singh gratefully accepted, taking a long sip before nodding back to the glass. 'What did they find?'

'A treasure trove. They found a wardrobe full of guns. I'm talking assault rifles, shotguns, pistols. Quite the collection.'

'Landlord?'

'Some Greek guy who was none the wiser. Said Sam kept himself to himself, paid in cash, and most importantly, on time.'

Singh took another sip.

'And that?'

'The coup de grâce. Crime spots, hideouts, safe houses, armouries. Sam had them mapped out. The High Rises were on there, which means he wasn't just out huntin' wabbits.'

Singh raised her eyebrow at Pearce's lame attempt at humour and found herself liking him more.

'He's smart,' she eventually offered.

'He's trained,' Pearce added. 'The man is trained to fight, kill, and survive. Thing is, the media want to portray him as a hero while Ashton and the higher ups want to portray him as a dangerous killer.'

Singh took a final long sip and looked thankfully at her senior colleague.

'How would you portray him?'

Pearce took a moment, rubbing his grey beard in thought.

'As a human,' he finally offered. 'As a broken man doing whatever he can to help those who need it.'

'You'd make a martyr out of him?' Singh said, clearly trying to provoke him.

'Nope. But I wouldn't drag him over the coals either.'

'Nor would I,' Singh said with a sigh. 'I think there's more to Sam's past than we've been allowed to see. Have you heard of Project Hailstorm?'

Pearce stepped in closer, his eyes widening slightly.

'Amy Devereaux mentioned it,' Pearce said, his voice a mere whisper. 'But Sam wouldn't speak about it.'

'Well, I found a form in Sam's file with a note about it and I searched the files. Then in the middle of the night, I get a visit from Sam's old commander. General Wallace.'

'General Ervin Wallace?' Pearce said, his voice an equal balance of regard and caution.

'Yeah. Do you know him?'

'I know he's a very powerful man. He has helped CID with a few cases that needed, how should I put it, certain doors opening.' Pearce shook his head. 'Whatever it is you think you stumbled on, shelf it. I wouldn't start digging in his garden.'

Singh stared at the empty cup in her hand, annoyed that the cautious words of Pearce were correct. Although the man had tanked his own career helping Sam, she knew this was different. Pearce had helped Sam take down a crime syndicate within the police.

She was potentially going up against a secret layer of the military.

Pearce was right.

Every sensible, logical fibre of her being was telling her to walk away.

A vision of the shipping yard flashed into her brain, of her on her knees, bleeding after fighting two men who were now aiming a gun at her. She was about to die in the pouring rain.

Sam saved her.

He'd saved her life and the lives of those innocent girls.

Because it was the right thing to do.

Pearce stood, hands on hips, a wry smile on his face as if once again, he could read her mind.

'I can't walk away from this,' she said firmly, before marching off towards the stairwell, a renewed sense of purpose pumping through her veins. Pearce sighed, feeling every day of his fifty-plus years. He chuckled, before following in Singh's direction.

'I didn't think so,' he said to himself, resigned to following Singh further down the rabbit hole.

CHAPTER TWELVE

Sam felt every single one of his cold muscles tighten, his body tensing as he listened to the Blackridge team discuss moving in on Marsden. Trapped all the way up on the third tier, Sam felt useless. Sims was staring out, a pair of binoculars held up to his eyes, watching his elite team stalk their prey. Behind him, Buck watched vigilantly, his arms folded, his massive frame blocking Sam from the stairwell.

To the other side of the walkway, three German officers stood, all of them watching with interest. All of them obstructing Sam's path to the escalator.

Sam needed to find the path of least resistance. And quick.

crackle target is approaching Coffee Shop on east side... *crackle*... on the move... *crackle*

Sims pressed his finger to his ear for more clarity and then gave the order.

'Any force necessary. I repeat, use any force necessary.'

The order to kill to his men was also an order to jump into action for Sam. Quickly, Sam stepped slightly behind Buck and gently placed his stolen mobile phone onto the ground. Silently, he stood back up, nudging the phone closer to Buck until the device was a few inches from his foot. With Sims peering out with his binoculars, not wanting to join the action, Sam knew he had one chance at incapacitating both of them if he stood any hope of reaching Marsden first.

Sam took a deep breath.

'Hey, Buck, is that your phone?'

Buck turned, his eyebrows furrowing with irritation at the sight of his phone. With a grunt, he turned to his side, arching down and reaching out for it with his thick, muscular arm. Sam quickly shot his arm out to Buck's waist, relieving his belt of its pair of handcuffs. Buck, off balance, shouted in dismay, but Sam used his balance to his advantage, Swiftly, he drew his right leg behind Buck's standing leg and swept him clean off the floor. The hulking man twisted in the air, landing awkwardly on the metal floor with a thud, yelling in pain and alerting his boss.

Sims turned, his face colliding with the ferocious right hook Sam connected with, knocking the man off balance. Behind him, Sam could hear the furious cries of the German police, their footsteps thudding loudly as they zeroed in on him. Sam snapped the cuff around Buck's wrist, pinning him face down to the metal with a knee. He yanked the man's shoulder back towards the barrier that framed the tier they were stood on. Sam slid the handcuff around one of the iron joints of the barrier and then slapped the other cuff around Sims's wrist, the commander still woozy from his vicious blow.

'Get the fuck off me,' Buck yelled, struggling against the pressure Sam applied. The German officers were less than ten feet away and Sam quickly stuffed his hand into Buck's pocket, found the key to the cuffs and threw it as hard as he could into the station.

Sam set off to the stairwell, the three German officers

on his tail and a bloodthirsty Buck attached to his commander.

———

On the ground, Evans, Ray, Alex, and the other lady, nick-named 'Rocky', were slowly following Marsden, watching as he weaved between the families and tourists that were quickly filling up the concourse. Evans clocked a few police officers who were also showing interest, pleased that the local authorities had been so helpful. He was sure Sims had promised them a generous bonus payment.

The man had his way of dealing with problems. Evans may not have liked Sims personally, but he respected the man's bullish refusal to accept no for an answer.

Evans motioned to Rocky to head down the subway stairs, wanting to ensure they had eyes below if Marsden decided to change direction or make a break for it.

Not on Evans's watch.

With careful steps, Evans kept to the edge of the concourse, cautiously walking across the busy doorways to a number of eateries. Customers rushed in and out and one young, attractive blonde woman almost covered him in piping hot coffee.

He offered her a curt smile and then moved past her. He had no time to flirt with the local talent. That had been a few evenings earlier, with him and Rocky seeing which one of them could take a German girl back to the hotel room. After several drinks and bumps of coke, they both managed it.

Stories for another time.

Evans watched as Ray moved across the other side of the concourse, his eyes fixed on the red and grey coat of Marsden up ahead. Somewhere in the crowd, Alex was also keeping her eyes peeled, but Evans didn't care. She wasn't like the rest of them. She was a driver; she didn't belong in the field, but Sims seemed to have some twisted delighted in keeping her on-board.

Something about her family.

Whatever it was, it pleased Sims and Evans didn't care enough about Alex to ask further questions.

Marsden approached a gate.

Evans raised his jacket cuff, where is mic resided.

Crackle… *Marsden is approaching gate nine … headed to Paris. *crackle*… Moving in…*

―――――

Through his earpiece, Sam heard Evans's update and pushed open the door to the stairwell, slamming it shut behind him. Instead of leaping down the stairs, Sam stepped to the side of the door, pressed himself against the wall and took a deep breath.

He wouldn't get anywhere with three cops on his tail.

Seconds later, the first police officer burst through the door and Sam reached out, grabbing the man by the back of the head and using his momentum to drive him head-first into the wall. As the man collapsed, Sam turned and the second officer charged into him, driving his shoulder into Sam's gut and pushing him back a few steps. Sam drove his elbow down hard into the man's spine, trying to break free, when the third officer raced through the doorway to join the mayhem.

Sam drove a hard elbow into his attacker's neck, weakening his grip and then raised a hard knee into the man's face. The man rocked back, stumbling backwards as the third officer charged forward with his gun aimed at Sam. Instinctively, Sam shot his hand out, striking the man's wrist and knocking his arm upwards.

Bang!

The gun fired, the bullet embedding itself in the roof of the stairwell. With his fingers firmly gripped on the man's wrist, Sam twisted it sharply, feeling the bone snap before pulling the man towards him and striking him viciously with his elbow. Without releasing the man's shattered wrist, Sam wrenched himself under the man's arm, twisting the tendons in the man's shoulder. As he stepped through, he thrust his boot right into the other guard's chest, sending him hurtling back into the wall of the narrow landing. As the second guard slumped against the brickwork, Sam then drove his elbow deep firmly into the back of the final guard's head, relinquishing his grip on the man as he flopped to the ground.

All three officers were unconscious, and Sam straightened his jacket and then bound down the steps three at a time.

————

Alex slowly followed roughly ten feet behind Evans, doing enough to be visible by the team but not to have any impact on what happened. After her night with Sam, she felt more inclined to help Marsden, to see if maybe her team could be reasoned with. Having witnessed them shoot a number of key targets, some of whom were only witnesses, she knew that Blackridge didn't deal in diplomacy.

They dealt in lead.

As she watched Marsden approach the barrier, he slid his ticket into the machine and the turnstile burst open, granting him access to the platform. A good thirty metres up the platform was the train to Paris, the large door already open to welcome the early arrivals onto the carriage.

Evans sent his command to the team, before hastily

making his way towards the platform, pushing past a few unsuspecting commuters who berated him in their native tongue. He clearly didn't care; he was moving in on his target and Evans was like a shark smelling blood. Across the concourse, Ray was forging a similar path through the crowds of people.

Suddenly, the echo of a gunshot filled the train station, causing an instant panic to spread through the public like a forest fire.

The earpiece crackled to life.

'Sam Pope has gone rogue. I repeat, Sam Pope has gone rogue. Shoot on sight.'

A smile crept across Alex's face as Buck's enraged voice barked out his warning, but then she saw Evans and Ray jump the barrier and race up the platform. Amidst the panic, Marsden was fast approaching the door to the train when Evans dropped to one knee, pulled his handgun from his shoulder holster, and in one fluid motion, aligned the sight with his eye.

He pulled the trigger.

The thunderous roar of his gun sent another shockwave of panic through the station, as well as a bullet which ripped through Marsden's right calf muscle. The treacherous old Sergeant fell forward onto the unforgiven concrete, howling pain as blood quickly pumped out of his leg. Ray raced forward, his gun drawn, aiming it at the body on the floor. With a rough kick, Ray turned Marsden over.

A young, mid-twenties Chinese man looked back at him.

Crackle... *It's a decoy. I repeat, it isn't Marsden!*

Infuriated, Evans raced back towards the barrier, scowling at Alex and demanding she follow him. Ray raced behind them, as they cut through the swathes of people all cowering on the ground, being reassured by the police that everything was fine.

Another crackle came through the earpiece, this time, Rocky's voice, clearly mid-run.

'I've got him…*crackle*… Platform twelve. South east side. Suspect is fleeing to departing train.'

At that moment, the shrill wail of the fire alarm broke out, taking the bubbling pressure of the situation over the edge and the commuters began to rush wildly towards the exits. As the police fought uselessly to control the situation, Evans and Ray used whatever force necessary to forge their runway to platform twelve.

Alex followed, as the station descended into chaos.

———

Sam stopped at the bottom of the stairwell, pressing his finger to his ear and listening intently.

crackle. *It's a decoy. I repeat, it isn't Marsden!*

A smile curled across his lips. Just as he'd expected, Marsden wouldn't walk blindly into a trap. The man was one of the smartest people Sam had met, and he knew Marsden would have seen this coming. All Sam had to do now was get to him before the others did. As Sam raced through the service corridor towards the door to the concourse, his earpiece crackled into life again.

'I've got him… *crackle*… Platform twelve. South east side. Suspect is fleeing to departing train.'

'Shit,' Sam said out loud, picking up the pace for the final few feet to the door. As he reached for the handle, he slowed himself. Beyond the door, the rising murmurs of panic echoed through the large station, the second gunshot moments before the decoy reveal had sent the station into a tailspin.

Sam reached out, smashed the fire alarm and decided to add to the chaos.

The glass shattered to the concrete below and instantly, the shrill ringing of the alarm roared through the station. Sam pulled open the door and stepped out, staying close to the wall as he walked against the tide of people being ushered towards the exit. An automated voice tried to battle the alarm for prominence, asking the German citizens and the plethora of tourists to remain calm.

Sam saw the sign for platform twelve.

With only a minute before the doors closed, the station had given the green light for the train to depart. As Sam raced towards the barriers, he saw Ray hop onto the back carriage. Assuming Marsden was somewhere on the twelve-carriage train, Sam hopped the barrier, immediately confronted by a German officer who thrust a hand into Sam's chest, his other hand reaching for the pistol strapped to his belt. Sam stepped forward, grabbed the man's arm, and hauled him over his shoulder, driving the man into the concrete and air from his lungs. As the guard wheezed in pain, Sam turned straight into the barrel of a pistol.

On the other side was Alex Stone.

Sam raised his hands and his eyebrows, staring intently at the woman he'd made love to the night before. Her eyes were watering knowing her family's safety and security was on the line and her orders from Sims would be crystal clear.

Stop Sam Pope.

A shrill whistle indicated the train was ready to depart, the final train for what would easily be a few hours after the mayhem Sam and Blackridge had caused. Alex's hand shook, the gun a few feet from Sam's chest. Sam took a step towards the train and Alex's arm followed him.

'I'll come back for you,' Sam said sternly. 'I promise.'

Alex gritted her teeth and then lowered her arm,

signalling for Sam to go. He did, exploding towards the train as fast as he could, as Alex turned towards the German police officers and shot a bullet into the air, sparking more panic and a healthy distraction. Sam shot a glance over his shoulder, watching as Alex gently placed the gun on the ground and began to lower herself after it.

She would be arrested and detained as a terror threat.

Sims would get her out of it. Just as long as he didn't find out she'd let Sam go.

As the doors began to beep and slide together, Sam bounded the final few steps and launched himself through the doors, onto the cold, solid floor of the carriage. A few of the passengers, already spooked by the events at the station, startled, but Sam held his hands up in surrender.

He racked his brains for any passable German diction.

'Ich bin hier um zu helfen.'

His calm declaration of help seemed to work, and a few passengers looked up the corridor, directing him to where Ray would have been. Sam nodded and began his journey through the train, the LED screen suspended from the roof telling him it was a non-stop train to Rome, Italy.

Sam marched towards the next carriage, ready to go to war.

CHAPTER THIRTEEN

The first carriage was clear, all the passengers were too engrossed in their tablets or books to even notice Sam as he marched through the walkway. Scouting the faces as he went, Sam made his way hastily through to the next carriage, passing through the two interconnecting doors and being blasted by the cold air between the carriages.

He closed it gently behind him, nodding an apology to a young man and his daughter, who shuddered at the instant blast of cold air.

Sam heard a feint cackle on his earpiece, but the message wasn't clear, the reception cracking as they moved further away from Berlin. Sam dropped it from his ear and continued down the carriage, noticing Ray slowly walking ahead of him, his hand ready to snap to his pistol at any moment.

They were not there to catch Marsden alive. That much, Sam was sure of. He was also certain that if they saw him, a similar fate awaited.

At the end of the carriage, the walkway narrowed down into a small waiting area, hidden behind the large, toilet cubicle. The light above the door was green, indicating it was vacant and Ray stepped through the narrow entrance, into the secluded space where commuters waited patiently for the doors to open to debark. Ray raised his finger to his ear, scowling at the interference. The train trundled on, entering a tunnel and bathing the waiting area in darkness.

Ray reached out and tapped the 'open' button, his hand racing to his pistol as the electronic door hissed, and then slid to the side.

The large cubicle was empty.

Sam made his move.

With all of his power, Sam shunted his shoulder directly into Ray's spine, sending him crashing into the empty cubicle. As Ray shot forward, his neck snapped back, the whiplash instant and his brain shook on impact. Seconds later, his face collided with the hard, laminate cabinet above the sink, the storage unit housing the water, hand dryer and soap, all within its magical confines. Sam stepped in behind Ray, pressing the 'close' button and allowing the door to slide shut behind them.

Ray tried to gather himself, his hand limply pulling the gun from the inside of his jacket, but Sam grabbed his wrist, straightened the arm and with his other palm, shattered Ray's forearm. As the bone snapped in half, Ray opened his mouth to scream in pain, but Sam pulled his jacket over his face, muffling the noise. With his fist gripping the jacket, Sam drove it downward, slamming Ray's head on the side of the toilet. Ray went limp, his unconscious body propped against the faux porcelain. Sam quickly dropped down to Ray's prone body, emptying his pockets onto the floor. Sam took the cash, about fifty euros before dumping the rest of it into the toilet and flushing. Whatever was left after, would be useless anyway.

Next, Sam pulled open the cabinet underneath the sink, revealing the extra supplies used to replenish. Quickly, he grabbed the roll of plastic bags tearing one free and then removing the thick, durable plastic string that comprised the handle. Sam pulled another bag and repeated the removal before tying the two pieces together with a tight, double knot. With a gentle shove, he moved Ray's motionless body to the floor and then pulled his arms up behind his back, carefully manoeuvring the shattered radius into position. With both hands pressed together, Sam wrapped the thin plastic around the wrists, binding them together. The plastic would be too difficult to snap, especially with the damage Sam had done to the man's arm. Next, Sam pulled a number of paper towels from the towel dispenser, and stuffed them into Ray's mouth, tying them in place with the rest of the plastic bag.

Lastly, Sam pulled Ray into position, so his feet were either side of the toilet. With quite a bit of difficulty, Sam managed to wrap a carrier bag around both ankles and tied them together with a firm, double knot. Ray was still motionless, lying on his front with a large gash on his head and his shattered arm pinned to his back. He couldn't move or call for help.

Sam hit the button, the door sliding open to reveal an empty walkway. Sam hit the close button quickly, shutting the devastation from the world. Beside the door, an out-of-order sign was tucked onto a small shelf. Sam smiled, pinning it to the door before moving on through the carriage as quickly as he could.

———

Marsden knew they had made it onto the train, so he rushed as quickly as he could through the interconnecting carriages, headed for the sanctuary of the private room he'd booked. At sixty-two years of age, Marsden didn't fancy taking on any of the Blackridge mercenaries in hand to hand combat. He kept himself in shape and was a dab hand in the boxing ring in his prime, but nowadays it would be useless. While he despised the notion of a privatized and monetized military regiment, he knew the men and women recruited to Blackridge were the best of the best.

Similar to Project Hailstorm.

The very thought caused his heart to beat faster, the realization of what he'd set in motion was heavy to bear.

But what Marsden had in his pocket wouldn't just change the war on terror, it would change the entire political landscape completely.

Weaving past a few commuters, Marsden flashed them an unreciprocated grin before venturing into the next carriage. Far longer than the one previous, the carriage was split out into a number of rooms, a thin slither of privacy that comprised of a bed and possibly a toilet. It wasn't luxury, but for a sixteen-hour train journey, it felt like five star. As Marsden walked through the thin corridor connecting the rooms, the train jolted into a tunnel, the murky view of the cold, windswept German countryside replaced by an empty darkness. Marsden caught his reflection in the window, his grey beard thick and unkept.

He looked a mess.

A long way from his smart, regimented army days.

No, his dark skin was showing signs of age, a few wrinkles taking up permanent residence at the sides of his brown eyes. His grey hair, always cropped short, was thinning to the point of mockery, offset by the thick, grey beard that adorned his strong jaw. Wearing a black jumper, jeans and boots, he'd tried to look inconspicuous, but he knew Sims's men would have located him sooner or later. As he weaved through the corridor, a young couple exited one of the rooms, a baby strapped to the chest of the father. The parents eyed Marsden with suspicion, and he offered his most comforting smile.

They stepped past him, the wife uttering something in German that Marsden couldn't understand. The idea of a young family being caught in the crossfire turned his stomach and made him think of all the other senseless deaths that had happened.

Could still happen.

He was certain that his mission would lead him to his death, but after what he'd exposed, what he'd uncovered, he knew he had to do what any good soldier would do.

His duty.

To protect.

Marsden came to his cabin, and he slid the key card into the door and a little green light accompanied the click. He slipped into the room, the tiny space offering him at least somewhere to think. The limited floor space lead to an uncomfortable looking bed built into the wall, a small door to his left opened up into a cubicle with a toilet and sink. A large window welcomed him, the darkness of the tunnel presenting him with his own reflection once more, before instantly blasting him with the light from outside as they emerged from the darkness.

The sudden change skewed his vision for a few moments before he eventually lowered himself onto the solid mattress, feeling every ache and pain in his aging body. Marsden had been a soldier for over three decades, engaged in numerous combat situations and had even fought for his life a couple of times. The toll on his body was slowly being collected by Father Time and he felt it with every creak of his joint, or every crack in his movements.

Despite his storied career, Marsden had never been severely injured, due to accepting a safer role as a senior figure, training and pulling together elite squadrons.

Project Hailstorm may not have been his baby, but he damn sure nurtured it to existence.

It was why he felt compelled to do what he was doing. All the pain and suffering it had caused. The realization of what he'd helped create.

The near death of Sam Pope.

Marsden knew he couldn't wash all the blood off his hands, but he knew he could at least try to wipe some of it clean. The USB stick in his pocket wasn't a clean slate, but it was at least a slither of redemption.

Because that was really what they were all after. Every soldier who had fought his way through Afghanistan. Every soldier who had shed blood in Iraq.

All the killing.

All the bloodshed.

All any of them wanted when the shooting stopped, was redemption.

Marsden knew he may not be able to offer it to them in person, but with what he had in his possession, he could at least make those in charge face their demons. When what he had was made public, Wallace and the rest of them would never get out alive.

It was why he was on the run.

It was why he had an elite team of mercenaries hunting him through Europe.

As the train shunted along the track, rain clattered against the window behind him, the thin glass rattling in its frame. Wind was escaping through the gaps, the pane almost sliding from its position. Marsden slid the rucksack from his back and dropped it between his legs, reaching over with a heavy hand to open it. Inside were his documents, a spare change of clothes, and some toiletries. He'd decided to travel light, it had been five days since he'd abandoned his post in Switzerland with the information and had been purchasing new clothes each day. He'd cleaned out his account, trading it all in for euros and ensuring there was little paper trail.

It hadn't mattered, as much as he had suspected.

They'd hunted him down and now, most likely, would eliminate him on the very train he sat on.

He reached into his bag and pulled out a Glock 19 pistol, the clip fully loaded and the grip a familiar feeling in his hand.

He'd spent his entire life fighting for the freedom, liberation, and safety of humanity.

Now, with the net tightening, Marsden was ready to fight for it one last time.

CHAPTER FOURTEEN

Rocky and Evans walked calmly through the centre of the carriage, offering welcoming smiles and assured nods of the head to any interested passengers. They knew they stood out like a sore thumb, their matching polo shirts and bomber jackets may as well have been a uniform and they were conscientious about their firearms. Both of them had a Glock 19 strapped under their arm, fastened into a leather holster.

The train whipping in and out of tunnels as it moved further away from Berlin had rendered their earpieces useless, but the two of them knew the mission.

Stop Marsden.

Blackridge would ideally want Marsden brought back alive. Sims was a political parasite, and the idea of handing Marsden over to the British authorities undoubtedly gave him a hard on. Evans didn't particularly like Sims, and he couldn't give a damn about the political ladder. His office was out in the field, gun in his hand and putting the bad guys down.

In his mind, sticking a bullet between the eyes of the

treacherous bastard was the most likely option. Plus, he was pretty sure Marsden would put up a fight.

'Hey, chief, the cabin is clear.'

Rocky grunted, her dark red hair tied back tight and covered with a bandana. She was without a doubt the toughest soldier, male or female, that Evans had ever come across. She hit harder than any man he'd met, and she was twice as vicious. If he wanted to put a bullet in Marsden's skull, she would want to carve it open and shred the insides.

'Let's go,' he uttered, offering a smile to a young kid who stared at him with fascination. Without raising suspicion, the two of them stepped forward into the small waiting area between the two carriages. Outside, rain splashed against the speeding train, rendering the vista nothing more than a wet blur. As Rocky reached out with a gloved hand for the connecting door, the door swung open and the conductor stepped through the gap between the carriages. Startled by the intimidating twosome, he tried to gather himself, straightening the creased shirt that clung to his rotund body and he cleared his throat.

'Ticket, bitte?' he asked, a small, black scanner in his hand. Rocky shook her head and dismissively waved him off. Evans flashed him a white grin, opened his jacket, and revealed the handle of his gun. The colour drained from the conductor's face and his eyes darted around in a panic.

'*Sprechen sie Englisch*? Evans asked calmly, knowing full well most Germans working in the tourist or transport industry were bi-lingual. The man nodded, sweat dripping down his brow and he patted his thin, whispy hair. Evans reached out and gently rested his gloved hand on the man's shoulder, with enough weight to intimidate. 'We are United States Special Forces. We believe a terrorist is on this train.'

'Oh dear,' the man stammered, his eyes watering as the fear set in. Rocky chewed her gum, looking at the pathetic man with disdain. Just another confirmation that men were useless for everything.

'The man is black, about six foot tall. Grey hair.' Evans gestured to his jaw. 'Grey beard too.'

'Ja. I see him,' the conductor said enthusiastically. 'He is in private cabin. *Nummer seiben.*'

The man turned and pointed through the door he'd entered through and instantly Rocky reached for the door handle. She yanked it open and bolted through, her hand reaching to the inside of her jacket as she stepped onto the next carriage. Evans held a finger up to his lips, demanding the man's silence, which he offered with a feeble nod of the head.

'*Danke,*' Evans said coldly, before following Rocky through to the next carriage, the door slamming shut behind him and protecting him from the short blast of freezing wind that he'd stepped through. The carriage was longer, with a narrow walkway along one side. The rest of the carriage had been separated into a number of small, private cabins. Although no bigger than a broom cupboard, having a bed and a private bathroom on a long-haul train was certainly appealing.

The walkway was clear, and Evans followed behind Rocky, who now held her pistol firmly between her fingers, aiming it low to her side as she strode along the carriage. Strapped to her waist was a seven-inch blade, her go-to weapon when Blackridge decide to have a little fun. Well, they did have a sixteen-hour train journey.

Evans chuckled at the idea and then slowly brought himself to a standstill. Rocky stood to the side of door seven. She flashed Evans a look with her dark-brown eyes and then reached forward with her left hand and gently pulled down the handle.

The machine clicked and flashed a red light.

'Fuck,' she uttered under her breath, before taking a

step back and with the force of a prize horse, shunted her foot directly onto the handle. Her military grade boot shattered the card reader and the door flew open, her momentum carrying her in, her pistol raised and ready to execute. She almost pulled the trigger, but realized it was just her reflection on the window.

The room was empty.

As she turned to open the bathroom door, it flew open, the door slamming into her wrist and smacking the gun from her hand. As she stumbled back in shock, Marsden leapt forward, colliding into her and both of them hit the wall of the cabin. The impact felt like it shook the entire carriage as they fell to the floor, Rocky's elbow slammed into the cabin door, driving it back into Evans who was fast approaching.

Angered, Evans readjusted, raised his gun and went to kick the door open to murder Marsden. It was that blind rage that had caused his guard to slip.

It meant he didn't hear the footsteps in time.

———

After disposing of Ray in the now defunct rest room, Sam had begun his march through the train. As ever with his training, he committed every detail to memory.

Thirty separate rows.

Four seats per row.

Seventy-six passengers.

Fifty-three steps to clear the carriage.

It was what made Sam so efficient, his attention to detail. Not just around his targets, but every aspect of his life. He studied and monitored everything and ever since he'd lost Jamie, he'd retargeted that focus on his quest for justice. It had brought down the High Rise and exposed the police bombing of the London Marathon. It had brought down the Kovalenko trafficking empire and severed their ties with the English political scene.

Now it had brought him to a train, speeding through Germany on its way to Rome, where two very dangerous people were zeroing in on his mentor.

Sam shot through the connecting door and into the next carriage, moving with haste among the seats. A few passengers raised their heads to watch, having already seen other people stride past. Nothing caused fear more than seeing people acting suspiciously on public transport and Sam held his hand up to try to lower the rising tension. As he passed through, he almost collided with a portly, middle aged man, his shirt covered in sweat. The man held a ticket machine in his hand and looked clearly flustered. Before Sam could speak, the man leant in, his body odour immense, as he whispered.

'Your friends are already at the carriage.' He jerked his head towards the door. 'Cabin *seiben*.'

Sam smiled and patted the man on his damp shoulder, marching towards the door as the conductor began speaking to passengers in his native tongue, trying his best to quash any fears. Sam pulled open the door and stepped through the cold and onto the next carriage, ahead of him he could see Rocky break the door down with a thunderous kick, before disappearing into the room. Sam walked as quietly as possible, keeping himself against the side of the cabin and hopefully out of Evans periphery. A large crash echoed from the room and the door slammed back, colliding with Evans who angrily stepped back. With a furious crack of his neck, Evans regripped his gun and stepped towards the door.

Sam broke into a sprint.

Evans turned at the final second, his eyes widening with a mixture of shock and rage as Sam launched his body forward, his shoulder colliding into Evans' chest and knocking the man to the floor. The gun fell from his hand and Sam immediately reached for it. Evans fell onto his back, but quickly shot a foot up, his boot slamming into Sam's chest as he bent forward. Sam stumbled backwards and Evans quickly scampered to his feet, raising his fists and locking his eyes squarely onto Sam. As he readjusted his feet, Sam pulled his fists up and, in that brief silent moment, both men agreed that this was to the death.

Evans launched forward with a barrage of rights and lefts, hammering Sam with the precision and power of a champion boxer. In the limited space, Sam raised both of his arms, taking the impact in his powerful muscles, before waiting for a brief opening. As he deflected one of Evans's stinging blows to the left, he drove his knee forward, ramming it firmly into Evans's midsection and driving the wind out of him. As his attacker stumbled back slightly, Sam drove a hard left into the man's cheek, rocking him slightly. He floored Evans with a striking right hook.

Inside the room, Rocky had kicked Marsden off her and towards the bed, angrily jumping to her feet and laying into the veteran soldier with some vicious kicks. Marsden protected himself well, catching her leg on impact and swinging her with all his might. Caught off balance, Rocky spun in the room and collided with the glass window, her face colliding so hard it left an imprint and speck of blood. With her eyes wide with anger, she slipped the knife from her belt and slashed wildly at Marsden, who dodged two swipes before blocking the third with his arm. Rocky stamped on his foot, weakening his balance, before she pressed forward with all her strength, sending both of them onto the solid mattress. With her low centre of gravity locking Marsden in place beneath her, her eyes sparkled with delight as she pressed down with both hands.

The blade was an inch or two from Marsden's neck and his arms began to shake as he fought for his life.

Sam turned, pushed open the door and as he went to enter, Evans spat blood onto the floor and chuckled.

'Is that all you've got?' Evans got to his feet, unsheathing a knife from his belt and wiping the rest of the blood away from his lip with the back of his glove. In two bounds he was right on Sam, slashing the knife towards him with murderous intent. In the close confines of the carriage, Sam managed to dodge the first slash, then deflect the next with a well-timed forearm, Evans drove a brutal knee into Sam's fresh stitches, causing his thigh to burn with pain and his leg to go limp. As he stumbled backwards, Evans slashed his right bicep with his blade, drawing blood and a grunt of pain from Sam.

'Oh, I'm going to enjoy this,' Evans boasted, his maniacal need to inflict pain emerging through the evil grin that dominated his face. Sam shrugged off the pain and as Evans lunged forward with the intent to kill, Sam dodged the blade. Quickly, he grabbed Evans's forearm and slammed it into the wall, his finger digging into the pressure point. Evans' gloved grip relinquished, and the blade dropped, which Sam caught with his other hand, turning on his heel and slicing the sharp blade across his attacker's thigh. Evans groaned in pain and stepped backward, his hands reaching for the bloody wound.

Sam rocked him with a few rights before swinging the blade with his left. Evans blocked it expertly, but Sam dropped the blade, catching it with his right, and plunged it deep into Evans's hip. The man roared with pain for a mere second, before Sam caught him with a vicious headbutt.

Evans crashed backwards to the floor, his brain rocked by the vicious blow, the knife still embedded in his side.

Sam pressed his hand to his injured bicep, his fingers

returning covered in blood. Ignoring the pain, Sam rushed into the room as Rocky applied more pressure to the handle of her blade.

The tip of it began to pierce Marsden's throat.

Sam hurled himself into her, dragging her from his old mentor and driving both himself and Rocky into the wall. Marsden rolled to the side, shocked at his saviour as Sam got to his feet, only to be caught by a vicious right hook that split his lip.

Rocky hit like her namesake.

As Sam stumbled back, she threw herself forward, blade ready, aiming for his chest. Sam managed to swivel on the spot, his leg almost giving way through the pain and as she darted past, he used her own momentum to launch her into the small bathroom. She hit the tiled wall hard, blood shooting from her nose on impact and as she woozily turned, she lazily swiped the knife towards the door. Sam dodged the swipe, slammed her arm against the wall, disarming her. As she tried to spin free, Sam pulled her bandana down across her face until it was wrapped around her neck, then with an almighty tug, drove her headfirst against the solid, porcelain toilet.

The impact was sickening.

Rocky stopped moving, her arm twitching slightly, and Sam stumbled back into the small cabin, a sudden blast of cold air greeting him. As he and Rocky had collided with the wall, it had shunted the wall with enough force to loosen the window panel, which had slid open.

As Sam turned to close it, Evans charged through the door, his hand pressed to his hip which pumped blood, his other hand wildly wielding the knife. He roared with fury, any sense of the mission game plan replaced with a blind rage and need to kill Sam. As he launched forward, he was blind to Marsden who had pulled himself to his feet and who caught Evans with a striking right hand, which knocked him off balance.

As he stumbled forward, Sam grabbed him by the lapels of his jacket and in a final push of strength, he hurled Evans through the open window and out of the train.

Evans instantly disappeared, ripped back by the speed and considering they were surrounded by a rough terrain of hard fields and rocks, Sam wasn't confident of his chances of survival. His body would hit that landscape at over one hundred miles an hour, the rough terrain would likely tear his skin to shreds and reduce his bones to dust.

Finally, Sam took a deep breath, before sliding the window back into place. His face and shirt were wet, the rain sneaking in for a brief moment. His leg ached and his right arm was now drenched with his own blood.

Just another day.

With considerable difficulty, he turned his aching body, coming face to face with an obviously shocked Marsden.

'Sam?' he asked, bewildered. 'What the hell are you doing here?'

Sam smiled; his teeth slightly covered in blood.

'Just a bit of sightseeing,' Sam replied and then quickly added, 'Sir.'

CHAPTER FIFTEEN

'Goddamn it.'

Pearce cursed loudly before reaching out and slapping the side of his computer monitor. He was a self-confessed technophobe and whenever a program he was using gave him the ill-fated white screen and 'not-responding' message, he yearned for the good old days of pen and paper. After slapping the screen, he took a moment, chuckling at himself for becoming his father. His dad had eked out a living selling old vinyl records in a small store just outside of Walthamstow.

Spinnin' Sessions.

Pearce could remember the smell of the shop, the incense his father burned as the speakers pumped out the likes of Marvin Gaye and Bob Marley. His father was a traditionalist, always wanting to preach about how his days where the 'good old days' and how his era of everything was better than the current. It was a conversation Pearce found himself having with the kids down at the youth club, finding his own soap box to talk about how the music he listened to in the seventies and eighties was so much better than the current shit on the radio.

It was a ridiculous circle that would be repeated by every generation, with the previous one lamenting the constant need for upgrading, always feeling like their time in the sun was the peak of humanity.

While he hated technology, he did understand the vast improvements it had made to his own detective work, the video cameras, mobile phones, even social media had all played a part in helping him uncover dodgy cops.

Move with the times or be consigned to the past with the other relics.

That's what Pearce told himself, although the fact he sat in nothing short of a broom cupboard told him the Metropolitan Police were keen to see him put out to pasture.

It was a price he gladly paid for doing the right thing and exposing the corruption that had infiltrated the veins of her Majesty's police service like a cancer and was killing it from within. He would gladly be shunted to the derelict toilets in the basement if it meant he could hold his head up high and say he did the right thing. After nearly thirty years of distinguished service, he knew when to push back and when to let the powers that be feel in control.

With age came wisdom and that would carry him through.

He feared for Singh.

He sat back in his chair and lifted his mug to his lips, recoiling at the stone-cold coffee that greeted him. Pearce was fond of Singh, enthralled with her persistence and clear distinction of right and wrong. Her record and reputation spoke for itself and he saw a lot of himself in her. She would make a fine internal investigator and he would have no qualms in handing over the Department of Professional Standards over to her.

But the rate she was going, she wouldn't make it beyond her current post. They'd already ostracized her for the Kovalenko scandal and as she ran headfirst into a collision with a powerful military function shrouded in mystery, he couldn't help but worry.

She was like him. Heart in the right place.

She was like Sam. Wanting to do the right thing.

Pearce knew he couldn't stop Singh from her mission but the least he could do was keep an eye on her. Be there for her and to help where he could. He thought of Theo Walker, Sam's friend who sacrificed himself to save a couple he'd just met for no other reason other than he was a hero.

He was a good man.

Pearce had tried to honour his legacy by continuing to run the Bethnal Green Youth Club and was petitioning to rename it in Theo's memory. It was the least he could do and while he knew Theo died for the right reason, he didn't want Singh to end up doing the same thing.

Some fights were not winnable.

A knock on the door snapped Pearce back into the room and he noticed his Word document had finished loading, reminding him that patience was a virtue.

'Come in,' he bellowed out, trying to look busy by arranging the stack of papers that polluted his desk, the tiny room looking more cluttered than ever. The door swung open, colliding with the edge of his desk with a mighty thud and in stepped Assistant Commissioner Ashton. Pearce immediately stood, the respect of rank as natural as breathing.

'Adrian, please. Sit.'

Pearce frowned in confusion, slowly lowering himself back into his leather chair. Ashton was a respected senior officer, known for her tenacity and cut-throat approach. The idea of her being cordial was unsettling.

'How can I help you, ma'am?' Pearce asked calmly, eyeing his superior with an uneasy glare. Ashton was in her late forties with sharp features. Her nose was thin and pointy, set between two fierce cheekbones. Her dark eyes burrowed into her small face, giving off a slightly gaunt look. Her short, dark hair rested messily atop her head as she clutched her hat tightly under her arm. AC Ashton was impeccable, the perfect senior officer but manners and friendly banter was not her forte.

'Oh, Adrian. Please, call me Ruth.'

Again, Pearce smiled, his stomach knotting with unease at the situation. Although he would never disrespect a senior officer unless he had due reason, he couldn't help but want this conversation over as quickly as possible.

'Forgive me, ma'am.' She shot him a look. 'Ruth. What can I you for?'

Ashton ventured into the tiny office, unable to mask her disdain at the compact mess Pearce called his office. She took a couple of steps to the plastic chair wedged up against the wall.

'Adrian, how long have we known each other?'

Again, the question sat uneasily with Pearce.

'Many years.'

'Exactly, and in that time, I would like to think we know each other well enough to know, we give a damn.'

'Okay,' Pearce said, his eyes narrowing, waiting for her motive.

'Your reputation precedes you, Adrian and trust me, I'm doing all I can to get you out of this closet and away from this busy work.' She offered him a warm smile. 'You've never been big on the politics of this place, have you?'

'Not one bit.' He shook his head. 'As far as I'm concerned, the law's the law and we are all pushing for the same thing. Playing the game, dicking people over to climb another rung up the ladder, it's something that we, as police officers, should be above. But, that's just my take on it.'

'No, a completely valid point and to be honest, if we had more people with your integrity wearing the uniform, we wouldn't need a Department of Professional Standards.'

The compliment caused a little smile to creep across Pearce's face and Ashton noted it. Pearce linked his fingers together and dropped his hands onto his lap.

'What can I do for you, ma'am?'

Ashton tutted, annoyed by his refusal to drop the formalities.

'I have reason to believe that DI Singh is investigating sensitive, military information that she should not be privy to. Now, as I'm sure you of all people know, reputations can be ruined pretty quickly, especially in conjunction with Sam Pope.'

Pearce sat forward, placing his hands on his desk.

'You want me to warn her off, is that it? Use my own shitty experience as a deterrent?'

'No, Pearce. Not at all.' Ashton stood. 'I want you to do what you do best. I want you to find something, anything we can pin on Singh so we can push her towards the exit.'

'Excuse me?' Pearce stood up, hands firmly on hips.

'Look, Pearce.' Ashton had dropped the niceties. 'You're in this situation because no one trusts you. Now Singh, she is starting to cause some people some problems. You bring me something that I can use to fix those problems, then those people will be very grateful. Like I said, you shouldn't be in this cupboard.'

Pearce shook his head, smiling at the audacity of the woman whose stare bore through him like a laser beam.

'And if I don't?' he said curtly.

'Well, let's just say Singh won't be the only problem I'll be finding a solution for.'

With that, Ashton took the few steps back to the door and let herself out, slamming it behind with just enough force to underline her point. Pearce sighed deeply, his anger at the political game sucking him was palpable and he launched his mug against the wall. The porcelain shattered, raining shards and ice-cold coffee onto his floor.

He dropped into his chair and massaged his temples.

He needed to help Singh.

But how?

———

Ashton marched through the New Scotland Yard office, appreciating the respect shown to her by her subordinates. She ruled with an iron fist, but she wasn't in the Met for popularity points. She was ruthlessly climbing the ladder, and the failure of the Sam Pope task force could be quite the stumbling block.

What mattered now was passing the buck, to pin it onto Singh as an overeager upstart who'd run before she could walk. Despite all of Ashton's guidance, Singh's reluctance to follow the chain of command was what had allowed Sam Pope to disappear.

It was an easy picture to paint and Ashton had already filled her pallet.

As she marched through the centre of the office, she shot a glance towards the task force incident room, the large board outlining all of Sam's armouries and safe houses rested proudly on the wall. It had been a great collar by one of her task forces, one which she would gladly take credit for. They were in the process of disarming Pope, cutting off his access to weaponry.

After that, they would tighten the net until they caught him then she would parade her catch as publicly as possible.

The public would adore her.

She would be a shoe in for the next Commissionership.

As her heels clicked across the laminate floor, she approached her office door, pushing it open and greeting her guest with a large grin.

'Consider Amara Singh taken care of,' Ashton said cheerily, striding across her neat, immaculate office to the drinks cabinet. A large decanter sat next to a few glass tumblers and she poured the whisky into two of them.

'Excellent.'

Ervin Wallace flashed his polished grin at her and graciously accepted the drink. Both of them admired the other's craving of power and their relentless quest for it. They both terrified any room they walked into and both of them knew, that breaking eggs was only the first step of the omelette.

'Give it a couple of days, and I'll have enough shit to bury her under, she'll need a goddamn ladder to come up for air.'

They clinked their glasses.

'Ruth, that is very pleasing to hear.' Wallace took a sip. 'Consider my help on the Sam Pope situation already underway.'

'Thank you, General.' Ashton sipped her drink, before taking her seat. 'I also trust, that when the time comes, I can count on your respected opinion to sway people to my direction.'

Wallace finished his drink and then flashed his grin again. His suit was tightly wrapped around his impressive, bulky frame.

'Ruth, if those idiots need me to point out that you're the only candidate to take the reins, then you have a hell of a job when it comes your way.'

They both raised their glasses again and Wallace placed his empty glass down. As Ashton sipped hers,

Wallace's inside pocket vibrated and he whipped the phone out. It looked tiny in his meaty hand.

'Hello?' Wallace's face dropped immediately. 'I see. I'll be on the first flight out.'

He clicked his phone off and stuffed it back into his pocket before turning to Ashton with a faux look of regret.

'Apologies, Ruth. I have to run. Something very important has come up.'

'Oh?' Ashton offered, hoping pathetically for the inside scoop. It didn't arrive. Wallace marched through the door to the corridor, walked at pace towards the exit. His phone buzzed again and this time the message simply said, *Am here.*

Wallace grinned sadistically, knowing full well what he was setting in motion. With his large fingers, he typed as he walked, arrogantly barging past the officers who passed him in the hallway.

He typed three words.

Do whatever's necessary.

———

Another evening alone.

Paul Etheridge sat the kitchen counter in his pristine kitchen, pathetically pouring himself a glass of MacMillan scotch. Usually, the thought of having such an expensive and luxurious drink would have filled him with an empty sense of pride, but now it just felt redundant. As a multi-millionaire who ran his own successful data security software company, the last few weeks had been surprisingly empty. Large, international organisations were frantically knocking on his door, begging him to sell them his game changing software at whatever price he demanded.

Somehow, after five years, the novelty of being a rich, flashy entrepreneur had worn off.

Etheridge knocked back the scotch and quickly lifted the bottle again, the warm, gold liquid crashing into the crystal glass with a gentle splash. Just over two weeks had passed since Sam Pope had turned up on his door, asking him for his help.

It had been a long time since Etheridge had served alongside Sam in the army, a role he wasn't cut out for but one that he still held proudly. One night, in the hot, mountainous terrain of Sudan, Sam had saved Etheridge's life after a routine mission nearly went awry. Etheridge had always been eternally grateful for that moment, as it was the catalyst for him to leave the army and make his millions in cyber security.

But when Sam had come knocking, urgently needing assistance to find a missing girl and bring down a sex trafficking rink, Etheridge had finally found a sense of purpose he'd long been lacking. The police had questioned him continuously, demanding he tell them where Sam was. Considering Sam had incapacitated an entire Armed Response Unit in Etheridge's house, he didn't fancy their chances when they found him.

Etheridge lied, told them Sam had held a gun to his head and made him hack a few security cameras. He omitted building Sam a new identity, buying him a multitude of open tickets to Europe and to manipulating the airport security systems to ensure Sam could safely transport his weapons to Ukraine.

Sam was going to war, and Etheridge had felt a sense of purpose for a long time, a feeling that stood high and proud above the materialistic life he'd forged for himself.

Regrettably, Kayleigh had filed for divorce. His second wife was twenty years his junior, and while he was under no illusion that his money was the magnet that had lured her in, they'd enjoyed a few rather passionate years together. In his early forties, Etheridge was no George

Clooney, but he'd hoped their time together had changed her motive.

When her divorce demands had landed on his doorstep earlier that day, he realized he was wrong.

Now, sat at his kitchen counter, he'd decided he was going to drink the night into a fuzzy oblivion, and then dedicate the next day to finding and helping Sam. The business would take care of itself, the share prices doubling each quarter and the fortune he sat upon would only grow.

It was time for Etheridge to do the right thing.

He could help Sam properly, use his expertise to equip Sam with the information that was just as vital as his own combat skills.

Together, they would be unstoppable.

The ringing of the doorbell cut through Etheridge's new-found focus like a knife through butter and, slightly perplexed, he looked at his watch. It was a little after eight in the evening, the winter darkness falling hours earlier. Etheridge couldn't recall ordering a takeaway and then begrudgingly walked across his impressive mansion to the front door, annoyed that the police were bothering him again. As he reached for the handle, he realized the buzzer for his gate had not been pressed and he regretted pulling the door from its latch.

A boot collided with the solid oak door, driving the sharp edge into his face and splitting his eyebrow on impact. As he fell back onto the marble floor of his hall-way, his vision blurred, and he felt a rising panic in his chest. He pushed himself up to a seated position, squinting through the pain and blood as a figure stepped through the door, backlit by his security light and framed by the falling sleet.

The man was tall, well-built, and decked out entirely in black, his long coat dripping cold water onto the floor.

On his face, he wore a black balaclava.

In his gloved hand, he held a gun.

Etheridge held his hands up in surrender, the blood trickling down his cheek.

'Look, take whatever you want, okay?'

The man took a few ominous steps towards him and then squatted down, meeting him at eye level. Etheridge could see the scarring around the man's eye, the lifeless pupils staring back at him. With a thick, Manchurian accent, the man in black spoke.

'Where can I find Sam Pope?'

CHAPTER SIXTEEN

TEN YEARS EARLIER…

The repetitive thud of the helicopter propellers was as welcoming as it was hypnotic, and Sam fell to his knees as they approached. The heat was unbearable, the unprotected sun relentless beating down upon the small village of Chakari, in the Kabul Province of Afghanistan. Around him, the seven dead bodies of the Taliban soldiers lay scattered, all of them slowly rotting in the baking sun. Sam had been trapped behind enemy lines, the shrapnel removed from his leg and waist by a local doctor, a man who had given his life to save him.

Through the pain and the searing heat, Sam's recollection of events was hazy.

There had been an explosion.

He'd lost someone close to him.

Sam had been left for dead.

As he tried to clear the fog that had settled over the last few days, he smacked his lips, trying to find hydration. His body ached, the bandages wrapped around his midriff were stained with blood. He felt a constant throb in his leg, and he thought of Lucy.

He'd almost died out here.

Alone in the heat.

The Taliban would never have returned his body to her, she would never have known what had happened. All she would have got was a knock on the door from Marsden, an apology and a cheque.

But Sam had refused to die, fighting through the pain barrier and eventually, the local Taliban unit that had been terrorizing the village.

They were dead.

Dr Farhad Nabizada was dead.

Now, as the chopper slowly lowered itself to the sandy clearing, Sam realized how close he truly had been to joining them. The engine roared, the propellers sweeping up gusts of sand, coating the entire area. At the controls, the pilot gently lowered it to the ground, before reaching up to the control panel and flicking a myriad of switches. The door slid to the side, and Sergeant Carl Marsden leapt from the helicopter, racing across the sand to Sam.

'Sam. Jesus,' Marsden said, dropping to his knees in front of him and wrapping his arms around him. Sam winced with pain but relented, his eyes watering at the comfort. 'We thought you were a goner.'

Sam wearily smiled.

'You can't get rid of me that easily.'

'Can you walk, son?' Marsden asked, refusing to let go of him. Sam nodded and Marsden clambered to his feet, easing Sam up as slowly as he needed. Both men were covered in dust as they got to their feet and Marsden draped Sam's arm over his shoulder, letting him dictate the pace. Each step was gingerly followed by the next, the heat and pain taking its toll on Sam. Marsden glanced around the campsite, the bullet-riddled bodies of the Taliban were sprawled out in whatever chaotic demise they'd met. Marsden shook his head slightly.

'You've made quite a mess here.'

'They deserved it,' Sam said through gritted teeth, watching as his friend Theo emerged from the helicopter with a handheld medikit. 'They killed a good man.'

'Well, they almost killed another one,' Marsden replied, gently patting Sam on the back.

'Theo.'

Sam greeted his friend, who didn't say anything, but wrapped both arms around him. Sam felt a tear fall from his eye as he embraced his friend, returning the hug with as much force as his weak body could muster. For a few moments, the two of them stood, both of them knowing how close it had been.

Theo pulled back shaking his head and wiping his eyes with the back of his hand.

'Fucking hell, mate.' Theo chuckled. 'You had me going then.'

'I'm sorry…' Sam began, before Theo stuffed a bottle of water in his hand.

'Don't you dare apologise.' Theo angrily remonstrated. 'It wasn't your fault. None of it was. We had bad intel and that nearly killed you.'

'Theo, enough,' Marsden interjected, raising his voice over the low hum of the propellers as the pilot slowly brought them to life. 'We'll debrief back at base. Let's get him in.'

Theo scowled at their superior but obliged, helping Marsden guide Sam up the step and into the cabin where another soldier greeted him and helped him to his seat. Theo followed, a look of concern on his face as he perused the brutal impact that the shrapnel had inflicted on Sam's body. Marsden was the last in, slamming the door closed and then giving the pilot the thumbs up.

The engine roared into the life, the main rotor blade whizzing into life and gently, the landing skids lifted from the dusty, derelict land below. As they rose into the scorching sky, Sam glanced one last time out of the window. Below, he could see the bloodstained sand surrounding the bodies he'd sent to the afterlife.

It had been an execution, his own had rage taken control and wiping out the evil squadron that had terrorized the village of Chakari.

It had left Tahir and Masood without a father.

Somewhere, through the shattered remnants of what had happened, he felt it had claimed someone else.

A friend. Perhaps?

Sam grunted with discomfort as Theo pressed a cloth of anti-septic against his wounds, but his friend's caring smile placated him. Sam pressed his head against the window, staring out at the vast, desert wasteland before them. He took another swig of water, his body craving the moisture like it was a drug.

'Sir,' Sam piped up. 'Why did you risk coming back for me?'

Marsden turned to Sam, the emotional weight of bringing him home was hanging heavy from him. His eyes, usually filled with conviction were red,

'You're one of my men, Sam,' he said softly. 'I would walk into hell to save any of you.'

Theo and Sam both smiled at him, nodding their appreciation. Theo went back to Sam's wounds, while Sam himself closed his eyes, resting his head against the cool glass. Before he dozed off, he quietly responded.

'Me too, sir. Me too.'

––––––––

The room was a fuzzy blur for the first few moments and Sam had to blink a few times to realise he'd been asleep. The mattress was as uncomfortable as the rocky mountains of Kirkuk and the shaking of the train meant the sleep had been just as tumultuous. With every muscle in his body aching, Sam eased himself to a seated position, swinging his legs around so they hung off the bed and cursed the burning pain emanating from his thigh. Despite the best work of Blackridge's doctors, the amount of strain he was putting on his bullet wound was causing him some serious damage. He stretched out his right arm, pushing through the pain of the knife wound Evans had administered before he took his one-way journey through the window.

The bandage Marsden had strapped to it was pulled tight, a little red with blood, but enough to stem the bleeding.

Marsden?

Sam's eyes shot around the tiny room and right on cue, the cabin door opened and in walked his comrade. Marsden had aged since Sam had last seen him; his usually clean-shaven face haggard with a matted, grey beard. Despite being in his sixties, Marsden was still as trim as ever, and Sam understood why Blackridge had sent so many people after him.

Marsden offered Sam a warm smile before handing him a cold bottle of Peroni. The red label indicated it was a different Peroni to the one in the UK, which was in fact an entirely different brew called *Nastro Azzuro*.

It still went down nicely and Sam finished it in three large swigs.

'It's good to see you, Sam.' Marsden smiled. 'Cheers.'

Sam blushed slightly as Marsden raised his full bottle and took a swig.

'You too, sir.'

'Can I ask you a question?' Marsden said, staring out into the room. 'What the fuck are you doing here?'

Sam nodded. It was a fair enough question.

'I came to help you, sir.'

'Help me?' Marsden sounded infuriated. 'Sam, do you have any idea how much trouble you're in? What I'm doing, what's going on here… there is no way back from it. No out. That's why I did this on my own.'

Marsden shook his head in disappointment, the situation angering him. Sam knew Marsden cared about him, but he refused to be berated for stepping in.

'With all due respect, sir. If I hadn't got involved, you would already be dead.' Marsden shot Sam a glare and Sam quickly spun his head to the bathroom door.

'She's alive. Not conscious. You gave her one hell of a concussion, I'd say.' Marsden drank once more, finishing his beer. 'You shouldn't have come.'

'I wasn't given a choice. They threatened Lucy.'

Marsden turned suddenly to look at his old friend, offering a compassionate nod of understanding.

'How is Lucy?'

'Well, I think. Remarried. Baby on the way.' Sam spoke through a deep breath. 'The life she deserves.'

The two men sat in silence for a few moments, the pain of Sam's plight hanging in the air between them. Marsden picked the label from his bottle before reaching out and patting Sam on the shoulder.

'Thank you, Sam. You saved my life.'

Sam reached up and patted Marsden's hand.

'Then we are even.' They smiled. 'Now… what the hell have you got yourself into?'

Marsden ran a hand across his short, grey hair and stood. Despite his age, he still walked with the command of a senior officer and he looked out of the window. They'd entered Italy a few hours before and were now in the final few miles of their journey. Marsden had thought about it long and hard while Sam slept. He'd known Black-ridge were stalking him, but his plan had relied heavily on giving them the slip in Berlin. The fact they'd embarked on the train with him meant they knew he was inbound and would undoubtedly be waiting for him at *Roma Termini*, guns locked and loaded. Sam had managed to intervene, scuppering their plans but now providing him with an option.

The last thing he wanted was to pull Sam into it. As he'd explained, there was no returning from what he was about to do. But he knew Sam, and the man would walk through hellfire and brimstone to do the right thing.

And this was the right thing.

Tentatively, he turned back from the window and faced his former protegee and folded his arms.

'Whatever they told you, they're lying.'

'Oh, I know that,' Sam stated. 'They're pinning you as a terrorist. You and I both know that's bullshit.'

'Thank you,' Marsden said, the appreciation genuine.

'Then once again, please tell me. What the fuck have you done?'

'I stumbled across something. Something hidden. Something a number of military forces want kept locked away. Believe me, I tried to walk away from it. I tried to ignore it, but the more I let it fester, the harder it became. I took the proof I needed, and I ran.'

'Sir, you're not making any sense. What did you find? Where were you?'

'I was stationed in one of our bases in Switzerland. Just outside of Zurich. There's a little town called Oirlikon and, anyway... I took the files and stuck them on this.' Marsden fished a USB stick from his pocket and held it up. 'This, Sam, this has the power to bring down a number of governments, end a lot of peace, and change the way we look at terrorism.'

Sam stood, his face writhe with concern.

'Sir, if it's that powerful, do you really want to be the guy to do that much damage to the world?'

'This has the names of everyone who has already damaged the world. Irreparably in some cases. This shows everything. Every lie, every dead body, every goddamn fucking traitor.' Marsden stopped, taking a breath. 'This is the truth, Sam. The truth about everything. Even Project Hailstorm.'

The final two words hit Sam like a lightning bolt and he shot round, his eyes meeting Marsden's. That night was still a blur to Sam, laid out on the cold concrete, feeling his life pump from the two holes in his chest. It was one of the few times in his life were Sam felt terrified, where his training and his instincts would have no say in the matter.

He should have died in that dark, abandoned warehouse.

It was Marsden who had pulled him out.

'Whatever you need, I'm in,' Sam said firmly. 'You don't have to tell me everything, I get that. But you saved my life. You were there when I was at the end of my rope and you brought me back. I've had some dark times, but it was you who saved me from losing myself to it.'

Marsden held out the USB stick and Sam took it, turning it over between his fingers like an expensive piece of jewellery. It always baffled him how the smallest objects could do the most damage.

A bullet from a sniper rifle.

A button primed for detonation.

A USB stick full of information.

Anything, in the right or wrong hands, could be world changing. The speakers kicked in and a notification in Italian drifted into the room, announcing their arrival into Rome station. A German announcement followed, and Marsden took a deep breath, contemplating their next steps.

'It's been a pleasure to serve with you, Sam,' Marsden spoke, his tone concerning Sam. 'You still know how to disappear, right?'

'Sir?'

'When the train comes to a stop, Blackridge will be all over this train. They can have me, but when you get your chance, you vanish. You hear me?'

'No, sir, I didn't get on this train to let you walk into their arms.'

Marsden stepped forward and rested his hand on Sam's shoulders. They both knew, that if Blackridge took Marsden, he wouldn't be seen again. Sam's face was pulled tight, his anger outweighing his understanding. Marsden, in his infinite wisdom, offered Sam his warmest smile.

'Sam, without that USB, they lose.' Marsden nodded and Sam reciprocated. He understood. Marsden then pulled his pistol from the back of his trousers and headed for the door.

'Good luck, sir.'

'And you, Sam.' Marsden opened the door. 'And you.'

With a gentle thud, the train came to a stop. The vast concrete platform was already filled with security in high-vis vests, as well as the unmistakable Blackridge uniforms. The doors dinged and Marsden and Sam exited their cabin, each man walking in different directions. There would be panic, Sam knew it and he needed to be in the crowd when it happened. A few moments later, the alarm began to scream its shrill, ear-piercing note and Sam felt the noise level rise instantly, the terrified public always seeming to be on the edge of a full-scale meltdown.

A scream of panic erupted, followed by a gunshot and a bullet embedding in the roof of a carriage.

Marsden had brought all the focus on his carriage and Sam knew all guns would be pointed on him. He just prayed there were no itchy trigger fingers. But Sam knew that Sims wanted the glory, and Marsden without the USB stick was no use to him dead. Marsden had willingly stepped into their arms.

The man had committed himself to the cause.

Sam had to do likewise.

As the hordes of passengers flooded onto the concrete, Sam slithered into the crowd, his head down, clocking instantly where the watchful eyes of Sims's crew were. He saw Buck, the bruised face scanning the crowd with a furious scowl. The security was all headed towards Marsden coach, ready to take the gun man down.

Sam knew he shouldn't just leave him, but with the USB stick safely in his pocket, he beeped his passport at the barrier and stepped off the platform.

CHAPTER SEVENTEEN

Pearce hadn't slept a wink.

Having spent the rest of his day contemplating AC Ashton's thinly veiled threat, he'd decided a long run would clear his mind. Although he ran almost eleven kilometres through the bitter, chilling rain of the December night, his thoughts were no more aligned. He knew that trying to urge Singh to step away from the Project Hailstorm investigation was useless. The woman was like a dog with a bone and he knew better than to try to wrest it from her.

How? Because they were cut from the same cloth.

Throughout his career within the DPS, Pearce had been told to back down more times than he cared to remember. Policing in the seventies was a different game entirely and being a black man hadn't helped. Instantly people distrusted him based purely on what they saw, which only aided Pearce's cause. The world had come on leaps and bounds since those heady days, but racism was still rife through all avenues of life and he knew Singh would hit those buffers, eventually.

If she even made it to the end of the week.

Pearce had spent the evening sitting up in bed, trying his best to devour the latest Dan Brown novel. He loved a good mystery, the detective in him loved to play the game, and the historical twist the author spun on his puzzles had always appealed to Pearce.

But even the historical adventures of Professor Langdon couldn't hold his attention.

Pearce needed to help Singh.

As he clambered up the steps of Embankment Station, he was greeted with another bitterly cold downpour, the weather doing its best to ruin the Christmas cheer London was trying to spread. The lamp posts were adorned with bright lights, which would light up the embankment with different colours when the sun went down. Considering the thick, dark clouds over head, Pearce wondered why they didn't just leave them on all day.

Hundreds of people squirmed past each other, a moving blur of suits, ties, and umbrellas as the professional world went about its business. Pearce looked up to the sky, letting the cold drizzle splash against his face and hoped it would slap him awake. It didn't help. He turned right from the station and meandered down the pavement, passing the Whitehall Gardens, usually so vibrant, which looked depressed and dark in the winter morning. The Embankment was a testament to previous times, with a number of military and London memorials lining the streets and littered throughout the gardens. During the summer, Pearce liked to do the rounds, taking in the vast history of the great city.

Today, he just needed to get to the office.

As he approached the famous sign of New Scotland Yard, he looked out to the Thames, overseeing the empty Westminster Pier. Not many tourists fancied a December trip up the Thames, and he didn't blame them. After quickly popping into Starbucks, he made his way into the building, leaving a trail of wet footprints up the stairs as he ascended to his office. As usual, nobody greeted him or made eye contact, the trust weathered by years of his internal investigations.

He didn't care.

He'd never cared.

Eventually, he came to his micro-office and with a sigh of relief, pushed open the door.

'Pearce!'

Singh's outburst caused him to nearly drop his coffee and he pressed his hand to his chest.

'Christ, you almost gave me a heart attack!'

'Sorry,' Singh offered, offering him a weak smile. He shook it off, sliding in through the door and closing it behind him. The office was small enough for one person, but with Singh hunched over the desk, her face in a stack of papers, there was little room to manoeuvre. Despite being purely platonic, he didn't want to encroach on her, so Pearce stood against the door and took a sip of his coffee.

'Everything okay?' he asked. 'You look like you haven't slept?'

'Ditto,' Singh barked back. 'I've been doing some digging, and you have to see this.'

'Digging?' Pearce asked, pushing himself from the door and politely moving Singh to the side so he could get to his chair. He dropped down into it, his wet coat slapping against the leather. Singh stared at him; her eyes were framed with dark circles. Her black hair was slightly frayed.

She'd never looked so determined.

'I found these files linking to Project Hailstorm, but surprise surprise, they were inaccessible. So, I did some cross referencing, running the names of the locations I have for the Project through the database and I found a few other 'missions' that fall under the same radar. Again, these files are locked down.'

'Singh...' Pearce began but was immediately cut off.

'Now usually, the military are pretty forthcoming with records. Obviously, if we need to know about someone's military history, it could be crucial in whatever our investigation is. But not only are these files locked down, but many of Sam Pope's military records are also off limits. I'm telling you, Pearce, something doesn't add up. Tie that up with Wallace coming to see me, and I think there's something there that people don't want coming out.'

'Singh, listen, you have to...' Pearce tried, needlessly, again.

'Well, I've managed to extract a number of files into a secure folder and have called in a favour with Jake in IT. I have the files saved on a private cloud. Now who was that guy? Etheridge? The one who clearly helped Sam but denies it. I'll get him to take a look and...'

'Singh, for the love of God, listen to me.' Pearce cut in, stopping Singh in her tracks and drawing a shocked look from her. 'You have to stop this. Please.'

'Stop this?' Singh checked the door was closed and then lowered her voice. 'Pearce, I've got senior military officials telling me to shut this down. I've clearly latched onto something and if it can help Sam in any way, then I need to do this.'

'But it's not your job, is it?' Pearce said, rubbing the bridge of his nose in frustration. 'Your job is to catch Sam.'

'No. My job is to do what's right. I made a solemn vow when I passed out to protect and serve, to uphold justice and above all else, do what's right.' Singh's voice cracked slightly, and Pearce looked at her with concern. It was if he could finally see the truth. The truth that she was trying to erase.

She was close to failing.

'Singh.' Pearce sighed. 'Amara. Ashton has blackmailed me to dig up whatever I can on you. She wants you out by the end of the week.'

Singh straightened, gathering her paperwork from the desk and turning to Pearce in his chair.

'I know I'm as good as gone. I was so blinkered for so long, the only thing I cared about was how far I could push myself in this place. How far I could go. How many people I could help.' Singh shook her head slightly, pulling her lips into a tight line. 'Somewhere along the way, I lost what was important.'

'What's that?' Pearce asked, casting a caring and interested eye over her. She took a deep breath before responding.

'Doing the right thing.'

Both of them smiled, knowing that Sam Pope, a man both of them had been tasked with catching at different points, had changed their view on the law. Had shown them another path to justice. It wasn't one they could take themselves.

But it was one they could both help him down.

Pearce stood, stretching his back and offering the soulful looking Singh his most charming smile.

'Well, we better take a trip to Farnham, eh?'

'Pearce?' Singh raised an eyebrow.

'Well, you want to go speak to Etheridge, right? I'm sure that computer nerd can sort you out.'

Singh felt her grip on his folder loosen and the weight gently lift off her slight shoulders. Having felt like she was losing herself it was good to find someone just as lost.

The most worrying thing was, there was no fear. Only a buzzing need to do the right thing.

As if she had a new purpose.

As she opened the door and slid through, she turned

back to Pearce, who was following suit, his drenched over-coat in his hand.

'But what about you, Pearce?'

'In for a penny, in for a pound.' He chuckled, locking his door. 'Besides, I'm pretty sure that bitch would kick me out ten seconds after you.'

The two of them laughed, their joy drawing a few disconcerting looks from the fellow officers. They were outcasts, but as they walked towards the exit, they felt a connection. A force of nature that had brought them together.

Justice.

———

It had been a long night.

Etheridge had lost track of the time, the measurement becoming redundant around the time his mysterious intruder broke his second finger. Now, Etheridge was strapped to a chair, his body aching, and his shirt stuck to his body through sweat. The back of his head was sticky with blood, the painful souvenir of a blow from the man's gun. After introducing Etheridge to the sharp edge of his own door, the man had proceeded to ask him where Sam was.

Etheridge pleaded ignorance, sat on the floor of the hallway, his eyebrow gushing blood and blinding his right eye.

The man had responded with a hard boot to the ribs, cracking one of them instantly and hammering the air from Etheridge's lungs. The man had repeated his ques-tion, his thick Manchurian accent laced with menace. Etheridge thought about it, for only a split second and real-ized that giving Sam up wasn't an option. His mind flashed back to the bottom of that mountain, just outside Egypt.

His leg broken.

Death only seconds away.

Sam had saved his life that day, dispatching three rounds expertly, eradicating Etheridge's would-be killers.

He owed Sam.

Refusing to speak, Etheridge had felt the hard, metal butt of the pistol come down on the back of his skull and turning everything to black.

When he awoke, a few hours had passed, and he was strapped to his computer chair in his loft-converted office. Although his spacious mansion had a number of rooms to accommodate a workspace, he liked the idea of being sat on the top floor. Pathetically, it made him feel like he was the top dog.

He already owned his own company.

Despite the egocentric reasoning, the loft had been converted into a lovely, light filled office where he worked on a number of highly profitable contracts. Now, under the winter moon, the slanted windows that adorned the roof were being hammered by the downpour. Whatever time it was, it didn't register with him and woozily he was confronted by his assailant.

The masked man asked again.

Etheridge again refused to answer.

The man took Etheridge's left hand and with his own gloved grip, snapped his index finger. Etheridge roared with pain, instantly receiving a jaw rocking right hook. The man asked again.

Same response.

Same outcome.

The man snapped Etheridge's middle finger, wrenching against its socket until his fingernail touched the back of his hand.

This happened twice more until only the thumb was left standing. Etheridge was crying, the pain of his hand buzzed through his brain like a bumble bee. His fingers were scattered across his hand, useless and shattered. The cable wrapped tightly around his body was beginning to rub, causing a slight friction burn on his skin. He wasn't a large man, and partook in badminton and squash to keep fit.

But he was trapped on the chair, as the masked man sat at his desk, his eyes scanning the multiple computer screens. The man was searching through Etheridge's files, hunting for any scraps of information that could take him to Sam.

Whoever he was, he was dangerous.

Etheridge knew Sam's world had always been filled with danger and violence. Pre and post Jamie's death.

But this man, he radiated a chaos that caused his stomach to knot and Etheridge knew that sending him to Sam would be like pulling the trigger himself.

But what would this man do if he continued to stay silent?

As if reading his mind, the man spun round in the leather chair, slightly slouched, his brilliant blue eyes glistened with impatience as he glared at Etheridge.

The man had hung his leather trench coat in the hall and was now just in his black jeans and jumper.

The only noticeable feature Etheridge had noticed, was the scarring around the man's left eye. The skin was charred and the eyelid itself was slightly crooked.

Whatever had happened, it was painful.

An agony that looked like it had been reincarnated as this mysterious man in black.

'I'm done playing games, Mr Etheridge.' The masked man spoke softly. He pushed himself up from the chair and walked towards the door, patting Etheridge on the side of the face as he passed. Etheridge flinched, then shook with fear as the man left the room. Immediately, he scanned the room, hoping beyond hope that he had a mobile phone or any means of sending for help.

Below, in his bedroom, he had a panic alarm that would notify the police of any intrusion. He'd installed it when one of Kayleigh's ex-lovers had tried to break in to see her.

Kayleigh?

A wave of panic crashed through Etheridge like the rising tide, the horror of Kayleigh returning home to make amends now would undoubtedly end with her death. The door swung open again, bringing Etheridge back into the situation and the man approached him, holding a white, Egyptian cotton towel in one hand and a large, two-litre bottle of water in the other. He placed the bottle down and then turned to Etheridge.

'These look expensive.' The man mused. 'What's the thread count?'

Before Etheridge could answer the man lunged forward, wrapping the soft, thick towel around Etheridge's face, pulling tight at the back to completely cover him. The man pulled the towel downwards, tilting Etheridge's head over the back of the chair. Terrified, Etheridge went stiff, his muscles tightening in sheer panic. The man leant in towards his ear.

'Now, I'm going to give you a brief example of what your next few hours look like, if you can hold on that long.'

With his hand still pulling the towel taut, the man lifted the bottle of water over Etheridge's covered face and tipped it. The water splashed down onto the towel, the soft, plush fibres absorbing it instantly. As it did, it began to soak through, the water filling the nose and mouth of the man trapped underneath.

Etheridge was drowning.

He squirmed and gasped and after a few more moments, the man released his hold and pulled the towel back. Etheridge lunged forward, gasping for breath, his eyes red with tears. Panicked, he took short, sharp breaths, betraying his body's need for a full intake. Etheridge felt the burning sensation of vomit forming the back of his throat, his nostril stinging. The man's calm voice echoed in his ear.

'Where can I find Sam Pope?'

Etheridge took a few more breathes, willing himself to be the soldier he set out to be.

'I...don't... know,' he finally responded.

'That's a shame.'

The man wrapped the towel over Etheridge's face again, ignoring the pleas for mercy and pulled it tight. Yanking it backwards, he tipped the rest of the water over the towel, emotionless as Etheridge squirmed and fought for survival. He waited longer this time, allowing Etheridge to edge a little further to death, before pulling the towel back and letting the air rush towards a terrorized Etheridge.

This wouldn't last much longer.

They both knew that.

The man in black sighed, shaking his head at the empty bottle of water.

'I'm going to have to get some more water,' he said coldly, as Etheridge stared vacantly ahead, accepting his slow, agonizing fate. Just as the man turned, the computer let out a rewarding ding, and a photo flashed up.

The man stopped in his tracks.

Etheridge lifted his head and felt a twinge of guilt course through his beaten body.

It was Sam Pope.

The name next to the photo said 'Jonathan Cooper', the forged passport completely undetectable. But Etheridge had been tracking it, ensuring he could keep tabs on Sam's whereabouts. It was that new-found drive to help Sam that could now, ultimately, lead to the exact opposite. The intruder leant forward, hand on the desk and inspected the image with a sneer on his face.

The passport had been scanned in at Rome Termini.

Pope was in Italy.

'There you are,' the man uttered grimly, his muscles tensing with fury at the very sight of Sam. He pushed himself away from the desk and turned back to Etheridge. The man was bloodied and soaked through, his hand a mess of broken bones.

But the man had not cracked.

He was impressed. Casually, the man in black pulled a pistol from the back of his jeans and Etheridge's eyes opened wide with fear.

'Please, don't kill me,' Etheridge begged, all sense of self-respect had long since dissipated. 'You got what you wanted.'

'I know,' the man said calmly. 'I'm not going to kill you.'

Lunging forward, the man pressed the barrel of the gun into Etheridge's knee and pulled the trigger. A large flash and Etheridge felt an instant burning, followed by the sheer agony of the bullet shattering through his kneecap and rupturing every ligament in its way. It burst out the back of his leg in a magnificent spray of blood before embedding itself in the floor.

Etheridge howled in agony, but a few seconds later, a combination of the shock and pain caused him to drop into a lucid unconsciousness.

The man in black had shot to wound, but as he left, he wondered if anyone would find the man in time before he bled out. As he made his way down the stairs, Etheridge slumped forward in the chair, the cable pulling tight.

He didn't have long.

CHAPTER EIGHTEEN

Another shudder of turbulence shook the private plane like a baby's rattle and Wallace gripped the fine, leather armrest. Despite being a man who was practically bathing in blood, he'd always detested flying. Control and power were two things he craved to the point of obsession but being in the hands of the pilot and the incredible technology never sat comfortably with him.

When he was a passenger, he wasn't in control.

The weather outside wasn't helping, the ferocious winter storm attacking the plane like an antidote attacking a virus, and his mind wandered to the likely outbreak of chemical warfare in the next few months. Obviously, this was unknown to the doughy eyed public, all of them living blissfully in their safety nets.

He knew the truth about what was happening in the dark corners of the world.

It was his job to prevent it.

With a self-satisfied chortle, he relaxed, allowing his broad shoulders to sink into the supple leather chair on the private jet. Being a man of considerable power, he was able to charter these jets for an emergency.

And this most certainly was an emergency.

It had been over a year since he'd last had any dealing with Carl Marsden and the name always triggered a trickle of regret. For over two decades, Marsden and Wallace had worked together, each becoming indispensable to the military in their own way. Marsden was a man of the people, a heck of a soldier who commanded respect and loyalty. Despite their philosophies differing radically, Wallace had always admired the way Marsden bonded with his troops.

They would run into hell for him. And beyond.

But while Marsden could spot a true talent and develop it into a ruthless, killing machine, he never operated with the same conviction as Wallace. While they were both dedicated to making the world a safer place, Marsden's ideals were too soft.

Marsden believed people were intrinsically good. That bad people were not born that way.

Wallace, however, saw himself as a realist. He knew that if you wanted to deal with the dirty you had to get into the mud with them. That's what eventually caused them to butt heads and ever since Project Hailstorm, they'd barely spoken. There was the unfortunate incident with Sam Pope and the even more tragic death of his child, but Wallace had seen worse happen to better people.

It was the way of the world.

Death and pain were inevitable and those who could use it as currency could dictate things.

It was a harsh truth, but one he stood vehemently by.

A truth that Marsden had never understood and one which broke their partnership. Since Sam went off the rails, Marsden had shipped himself out, working out of a military base in Switzerland for the past year. Wallace had kept tabs on him, as well as Sam. It had always paid to keep an eye on those who were involved in Black Ops missions. Although they were off the book, should anyone start sniffing there was always an opportunity to hang one of them out to dry.

That irritating Amara Singh had started digging in the wrong garden and Wallace was pleased he'd already snuffed her out. AC Ashton was a strong, powerful woman and he was aroused by the idea of bedding her. It would happen. The woman was desperate to take the reins of the Metropolitan Police and he would ensure that his gratification would see her ascend to the throne.

Plus, he knew the power he wielded was like a magnet for women who craved the very same.

The jet shook again, and Wallace felt his knuckles whiten over the arm rest. On the table in front of him, his coffee shook slightly, next to the tablet which was jam packed with confidential files.

Most of them were about Marsden.

Others about Sam Pope.

He'd been informed that Trevor Sims, the Head of Field Ops for Blackridge had apprehended Sam at Kiev airport. Under an assumed identity, Sam had brutalized one of Ukraine's most notorious crime families. Wallace couldn't care less. As far as he was concerned, Sam could eradicate every worthless piece of criminal scum this side of the equator. But Blackridge had been hired to find Marsden, who had recently gone on the run with vital files.

It was being treated as treason and potentially, as a terror threat.

Wallace knew Marsden, had known him for years and was concerned at how this could end for him. While their differences had long since severed any ties of friendship, Wallace needed to be there when Sims finally apprehended him.

Sims, while being as ambitious as Wallace, always craved money over power. It was a trait that Wallace found repugnant and the man was so slimy he should come with his own hand sanitizer. But while he was never the soldier Wallace was, Sims was able to make the right connections, put together the most effective teams and had transformed Blackridge into an unstoppable machine.

The reports had come in.

Marsden was on his way to Rome.

CCTV had confirmed that Sam Pope had also made it onto the same train headed out of Berlin train station.

That very train would be arriving into Rome within the next few hours and with Sims's vast funding, there was no doubt he and his men would be waiting at the gate.

Marsden would be taken in at gun point.

Sam, too.

While bridges may have been burned, Wallace knew he had to be there. Whatever Marsden was doing, Wallace needed to know. He couldn't believe Marsden would betray his country, but there was no smoke without fire.

As had been the case, for so many years, Wallace was the man you called to put those fires out.

As the plane rattled on towards the Italian capital, Wallace sat back in his chair, took a deep breath and once again cursed the world for always bringing out the worst in people.

———

Rome Termini had come to a complete standstill.

After the news of a gunshot had done the rounds on the radios, the security and *Polizia di Stato* immediately shut down all platforms. Commuters were slowly being asked to make their way towards the exits, a task proving more diffi-cult than it needed to be.

With armed men in black shirts surrounding the recent arrival from Berlin, the gossip hungry public had converged towards the platform, phones ready to try to share their experience with the world through any means necessary. The local authorities had cordoned off the platform, with two young officers sternly yet pointlessly telling the public to evacuate the building.

On the platform itself, a number of armed men in black polo shirts stood, their black bomber jackets concealing automatic weapons which had caused a stir of excitement. The initial fear of a potential gunman had subsided with the arrival of Blackridge, with four men and a woman marching onto the platform the second the train began its slow crawl alongside the concrete. As it had come to a stop, the team had begun to spread out, but the bellowing gunshot had changed their plans.

Now, with their hands at the ready, they waited for the police officers who had embarked the train to return with their gunman. A search of the other carriages by the other officers had discovered two brutally beaten passengers, both of whom were wearing the same uniform. Sims, stood at the front, his brown trench coat shielding him from the cold, was furious.

Marsden was good, but he wasn't that good.

This was clearly the work of Sam Pope.

Rocky and Ray had both been incapacitated. There was no sign of Evans, which lead Sims to believe there was probably a job of scraping up some remains somewhere between here and Berlin.

It didn't matter. Not really.

These soldiers knew the drill. They got paid handsomely and were given the freedom to do whatever they liked, within reason.

What mattered was they had Marsden and sure enough, to a new wave of excited murmuring from the crowd behind, Sims watched with a smug grin as Marsden was roughly led from the train to the platform.

Sam watched from the crowd.

Knowing he was skating very close to the edge; Sam just couldn't leave. As soon as he'd beeped through the barrier and saw the large, glass exit to the station, he felt his legs lock in place. Yes, Marsden had been very clear on his instructions. Whatever was on the USB, whatever dark secrets it held and whatever world changes it would enforce, Sam just couldn't leave him behind.

They didn't leave men behind.

While his mentor had been right in creating the diversion to allow him to escape, it had also given Sam the opportunity to begin to formulate his plan. Ever since he'd stormed the High Rise six months previously Sam had realized his recklessness would soon catch up with him. It almost happened when he rescued Aaron Hill from the second High Rise.

It very nearly did at the docks. He still had the bullet wound in the leg and the battle scars from his brutal fight with Oleg Kovalenko to show for it.

But now, he needed to act quickly but with restraint.

Ensuring he was hidden by a large, concrete pillar that held up the second floor of the grand central station, Sam peered over the crowd at the situation unfolding before him.

With an almost limitless bank behind him, Sims had chartered a private jet to Rome the second their train left. They were lying in wait and the smug look on Sims's face told Sam that Blackridge thought the battle had been won.

That the fight was over.

Sam would be more than happy to disappoint them.

As the officers led Marsden towards Sims, Buck stepped in, removing their prisoner and shunting Marsden roughly towards his boss. Buck's face wore the dark, purple bruises of a man who had overstepped his boundaries. Sam smiled at his handiwork. Although he was too far away to hear the conversation, Sam knew Sims was gloating, most likely threatening Marsden with the similar threats he'd made to him in a Ukrainian airport a few days earlier.

The man was a parasite, but one who had manoeuvred himself into a position of untouchable power.

Again, Sam would be happy to disappoint.

With a curious eye, Sam scanned the rest of the platform, noting the two new members of the team, both as unrecognizable as the others. Buzz cuts, bulging, tattoo-covered arms, and the steely gaze of someone who would shoot first and ask never.

The prime Blackridge candidate.

Standing nearer the crowd was Alex, her hands on her hips and a look of pained regret on her pretty face. Her taut, muscular frame was covered by her own bomber jacket, but alongside the armed and dangerous soldiers, she looked every bit the prisoner she was.

Sam needed to take a risk.

He began to squeeze through the crowd, careful not to draw any attention from the surveilling police officers. As he moved, a young lady swung her bag backwards, the thick leather crashing into Sam's leg and causing him to wince. She spun around, her worried face framed by dark, wavy hair and she offered an apology in Italian. Sam nodded his acceptance and then slid past, making his way to the front of the row. Luckily for him, about five people to his right, an elderly man was barking at the officer with a rising agitation.

Sam called out Alex's name as hushed as he could.

A confused frown burrowed across her brow and Alex turned, unsure of whether she'd been summoned. She scanned the crowd and then stopped, her jaw opening slightly with shock.

It was Sam.

Peering back at her crew, she knew she had a small

window. Sims was still gloating, and the others were now chaperoning the medics as they carried the battered body of Rocky from the train. She stepped backwards four times and then quickly turned on her heel, coming face to face with Sam. While there was no future for them, a fact they both knew, they smiled as their eyes met, both flashing back to the night of passion they'd shared.

'Sam,' she spoke quietly, shaking her head at the audacity. 'What the fuck are you doing?'

'Where are they taking him?'

'You need to go,' Alex demanded, glancing back, her face wild with worry.

'Trevi Fountain. Four o'clock.' Sam stated. 'Bring the guys. Make it look legit.'

Alex went to challenge him but stopped herself. For the first time since meeting him, she saw the cold, ruthless killer that Sims had described him as. They had someone he cared deeply about and she could see, through whatever means it took, Sam would get him out. With a deep sigh, she nodded, agreeing to the terms.

'What are you going to do?' she eventually asked, peering once more over her shoulder. The crowd collectively gasped as the beaten body of Ray was pulled out by the medics.

'What I do.'

With that, Sam turned and forced his way back through the crowd, his hand reaching into his pocket and his fingers wrapped around the USB stick. It was what had brought all of this together, this small, thin implement that Marsden was willing to lay his life down for.

Well, Sam wasn't willing to let him.

He would take care of the USB, ensure that the mission, regardless of its ending, would never be in vain.

Then, he would find where they kept Marsden and he planned on burning it to the ground.

With a few hours until his rendezvous, Sam felt his stomach rumble, the sheer intensity of the last twenty-four hours threatening to derail him with hunger. As he strode through the exit and out into the busy, freezing streets of Rome, he stuffed his hand into his other pocket where he had his passport and the money he'd liberated from Ray. Behind him, the large 'Roma Termini' stood proudly above the large, automatic door.

His stomach rumbled again, and Sam headed for the first sign that was marked *Pizza*.

Well, when in Rome.

CHAPTER NINETEEN

The journey to Farnham had been uncomfortable.

While getting the train back to his was always a nightmare due to the inhumane commuter crush, Pearce and Singh had realized that a tension had arisen between them. It was nothing sexual, Pearce was twice her age and felt more paternal than anything else towards her.

No, the tension was due to what they'd decided.

While it may have been slightly jovial when Pearce had agreed to help, they had both decided to cross that line. They were both acting against the wishes of their senior officer.

The wishes of the Metropolitan Police.

With sterling careers behind them, their commitment to the law and the justice system had never been in doubt. Pearce had even directed his career to the corrupt behind the badge such was his belief in it.

Now, it had changed.

And as they'd driven the forty miles out of London and to Farnham, the gravity of their situation dawned on them. The silence between them a white elephant, with neither of them able to talk the other out of it. While

Pearce was on the wind down of his career, he'd been offered a reprieve that involved tarnishing Singh.

He would not and could not do it.

Singh knew she was being ushered towards the door, her perceived failures in charge of the Sam Pope Task Force had seen her loyalty, quite rightly, questioned. They were hoping she would hand over her badge and walk away from it all.

She would not and could not do that.

As they'd sped down the M4, the rain had lashed down upon the motorway with a vengeance. The torrential downpour reduced the visibility and the traffic gave in to the elements. Cars slowed down and Pearce found himself frustratingly doing forty, ensuring the correct distance was maintained. The added time wasn't welcome, as the longer they drove, the harder it was to break the silence.

The hour-long journey took a little over ninety minutes and both were relieved as they pulled up outside Etheridge's gate. The large, iron gate stood in their way and Pearce huddled under his jacket as he reached up for the intercom.

It buzzed but there was no response.

Peering through the rain, Pearce could see Etheridge's Porsche 911 Carrera GTS parked up the drive, along with a state-of-the-art Range Rover, the rain shimmering off the fresh, black paint job. The man was a self-made millionaire, but when Pearce had met him a few weeks back, he'd found him rather affable.

He buzzed again and again no answer.

Strange.

Pearce turned back to the car and shook his head, alerting Singh to the situation. She pushed open the passenger door and was greeted by the freezing rain, grimacing as it seeped through her thin blazer. Within seconds, her jet-black hair was pinned to her head and she rushed towards the gate.

'No answer?' she yelled, the crashing water on the pavement echoing like white noise behind them.

'Nope.' Pearce nodded to the car. 'Both cars still here.'

Singh didn't need a second look and within moments, she was scaling the slick, wet iron gate, carefully skipping over the points that ran along the top. She dropped down to the other side, a slight ache shot up her spine.

No doubt her body reminding her of the beating she took among those shipping crates.

Sighing deeply, Pearce followed, his older joints refusing to allow his ascent to be as straight forward. As he tried to clamber off the top, his loafers slipped on the metal bar, sending him crashing the six feet to the cold, hard concrete,

'Shitbags,' he cursed loudly, drawing a chuckle from Singh who offered him a hand up. He quickly saw the funny side and gladly clasped her wrist and she hauled him to her feet. The tension had been washed away, the rain slathering both of them and they realized why they were there.

To help Sam and find the truth.

It didn't matter about how they'd arrived at this point.

Singh rushed towards the door and just as she went to thump her fist against it, she stopped herself. Pearce turned to her in confusion before following her eye line.

Singh was staring at the side of the door.

It was slightly ajar.

Carefully, Singh pushed it open, revealing the plush, well-decorated hallway. The rain followed quickly, splattering the floor as Singh and Pearce carefully stepped over the threshold.

The specks of blood across the floor instantly put them on high alert.

'Paul!' Pearce shouted, his voice echoing off the high ceilings. 'Paul, it's Detective Pearce.'

They ventured further into the house, past the expensively furnished living room which housed a glorious ninety-two-inch flat screen TV. It adorned the wall like a trophy.

Pearce headed for the stairs, his mind returning to the visit he'd paid Etheridge after Sam had taken down the Kovalenko's. Someone had helped Sam, the technical work it took to track the bank accounts of the Acid Gang required certain skills that he knew Sam didn't possess.

But Etheridge did and between the two of them, they'd shared an unspoken moment of confirmation.

Singh had also been to the mansion as well, although her memories were clouded with failure.

She'd sent an Armed Response team into the house to take down Sam, yet all of them were removed with bullet wounds. He'd shot to wound, aiming for the centre of the shin bones, but still, she had more than enough on her mind to be reminded of the pain and anger that hung heavy on her conscience.

That was when she'd first met Sam, as he incapacitated and then restrained her.

Life had taken a strange path since then, but the idea of walking across the landing where a number of her friends were shot still made her stomach turn.

Sam was still a criminal. She had to remind herself that. But the line between right and wrong had blurred so much, it resembled a smudge.

As she thought about that regrettable night, she collided with Pearce, who had stopped on the landing before the next staircase which led to what she believed would be a sizeable loft extension.

'Paul!' Pearce yelled again. There was no answer, although the ping of a computer could be heard. The light from the office crept over the landing, beckoning them up. The signs of life were not accompanied with any sounds of movement and Pearce purposefully stood in front of Singh, much to her amusement. She was one of the toughest officers on the force, with an extensive background in martial arts and Armed Response.

She could handle herself.

Pearce crept up the first few steps, his hand clutching the bannister, his eyes locked on the landing ahead. He called out again, edging up step by step. Again, he was met with silence and with Singh close behind him, he stepped uneasily onto the landing.

The door to the office was slightly ajar, the low hum of several computers eking out through the gap. Pearce took a breath and pushed the door open.

Both of them froze in shock.

Strapped to a chair, was an unconscious Paul Etheridge. His entire head and upper body were soaked, with two empty bottles and a towel surrounding the puddle of water beneath him. Pearce stepped in quickly, shaking his head at what clearly looked like a torture scene. More worrying was the blood pooling around the base of the chair, the trail leading back up Etheridge's leg to the shattered knee cap. One of his hands had been maimed, the fingers snapped and sticking in different directions.

He wore bruises and cuts on his motionless face.

Etheridge had been beaten, tortured, and then left for dead.

Pearce felt sick, having met the man a few weeks before and finding him rather charming. As if snapping back into the room, he dashed forward, past the computer screens and straight to the prone Etheridge, immediately reaching out pressing his fingers against his wet neck.

'He's alive,' Pearce confirmed, looking back at Singh

who was carefully walking into the room, her hands in her pockets so as not to tamper with any evidence.

'Who the hell did this?' Singh asked, her eyes darting around the lavish office. Something on the screen caught her eye.

'I don't know,' Pearce began, pulling his mobile phone from his pocket and hitting the screen three times. 'You need to leave, Singh.'

'Adrian. Look,' Singh said, ignoring Pearce as she leant in towards the screen.

'Singh. You need to go now,' Pearce began before his call connected. 'Hello, this is Detective Inspector Adrian Pearce. I need an ambulance and police assistance at 15 Collington Close. Male, early forties, alive but unresponsive. Potential gunshot wound to the leg.'

As Pearce finished his distress call, Singh yelled for him again.

'It's Sam.'

'We can't jump to conclusions, Singh. Etheridge owns a private online security company. He might have enemies.'

Singh beckoned him over then pointed to the screen, her face alive with excitement.

'It's Sam. Look.'

'Well slap my sausage,' Pearce said in exasperation. 'You don't think he did this, do you?'

'No. But I think he's the reason for this. Whoever it was, they wanted Sam and that poor guy was helping the wrong guy at the wrong time.'

'Fuck. He's in Rome,' Pearce said, to nobody in particular. 'Anyway, Singh, you have to go.'

'I'm not leaving. We need to get him to a hospital.'

'The ambulance is on its way and what the hell do you think Ashton will say if she finds out you were here searching for more Sam Pope clues?'

'But what about…'

'Don't worry about me.' Pearce waved her off. 'I'll say I was following up on a lead or some crap. You need to go. I'll call you.'

Singh nodded and then glanced once more at the battered Etheridge, still strapped to his chair. It was a dangerous world she was stepping into, where innocent civilians were treated as after thoughts. Whoever was hunting Sam had been cold, cruel, and calculated. Both her and Pearce shared a worried look, both of them wondering how much danger Sam was in.

Singh took her leave, concerned for Etheridge's health but just as frustrated that he couldn't help.

She couldn't help that all of this was connected. That there was a link between it all.

It sat with Sam and it resided somewhere on her files.

She bound out of the house and into the rain, walking briskly past Pearce's car and headed towards the main road they'd ventured down previously. She would need to find somewhere to reconvene and then hopefully, once Etheridge's survival was confirmed, she and Pearce could get back to hunting the truth. As she strode through the downpour, Singh didn't notice the black 4x4 which was station further down the road.

She certainly didn't see the two men sat in the front seat, one of them staring at her through his military issued binoculars.

With the rain lashing against their windscreen, they brought their car to life once more, indicated and slowly pulled out onto the road, continuing their surveillance of the plucky detective.

———

The narrow streets of Rome opened up onto the splendor of the Trevi Fountain, which in spite of the inclement weather, was still a hot bed of activity. A smattering of drizzle was lightly dusting the groups of tourists, who eagerly gathered around the iconic fountain, selfie sticks at the ready. The magnificent travertine stone structure that stood behind the pool of water loomed proudly; a coat of arms sat atop. The fountain itself was centuries old, but over time had been renovated numerous times. The most recent was in 2014, the work involving the inclusion of over a hundred LED bulbs to maximize the drawing potential at night.

While it improved the visibility of the stunning struc-ture and the lights shimmering across the water created a magical view, it hardly fit in with the aesthetic.

But everything moved on eventually.

Everything needed fixing.

Saving.

Which is what Sam told himself as he stood, his back pressed against the stone barrier that surrounded the water. Behind him, the great structure shot up to the greying sky, with sculptures of impressive men in white marble towering over everyone. To his left, a group of Japanese tourists were taking turns to have their photo taken, before tossing a few euros over their left shoulder with their right hand. It was a well-known tradition, one that Sam was sure had been spread by the Italian government itself.

With the amount of coins being launched into the water, Sam understood how they'd paid for the fancy new light bulbs.

Chuckling to himself, he pushed his hand into his pocket, wincing at the pain that hummed in his thigh and returned with his final few euros. The money he'd stolen from Ray had gone, all that was left was a handful of coins and his receipt.

Sam didn't believe in luck or in superstition. Years out in the deserts, staring down the sniper scope had taught him that the world didn't run on it either. Everything was managed by the smallest of margins. The smallest details, even when slightly tweaked, could send ripples of change.

Whether it be caused by a bullet or a USB drive.

There was no luck. No coincidence. Sam knew that what he was planning to do had only two possible outcomes. The most likely would see him in shackles, stuffed away in a hole where he would never see freedom again. The risk he was about to take was monumental, but there was no other option.

Eventually everything needed saving and right now, that was Marsden.

A man who had done everything he could to bring Sam back from his own darkness.

The rain picked up slightly, the thicker drops colliding harshly against his cut face. A woman strode by, wrapped up in her winter best with her arm aloft. Her fingers gripped a flag which she held up as a beacon, yelling something in Italian as a group of spellbound tourists approached the fountain, phones at the ready.

It was a beautiful structure, Sam had to admit. It was even more beautiful when it wasn't viewed through a phone screen.

The buzz of excitement increased, and Sam watched the eclectic tour group all gawp and marvel at the wonderful attraction. Beyond the newest group to approach from the main road, Sam saw a black 4X4 roll to a stop. The windscreen wipers were frantically battling the recent onslaught and the driver window slowly slid down.

Alex.

Sam glanced at his watch.

Four o'clock.

Right on time.

As her eyes scanned the courtyard, they eventually rested on him and she offered a half-baked smile. Right on cue, the two rear doors opened, and the two new guys that Sam had seen at the train station stepped out. Decked in the usual get up and wearing cocky expressions across their clean shaven, squared jaws, Sam felt his blood boil at the idea of them once being actual soldiers.

Now they were just hired help.

With an undeserved swagger, both men stomped through the crowds, roughly moving people out of their way. Sam rolled his eyes at the dick swinging and as they approached, one of them sneered.

'You got a problem?' the man barked; his eyes shielded pathetically behind his shades despite the darkening sky.

'Plenty,' Sam responded confidently. 'I doubt you'd be one of them.'

'All right, smart-ass.' The other one cut in, a southern twang to his American accent. 'Let's go.'

Sam nodded and then casually tossed the coins over his shoulder, as if he'd just spilt some salt. The two guys chuckled.

'That ain't gonna help, buddy.' The first guy smirked. 'You're shit out of luck.'

Sam nodded and as he neared, one of them roughly reached for his arm and twisted it behind his back. The other marched ahead, clearing a path as if Sam was some sort of celebrity. The onlookers watched with intrigue, their visit to the historic landmark enhanced with this sudden exchange. The guy in front pulled open the rear door of the 4X4 and Sam was roughly shoved onto the back seat. His chaperone followed, pulling the gun from the inside of his bomber jacket and pointing it directly at his face.

They slammed the door and the other guy raced around the car and jumped into the passenger side, barking an order for Alex to drive.

'Sam,' Alex said, nodding into the mirror.

'Alex,' Sam responded, before his captor flicked his wrist forward, catching him on the side of the head with the handle of the gun. Sam rocked back, his head spinning from the blow and the man reasserted his aim, the gun pressed against Sam's skull.

He felt like his brain was spinning.

The jock in the front seat turned, impressed at his friend's attack.

'You just shut the fuck up,' he said confidently. 'Alex, let's go.'

Alex shot another glance into the mirror, making sure Sam was okay and then she slid the car into the gear and pulled out onto the Vespa filled streets of Rome. Sam took a deep breath to recompose and he tried blinking away the pain.

He needed to be ready for the next time they attacked.

And there would be a next time. He was certain of it.

With the honking horns of inner-city traffic providing the background music, they slowly began their drive through Rome.

CHAPTER TWENTY

When the bag was pulled off Marsden's head, the brightness of the room almost blinded him. After he'd been publicly arrested, Sims had demanded his crew find Sam immediately. The beatings two of his soldiers had taken had confirmed to Sims that Pope was on-board the train, but Marsden was thrilled when Sims's goons reported he'd gone.

Sam was in the wind, with enough proof to bring everything down.

What happened now was inconsequential.

Sims had angrily ordered Marsden into one of his 4X4s, and once in, two of Blackridge's burliest men punched him in the stomach with hammerlike fists. Marsden had coughed up blood, but before he could hunch over to spit it out, Sims shoved a gun in his face, telling Marsden he had two minutes to appreciate the sun, because it was the last time he would see it.

As they ascended a hill just outside of Rome, Marsden caught a glimpse of a beautiful skyline, the stylish buildings that lined the streets of the iconic city shimmered under the wet gloss of rain. While the sun was hidden behind darkened clouds, the city emitted a gothic feel that Marsden found breathtaking. A tear slid down his cheek, his final view of the outside world was one of true beauty.

He'd never had a family.

His entire life had been to serve his country.

Now his death would be in service too.

A black sack was roughly shoved over his head, blocking his vision. His consciousness soon disappeared, as a clubbing blow rocked his skull, sending him into a deep blackness.

When he'd come to, he was sat up, an uncomfortable metal chair beneath him. His hands were bound behind his back, the cold metal of the cuffs digging into his skin. The room was cold, and the dank smell that filtered through the sack told him it was underground. Marsden had been in many rooms like this before.

Covert. Off the books.

This was a place where those with access were given permission to do whatever they wanted.

Whatever was necessary.

As he'd sat in the dark, he could hear Blackridge moving around, a few people entering the room and placing items on the table in front, no doubt tools that would be used to extract either the information or some sick satisfaction from him. The man known as Buck, who had been stuck to Sims's side like a lap dog, had decided to get in some practice on Marsden's trapped body, rocking him a few times with hard strikes to the kidneys before cracking his nose with a vicious right hook.

That was when the sack was whipped from his head, exposing him to the bright, halogen tube which buzzed almost as loudly. Marsden blinked through the pain, his shattered cartilage making it hard to breathe in.

The room was just as he'd pictured it, dark, with no

distinguishing features. Just four walls, with a metal door on the far side.

In front of him was a metal table.

On the other side, sat Sims.

Marsden turned his head to the side and spat on the dusty, concrete floor, sending a splatter of blood to the ground. It had been a few years since he'd seen Sims, and time hadn't been kind. The hair was thinning, and gravity was having its wicked way with the skin under his chin. The years of politicking from behind his desk had caused his gut to grow and it pressed against his sweat covered shirt.

Despite the bitter cold, Sims was nervous.

'Nice to see you, Carl,' Sims said, his chunky hands clasped on the table.

'I can't say the same,' Marsden retorted, noticing the scowl on Buck's face as he stood behind Sims, his back pressed against the wall. His face was covered in bruises, no doubt from an altercation with Sam. Marsden was pretty sure he knew how it went.

'Well, I don't see why we can't at least talk like adults.'

'Adults?' Marsden chuckled. 'You had your boy go to work on me while I was strapped to a chair. You had people chase and try to kill me on that train. I have nothing to say to you except go to hell.'

Sims sighed and sat back in his chair. He pulled a cigar from his pocket, followed by a chrome cigar cutter. With a quick snap, he took the end of the cigar off before slamming it on the table. Striking a match, Sims puffed a few thick, poisonous clouds into the already stuffy room.

'Where are the files?' Sims asked calmly.

'What files?'

'Let's not do this, Carl.' Sims sat forward. 'Look around. You're a long fucking way from home with a long fucking night ahead of you. Now I've got a few guys in the hospital and one guy missing, just trying to bring you and your boy, Sam, in. In one piece, I might add. Now I really don't want to put you through any more pain than I already have, but you have to work with me. So, I'll ask again. Where are the files?'

'Trevor, believe me when I tell you, I've been threatened with a lot worse, by a lot tougher.' Marsden smiled; his teeth stained with blood. 'So, I'll answer again, what files?'

Trevor lifted his right hand and immediately, Buck stomped across the room, his boots echoing off the walls. The edges of the room were shrouded in darkness and Buck reached forward and picked up the cigar cutter. Buck stepped behind Marsden and wrapped the loop around the top of his left index finger. Marsden took a breath, ready for the pain and stared Sims directly in the eye.

Sims shuffled nervously and nodded, and Buck slammed the cigar cutter shut.

Marsden gritted his teeth and grunted in pain, as the top of his finger fell to the floor, the razor slicing through flesh and bone like a knife through butter. The blood dripped to the floor with a gentle patter, pooling around Buck's feet. The burly henchman slid the lid open again and this time, he slid the cutter down to the knuckle.

Sims puffed his cigar impatiently.

'This is going to be a hell of a long night for you,' Sims threatened. 'Now if you're trying to be brave to protect Sam Pope, then I suggest you think again. We will find him, so why don't you save yourself anymore pain. Where are the files?'

Marsden took a moment, considering the excruciating pain he was about to experience. Chances are, they would kill him anyway, so why draw it out? Marsden nodded dejectedly, bringing a terrifying smile to Sims's face.

'Okay, okay. I'll tell you.' Marsden arched his neck

back to look at Buck. 'But you're gonna need a rubber glove to retrieve them.'

Fury lit up in Buck's eye and he snapped the cigar shutter as hard as he could, the blade cutting through the knuckle. Marsden yelled out in pain and Buck reached forward and slammed him face first against the metal table. More blood exploded from his nose and Marsden rocked back in his seat, his ears ringing and his finger pulsating. Sims watched uncomfortably as Marsden took a few moments to gather himself.

They'd both been respectable soldiers at one point.

Now one was ordering the slow torture of the other.

Buck stood stoically behind Marsden, his eyes locked on Sims and awaiting his next order. Sims took a few more puffs, contemplating his next move. Marsden took another intake and then spat another mouthful of blood onto the floor, before returning his gaze to Sims.

'You may as well just kill me,' Marsden said calmly. 'Because I don't know where those files are.'

'Look,' Sims replied, lowering his voice. 'I don't want to put you through more of this. But you need to give it up. Whatever it is you're trying to do or whoever you're working for.'

'I'm not working for anyone,' Marsden stated. 'You have me labelled as a terrorist, when I'm the only one trying to save this goddamn world.'

Sims flashed another glance to Buck, who obediently reached down, grabbing at the next finger along. Marsden helped him, ignoring the pain from his bloody stump to give Buck the finger.

'There you go.' Marsden smirked. 'Good dog.'

Buck roughly shoved the cutter over the finger, but before any further mutilation could take place, three thunderous knocks on the metal door shook the room. Buck released his grip and turned to the door; his eyebrows raised in confusion. Nervously, Sims scurried from his chair, marching across the damp chamber to the door.

With a slight struggle, he heaved it open and his body stiffened.

He was greeted by General Ervin Wallace.

Wallace's face was distorted with a furious scowl and Sims swallowed.

'General.' Sims almost bowed. 'I didn't think…'

'You never do.' Wallace dismissed him, stepping into the room. 'Carl. Are you alive?'

'Just about.' Marsden chuckled.

Wallace smiled. It quickly faded as he turned back to Sims, who he towered over both in size and stature.

'Follow me.'

'Sir?' Sims stammered, his voice quivering.

Wallace ignored him, marching back through the door and out into the dark corridors of the underground base. As they passed a few more empty rooms, Wallace stepped into the larger communal room, where a few of the Blackridge Squadron were sat around a table, a pile of cards and cash on the table between them.

They all stood as Wallace walked in.

Sims followed meekly behind.

'This is some fucking mess,' Wallace said, shaking his hairless head.

'I'm sorry, sir.'

'Keep your apologies to yourself, you sissy little prick. This is now an international incident; do you hear me? When you asked to take a UK Soldier into one of my locations, I was fine with it. But you have left a fucking trail of breadcrumbs the size of fucking walnuts.'

Wallace reached out and slammed his fist into the metal lockers that ran across the room. The sound reverberated around the room and Wallace's eyes locked onto Sims like a hungry predator circling its prey.

'What do you want me to do, sir?' Sims asked pathetically.

'What I fucking well hired you for.'

Sims and Wallace stood silently for a moment, both of them aware that the situation had escalated beyond critical. Wallace shook his head, planting his meaty hands on his hips and he turned away from Sims, almost with embarrassment.

'Marsden may be on the wrong side of this one, Sims, but he is still a good man. The job was to take him quietly and expertly in Berlin. Then deliver both him, Pope, and the fucking files to me.' Wallace turned back, baring his teeth like a rabid dog. 'You better have a better fucking plan than torturing that man to death.'

Before Sims could respond, one of the men across the room approached, his phone in his hand.

'Excuse me, sir. But I've got a message from the field team. They have Sam.'

Wallace snatched the phone from the young soldier's hand and ran his eyes over it. He turned to the man, staring coldly at him until he walked away. As the man retreated, Wallace turned back to Sims and slammed the phone into his chest.

'Saved by the fucking bell.'

With heavy stomps, Wallace moved to the other side of the room, where two sports bags adorned the table. They were unzipped and while one of them was filled with clothes, the other was stuffed with weaponry. An army issue assault rifle, as well as two Glock pistols. A few cartridges, all loaded, and a bulletproof jacket.

All of it in pristine condition.

'This Pope's bag?' Wallace snapped.

'Yes. We intercepted it at Kiev airport. How the hell he got it through, I'll never know.'

'He's got a guy. Etheridge.' Wallace reached into the

bag and picked up the Glock. He smoothly discharged the clip, reminding Sims of the brutal Special Ops missions he'd led before his life of bureaucracy. Wallace was an exceedingly powerful man with an enviable reach. But behind it all, he'd been a relentless and efficient killer.

Out of nowhere, the phone in Sims's hand pinged. The screen lit up with another message from the field team.

ETA. 30 mins.

Before Sims could read it out, Wallace snatched the phone from his hand. After reading it, he tossed it onto the table and took a step towards Sims.

'I want to speak to Carl,' Wallace sneered. 'And I want your guys out of here.'

'Yes, sir.' Sims nodded. 'We'll wait for Pope outside. Any smart moves and we'll tag him.'

'No, you little fucking weasel.' Wallace reached out and grabbed Sims by his sweaty collar. 'You're coming with me.'

With that, Wallace barged past Sims and headed to the door, demanding that the rest of Blackridge clear out. Sims sighed, angry at his own pitiful reaction to Wallace and then did as he was told, scurrying after his employer as they headed to have one last chat with a dear old friend.

Then soon, they would have Marsden, Pope, and the files and Sims would live to see another day.

CHAPTER TWENTY-ONE

THREE YEARS EARLIER...

'Hello? Sam?'

Marsden called out hopefully into the dark hallway, the front door had opened after two gentle knocks. It had been a long time since Marsden had visited Sam at his house. The last time was to check how his recovery was from his gunshot wounds which had ended his military career. It was a damn shame, the country had lost its most dangerous weapon, but a loving wife and adoring son had gained a full-time member of their family.

But the world was a cruel place and Marsden needed no further proof of that.

All he had to do was think about what had happened to Sam.

Nearing the end of his police training, his rise through the police ranks was as certain as the sun setting. His son, Jamie, was incredibly intelligent. His wife, Lucy, was as stunning as she was kind.

Sam had the perfect life that he fought, literally, for.

But it had all been taken away in a few seconds.

His son, cruelly taken by a drunk driver. Although this was the first time in a few years that Marsden had been to the Pope residence, *he'd seen both Sam and Lucy at the funeral. For a man who had seen countless atrocities across many countries, who had attended many funerals of young men shot down in the line of duty, watching these two good people grieve for their son was hard to watch.*

Now, six months on from that, Marsden stepped into the dark hallway of Sam Pope's house.

All the curtains were drawn, and a muggy smell had infested every room. Dirty plates and mugs sat on the table in the front room, thick skins of mould wrapping around the food remnants like a winter jacket.

Every photo had been placed face down.

Every mirror had been smashed.

'Sam?' Marsden called out again, finishing his sweep of the ground floor before moving towards the stairs.

As he made his way up the stairs, Marsden could hear the thudding sound of running water. Stepping onto the landing, Marsden was greeted by a pile of broken glass. Among the wreckage were a number of Sam's medals, relics from a previous life he was once proud of. Marsden could feel his heartbreaking for the man and he squatted down, carefully sweeping the glass to the wall and picking up a picture.

It was a picture they'd taken many years ago on a secret mission to the borders of Egypt. It was the night before a man called Etheridge had fallen and broken his leg. Sam had saved his life by eliminating a patrolling enemy squadron who had zoned in on his fallen comrade.

They were all sat on the rocky terrain under the sun. Sam sat with his closest friend, Theo Walker, who hadn't left his side through his injuries.

Corporal Murray and Private Griffin were also in the photo, a few of them holding up the peace sign.

Marsden cracked a smile at the memory.

'What are you doing here?'

The croaky voice came from behind him and Marsden stood, twirling to face Sam. His heart sank.

Stood in the doorway to Jamie's room was Sam, but not as Marsden had ever seen him. He wore an ill-fitting jumper and track-suit bottoms, his weight loss apparent. Sam had always been muscular but now he looked frail, the jumper hanging from his tiny frame and his cheek bones were pressed against his gaunt face. His hair was longer, unkempt and his face was covered in a scraggily, patchy beard.

The man looked like hell. Understandably.

The stench of alcohol was undeniable.

'Sam,' Marsden said warmly. 'It's good to see you.'

'Why are you here?' Sam said sternly, his eyes flickering to the open door to the bathroom.

'I came to see you. Theo said you weren't doing so good.'

'I'm okay.'

'I'll be honest, mate. It doesn't look like it,' Marsden said, his voice heavy with sadness.

'Thanks. I guess losing my son and my wife isn't the best look.'

'I didn't come here to upset you, Sam. We're all just worried about you.' Marsden looked past Sam and at the floor of Jamie's bedroom. It was covered with his books which Sam was obviously reading through. The man was torturing himself and Marsden shook his head.

'Why don't we let some light in here?'

Marsden stepped into the bathroom and pulled the blind down, just as a panicked Sam raced across the hallway, stopping at the threshold.

Marsden had already seen it.

On the side of the bath, two straight razor blades were resting.

The realization of what he'd interrupted had dawned on Marsden and with tears forming in his eyes, he turned to Sam. Before him, the man who was once the deadliest soldier he had ever had the honour of mentoring, stood sheepishly to the side, his frail arms wrapped around his body and his eyes firmly on the floor.

'Jesus, Sam.'

'You need to leave,' Sam said timidly.

'What? And let you kill yourself?'

'You don't know what it's like, sir. To be so alone and so lost and know that you could have stopped it. What it's like to bury your son. To lose everything.'

Sam dropped to his knees, tears flooding from his eyes. Marsden took a deep breath and turned off the taps, before kneeling down in front of Sam.

'I don't know what it's like? Sam, do you know how many good people I've lost in this lifetime? Sure, I may not have had a wife and kids, but I looked upon all of you as my own. I've knocked on too many doors to tell spouses they've lost the one they love. I've attended too many funerals, all for great soldiers who just wanted to make the world a better place.' Marsden reached out and rested a hand on Sam's bony shoulder. 'I can only imagine the pain you're going through, and you may be lost. But you're not alone.'

Sam took a few moments to compose himself, the anguish of losing his family shuddering through his body with each intake of breath.

The man was at the end of his rope.

'I don't have anything left,' Sam spoke softly. 'There is no reason anymore.'

'Then find one, soldier,' Marsden spoke with authority. 'Don't let what happened consume you. Let it drive you.'

'Sir?' Sam lifted his scruffy face, looking at Marsden with red eyes. Behind them, Marsden could sense the smallest fraction of hope.

'This world is a better place with people like you in it, son. What has happened to you is devastating. But Jamie knew his dad to be the bravest, strongest, most fearless man he knew. So be that man.' Marsden stood to his feet and extended a hand. 'The world needs Sam Pope.'

After a few moments of silence, Sam lifted his hand and took Marsden's paternal grip, hoisting himself to his feet. A moment of clarity had danced through his body and although he didn't quite know what it meant; he knew it would keep him alive for another day. Through deep breaths, Sam wrestled back a modicum of composure.

'Thank you, sir.'

'Don't thank me.' Marsden offered him a friendly grin. 'Have yourself a bath, clean yourself up, and I'll get us some food, eh?'

'Thank you.' Sam stepped forward and hugged Marsden, holding him tight. 'For everything.'

'You're welcome, son.' Marsden stepped back into the bathroom and lifted the straight razors. Their original destination had changed as Marsden stuffed them into his pocket. 'I'm keeping these.'

Sam nodded, wiped his nose with his sleeve and then stepped past Marsden into the bathroom. As the door closed behind him, Sam didn't feel so alone. He knew people like Theo and Marsden were always going to be alongside him. They were bound by the wars they'd faced together.

When one of them fell, they all did.

But they always pulled each other back up.

With a silent apology to his son, Sam got into the bath, determined it was the first step on the road to recovery.

———

It was that moment that had filtered through Sam's mind when he decided to hand himself back to Blackridge. Marsden had wanted him to disappear, to see his mission through to the end. But Sam couldn't leave him to the mercies of Trevor Sims and the authorities. If what they were saying were true, and what Marsden had claimed to have found, then they would do unspeakable things to find out where the files were.

Sam had to go back for him.

They'd just left the hustle and bustle of the inner city, the Rome traffic an entirely different beast to what Sam was used to in London. The reckless abandon that the Vespa drivers overtook with was as impressive as it was heart stopping.

Now, the road had cleared, and they were driving through a large, derelict area, with waste land surrounding the road, veering off towards the surprising mountainous landscape. It baffled Sam how tropical Italy could be, but at the same times, there were parts of the beautiful country which had been neglected beyond repair. Half built buildings littered the long roads, all of them covered with graffiti and the ever-lasting effect of the credit crunch.

They were heading into the middle of nowhere and Sam knew they didn't intend to bring him back.

Alex drove carefully, her face as stoic as possible beyond the odd cautious glance in the rear-view mirror. Every time she did, Sam looked her dead in the eye, hoping his eye contact would ease her concern. That concern wasn't unfounded, considering he had a gun pointed to his temple with a trigger-happy mercenary on the other end of it.

As they drove, the two American men spoke loudly about Sam and Marsden's fate in a pointless attempt to scare him.

'Yeah, Pops is probably screaming in agony right now. Begging our guys to stop.' The one in the passenger seat spoke jovially. 'They'll probably start removing his teeth next. Did Buck bring his pliers?'

Sam couldn't help but interject.

'Does he need those to help pull his nose from Sims's arse?'

Thwack!

The man next to Sam jabbed him in the side of the head once again, the hard metal of the gun sending him across the leather seats of the 4x4. As the two men laughed, Sam gently unclipped his seat belt, covering the end with his hand. Slumping forward with pretend wooziness, he also unclipped the passenger seat belt and held onto it. As he woozily sat back up, the man in the passenger seat was still laughing.

'Good one, dip shit,' the passenger spat through his chortles.

'Sam, you okay?' Alex asked, flicking her eyes to the mirror.

'Who gives a fuck if he's okay?' The passenger angrily yelled. 'We could put a bullet in his fucking skull right now and just say he tried to break free. Isn't that right?'

'Yes, it is,' Sam said clearly, catching both of them by surprise. 'Alex, now.'

Instantly, Alex slammed her foot down on the brake and Sam let go of the seat belt. The passenger lunged forward, his face colliding hard with the windscreen, cracking the glass and shattering his cheek bone. The man next to Alex shunted forward, his grip on him loosening. With his own seat belt loose, Sam rolled back on the seat and rammed one of his boots into the man's wrist, crushing the bone against the door panel and relinquishing the weapon instantly. The man howled with agony at his shattered wrist, but Sam then shunted his other foot into the man's face, smashing his head through the glass window in a spray of glass, blood, and loose teeth.

With the man dazed, Sam looped his own seat belt over his head and pulled it tight around his neck, before rolling onto his front and pulling with all his might. The man arched back across Sam's spine, wildly grabbing at the belt which rapidly crushed down his windpipe and strangled him.

The passenger, trying to regain his bearings, saw what was happening, but before he could react, Alex rammed her elbow as hard as she could into his temple, slamming him limply against the car door.

He was unconscious.

The man in the back stopped struggling and Sam pulled once more, draining the life from his captor, and eventually relinquishing as the man went limp. Sam pushed himself to a seated position and reached across the man he'd just killed for the door handle. He pulled it, welcoming in the harsh, wet outside world and kicked the limp body from the car and sent it crashing to the hard pavement below.

Alex looked on; her eyes wide with adrenaline at the situation that had just unfurled. As Sam followed the body out of the car, she panicked about any onlookers, her mind processing they had been immobile on the street for what felt like half an hour.

In reality, Sam had dispatched the man in less than two minutes and as she watched from her seat, he heaved the body across to the thick shrubbery. Ditching it behind the plants, Sam hobbled back towards the passenger side of the car, hauled it open and let the unconscious man drop from the car to the concrete. His face was heavily bleeding, and Sam imagined a few broken ribs from his hard collision with the dashboard. Within twenty seconds, the two bodies were out of sight, unlikely to be spotted in the darkening evening light. It was nearly six o'clock and the only lights around were from a few houses that adorned the hills in the distance, and the full beams that poured from their own vehicle.

Alex took a deep breath, trying to calm her heart rate. She was used to the adrenaline rush of a car race, zipping through closed, narrow streets at over a hundred. But watching a man kill and dispose of someone was something new.

Sam reached into the back of the car and lifted the pistol that had been used to batter him. Then, with visible discomfort, he dropped into the passenger seat next to Alex and slammed the door. He groaned with pain as he clipped in his belt.

'Drive,' he said through gritted teeth.

'You don't have to do this, Sam,' Alex said, her words fraught with fear. 'You could just go. Disappear.'

Sam shook his head and offered her a pained smile.

'That man saved my life. I at least have to try to do the same.'

Alex turned the key, shaking her head at the fool hardy stubbornness of the man beside her. Despite living up to his reputation, he was clearly wounded and racing head-first into a battle with Blackridge was suicidal.

But loyalty was a strange concept. She understood that, especially as hers had quickly formed for the man beside her.

They drove into the darkness, towards the complex that housed Marsden.

As the rain clattered against the windscreen, Sam slid the clip from the pistol, checking how many bullets he had.

Alex watched out of the corner of her eye.

'You know there will be more of them, right?' she said, trying to persuade him. 'Sims has a bunch of guys all willing to die for him.'

Sam slammed the clip back. His eyes, coldly staring straight ahead.

'Good.'

CHAPTER TWENTY-TWO

With a confidence draining clunk, the coffee machine whirred into action, spewing questionable coffee into the paper cup. Pearce watched with caution as the powdered milk followed, before retrieving his drink and taking an apprehensive sip.

It didn't taste good.

Pearce had been in a number of hospitals; it was all part of the job. It didn't surprise him how many dirty cops ended up in hospital, and once they'd seen the physical side of their partnerships with organized crime, they were much more cooperative.

But this trip had filled him with little satisfaction.

As soon as the ambulance had arrived, the paramedics thanked Pearce for applying pressure to the gunshot wound that had decimated Etheridge's knee cap. Pearce had let them do their job, and they quickly moved Etheridge to the ambulance and shot back towards Farnham Hospital with their sirens wailing. Pearce had followed behind, feeling a sense of dread for what he and Singh were looking in to.

Whoever had done this to Etheridge, had taken their time and used a certain level of skill that he found barbaric. Sure, he'd seen the odd piece of gang torture when he was on the beat, with rival thugs wanting to send a message. A cruelly beaten or sliced up rival usual only sends the message to fight back.

This was torture for a purpose.

To find Sam Pope.

Despite his background, Etheridge wasn't built for combat. Pearce had done his own investigating when Etheridge came into the picture a few weeks earlier and despite the man's clear genius and business acumen, he wasn't a soldier. He wasn't built or trained to eliminate to the same prolific level as Sam.

The damage done to his right hand was potentially permanent. The impact of the bullet on his knee definitely was. Etheridge wouldn't walk properly again, that much was clear but after a few hours of surgery, the doctor had assured him that he would pull through. Etheridge had lost a lot of blood, but they had him hooked up to a steady supply and had reset his hand as best they could. The operation on his knee was a success but would require a painful rehabilitation.

All because he'd helped Sam Pope.

It hadn't escaped his mind that a similar fate could befall him. What concerned him more, was the fate that could soon be coming for Singh.

She'd clearly riled the wrong people, her digging into Sam's past had drawn the attention of one of the British Military's most powerful men. Along with that, the Assistant Commissioner was strong arming him into digging up enough dirt to bury her under. A promising career, a true asset to the Metropolitan Police, was heading down a dead end.

Pearce sipped the coffee, grimacing as the sour taste slid down his throat. The hospital was on its last legs, the continuous struggle of the NHS evident by the rickety chairs in the waiting room and the over worked staff scuttling through the corridors. Pearce found one of the rickety chairs and sat down, his body aching.

Was this getting too dangerous?

It had crossed his mind a few times.

What had started out as a routine investigation into an employee had taken him on a path of aiding and abetting a wanted vigilante. He had enough leverage with the Inspector Howell fiasco in the High Rise, but even then, that wouldn't last forever. It was unlikely he would betray Singh, which meant by the end of the week, Ashton would want his badge.

But would that be the end of it?

It wasn't beyond those in power to fabricate evidence to link him to Sam, and then they would set their lap dogs on him as they had Etheridge.

They would most likely do the same to Singh.

Pearce reached into his pocket and pulled out his phone.

He had three missed calls.

Two from Singh.

One from Sean Wiseman.

Pearce smiled. Sean had been at the youth centre every day, working tirelessly with the kids to push them away from a life on the streets. As someone who had been forced into a gang at a young age and had been hospitalized after a brutal attack, the man was committed to turning his life around. It was a true reminder that sometimes, what they did at the centre, actually made a difference.

Pearce had only taken on the role of organizing the youth club after Theo had tragically given his life to save Amy Devereux, Sam's psychiatrist, and since then, Sean had stepped up to alleviate some of the responsibility.

But again, all the stories were tinged with violence.

All towards people who were helping Sam.

Pearce rubbed his chin, his fingers combing the well-groomed, grey beard and he contemplated his next move. A woman had barged in, her mascara smudged through tears and she spoke to the doctor about Etheridge's condition. She claimed to be his wife, but Pearce hadn't noticed much of a woman's touch in the house. But what went on behind closed doors was not his concern and while there wasn't anything more he could do to help Etheridge for now, he made a silent promise to ensure he would be there when Etheridge was ready to talk.

The man had been put through hell, all because he thought he was doing the right thing.

The line between right and wrong was blurring for a lot of people.

Blurred by Sam Pope.

As Pearce headed for the exit, he knew he was too far gone in his quest to help Sam.

But he wouldn't let anything happen to Singh. He couldn't live with himself if he did.

As he approached the front door of the hospital, the rain awaited him. A thunderstorm had begun to rattle in the sky above.

It was a little on the nose, but he saw the meaning.

As he headed for his car, he found Ashton's office number on his phone and clicked dial.

———

As the metal door slammed shut with a mighty thud, Marsden's brain shook. The beating he'd taken from Sims's men had left his head rattling and every loud noise hit it like a clap of thunder.

Heavy footsteps echoed through the room and Marsden waited patiently as the stocky frame of Ervin Wallace passed him and made himself comfortable on the small chair on the other side of the table. Wallace refused to look at his former colleague, instead looking at the pistol he held in his hand. Behind him, Sims followed, his shoulders slumped like a naughty child who had been caught cheating on his homework. The cocky swagger of a man in charge of his own personal army had gone, replaced by a man who had recently been reacquainted with where he existed on the food chain.

After a few moments, Wallace placed the gun on the table, turning it so Marsden could see there was no clip. The light bounced off Wallace's bald head and the mountainous man flashed his well-rehearsed grin.

'It's good to see you, Carl,' he spoke, his words almost sincere. 'It's a shame it has come to this. Can I get you anything? Water? Coffee?'

Marsden just stared at the man he'd served with for decades, a look of disgust on his beaten face. Wallace clicked his fingers at Sims, treating him like a waiter.

'Take his cuffs off, for Christ's sake.'

Sims obliged, reaching down behind Marsden and unlocked the bloodstained cuffs. He recoiled at the sight of his severed finger on the floor but tried his best to hide it from the two men sat at the table.

He couldn't and they both shook their head at him.

Neither of them saw him as a soldier and all the power he'd once held in this mission had completely dissipated, like a tyre with a slow puncture.

Marsden gingerly lifted his mangled hand onto the table, allowing it to rest on the cold metal. Wallace looked at the wound as if he was inspecting an antique and tutted.

'Barbaric.' He flashed a glare at Sims who looked away. 'You goddamn Yanks and your torture.'

'What are you doing here, Ervin?' Marsden asked calmly. Despite the pain and the situation he was in, Marsden did not shake. He'd made his decisions and both he and Wallace knew he was a man of complete conviction.

'Carl, we've known each other a long time. You have no idea how angry or shocked I was when news came through that you were being hunted for acts of espionage and potential terrorism.' Wallace shook his head in disbelief. 'I mean, you? You're a fucking boy scout. Word came through that you were on a train to Rome due to the, how should we say, heavy handed way these Blackridge punks went about their business?'

Sims stepped forward, hoping to wrestle back some respect from the room.

'Sir, we acted with complete tact and sensitivity so as not arouse public panic.'

'Bollocks,' Wallace snapped back, slamming his hand on the metal and causing another striking pain to slither through Marsden's skull. 'You boys are the equivalent to using a sledgehammer to crack a walnut.'

'Then why the fuck did you hire us?'

Marsden suddenly jolted up right, his eyes fixed on Wallace who ran his tongue on the inside of his lip, contemplating his next move. Sims, realizing the tension raise in the room, stepped back towards the room again.

Marsden spoke with clarity.

'So, it's true. Everything on those files. It's true.'

'Carl, let me explain…' Wallace began.

'No need. Soon, everyone will know, and then you can explain to the whole world that the biggest terrorist in the world is the guy at the forefront of stopping it.'

'You think I'm a terrorist?' Wallace chuckled. 'You have no fucking clue what I am. Do you think we really keep the world safe by popping on the camo and walking through some shit-hole country decimated by bombs? That's for the cameras, Carl. Even you know that.'

'We fight and protect those that need it,' Marsden began, his voice cracking with anger.

'That's what I have been fucking doing. How do you think this all works? What, you don't think these Yank bastards were plying the fucking ragheads with enough gear to start the Taliban? Or that the higher ups didn't know a plane was going to be slammed into a fucking building? It's all known, the thing is, Carl, what people don't understand is we need things like that to happen for the good of the world.'

'You're insane,' Marsden said defiantly. 'Listen to yourself. You're saying the world needs terrorists?'

'You're damn right it does. It needs the boogeymen. Because ninety-nine per cent of this planet need to know they're safe. They need to know that we are on the edge of a fucking war because it gives them meaning to their lives. The idea of things ending like that—' Wallace clicked his fingers '—it keeps the world ticking and it's men like me who keep it all in check. So, I need you to tell me where the fuck those files are.'

Marsden chuckled quietly and shook his head.

'You know, for years, Erv, I thought you were a good guy. A bit of a prick. A bit rough around the edges, but ultimately, a good guy. But this is beyond delusion. You're a monster.'

Wallace leant forward; his lips pulled back as he snarled.

'The true monsters are those who want to disturb the peace. Those who want to scare and derail society and the very fine threads that hold our countries together. Terrorists.' Wallace jabbed a finger at Marsden. 'Which is what you will be if you release those files.'

'What, and let the world know the truth?' Marsden yelled in exasperation.

'The world doesn't need the truth. It needs a fucking

roll of cotton wool to be wrapped up in. So, I'm only going to ask you one more time, where are the fucking files?'

'I don't have them. Sam does,' Marsden said triumphantly. 'And he's in the wind.'

'Really?' Wallace smirked. 'See, we got word about half an hour ago that he was picked up by Sims's men and they're on their way back here. Now despite this little crusade he's been on, Sam is still a soldier. He will see sense.'

'You're bluffing,' Marsden barked, a hint of nervousness in his voice. It was like blood in the water for Wallace.

'You're fond of Sam, aren't you, Carl?' Wallace said, reaching for the empty gun. 'This is his, by the way. We picked it up in Kiev. So, he's unarmed. Now, do I try him for treason the same way you will be tried, or will you do the right thing by him and tell him to give me the files?'

Marsden could see the chess pieces moving and despite everything he'd tried to do he knew Wallace almost had him at check mate. But Marsden knew Sam.

Sam wasn't just a soldier.

He was a good man.

Despite walking on a darker side of the law, Sam would always do the right thing.

'Fuck you,' Marsden said. 'You'll put a bullet in us both the second you have those files.'

'On the contrary, I intend to keep Sam very much alive,' Wallace said cheerily, sitting back in his chair. 'I've got the Met Police in my pocket and delivering Sam to them is a good favour to have in the bank. Especially after all those people he killed.'

'Those people were criminals,' Marsden responded defensively.

'What about the senior member of the US Military he murdered in cold blood?'

Marsden frowned, trying to place the proof against

Wallace's allegation. Before he could connect the dots, Wallace slammed a clip into the pistol, span on his chair, and pulled the trigger. The bullet ripped through Sims's forehead and exploded out the back of his skull, painting the walls behind him in an upward splash of blood, bone, and brain matter.

Sims fell to the floor dead.

Marsden sat still, taking a few deep breaths and remembering the incredible job he'd been honoured to have, the differences he'd made, and lives he'd saved.

Like Sam's.

Wallace turned back to Marsden; his eyes heavy with regret.

'And when his crimes became too much, the broken Sam Pope tragically turned the gun on the man who made him.'

Before Marsden could speak, Wallace pulled the trigger. The bullet hit Marsden just below the rib cage, burrowing into his intestines. Instantly, blood pumped out over his hands and he pressed them against the wound in a helpless attempt for survival.

Another gunshot exploded into the room.

This bullet ripped through his right lung, knocking him back off the chair and onto the bloodstained concrete behind. The air immediately began to filter from the wound and blood slowly began to fill the cavity. With his own life force drowning him, Marsden reached under his shirt with a shaky hand and clasped his dog tags.

He would die in this room, painted as a terrorist.

But he was a soldier. And he would die as one.

As he struggled for breath and the blood pooled over his stomach, Marsden heard the footsteps of Wallace moving towards the door. To his right, he glimpsed the motionless body of Sims, who had died instantly.

The metal door creaked loudly and just before he left, Wallace turned back to his dying comrade.

'Goodbye, old friend.'

The door closed, and Marsden rested his head back against the concrete, awaiting death.

CHAPTER TWENTY-THREE

The passport check at Rome airport was surprisingly busy for the evening flight that the man in black had arrived on. Underestimating the number of tourists wanting to flock to the historic city during the horrible winter season, the airport had only scheduled one put-upon guard to process those crossing over into the country.

Patiently, he waited, taking a few marginal steps forward every few minutes. Behind him, a young French couple were discussing their plans for the week ahead. Although his French wasn't as strong as some of his other languages, they were running through the list of tourist attractions with relative excitement. In front, an English couple were bickering, just another by product of a mundane, middle-aged existence. Their two kids stood agitated, continuously glancing back and staring up at him.

He was used to it.

The mother had turned around once, startled at the disfiguring burns that covered the left side of his face and apologized for her kids' manners. He'd offered an accepting smile, but the mum kept yanking her kids forward whenever they glanced back.

People always stared.

Just stood in the queue, he could feel the eyes of several people locked on him, all of them speculating how he'd ended up with his horrific injuries.

Sam Pope.

With another step, he came closer to the booth and ready to pass through and meet his maker. It was what had driven him to this moment. That unrelenting need for revenge.

The family were called forward and the dad fumbled with the passports, drawing the ire of his wife and a frustrated frown from the portly man sat in the booth. The kids looked back, sniggering at the monstrous man behind them.

He didn't mind.

He was a monster.

The brutal torture of a man associated with Pope was a testament to that.

But it was all he knew.

After a few more frustrating minutes, the man waved the family through and they stormed off towards the baggage claim, the parents bickering like the children they were supposed to be parenting. The kids looked back one last time, the little girl pulling a face at him.

He smiled.

'Come,' The man in the booth called out in a thick, Italian accent, not looking up from his desk.

He approached.

The man in black slid his passport under the glass, the picture as horrifying as the real thing. The man lazily looked at it and recoiled, before slowly looking up with an apologetic smile.

The burns ran from the left side of his head, cutting through his hair line and wrapping around his left eye. There was no eyebrow, the hair follicles obliterated. The smooth, white skin ran across his cheek to his nose, his left nostril a distant memory. The top part of his lip was also mutilated, and the scarring ran down the left side of his neck and disappeared under the crew neck jumper he wore.

The man cautiously looked back and forth at the hideous man before him and his shocking photo. While the burns were a cause for concern, he knew he couldn't be discriminated against for being a burns victim.

Or for the other painful, abhorrent trials he'd been put through for years.

If only they knew.

The man coughed nervously and then handed him back the passport with a patronizing nod. He took it, reciprocated, and then marched towards the exit. He was travelling light, only his passport, phone, and a wad of euros in his pockets.

He didn't need anything else. The rest would be taken care of when he arrived. With the eyes of the airport on him, he strode purposefully towards the exit, ignoring the sickened expressions of the general public.

He had the location.

A gun would be waiting for him on arrival.

With the excitement of finally being able to come face to face with Sam Pope building, he headed for the nearest Eurocar, knowing the roll of fifties in his pocket would put a key in his hand in no time.

———

Alex had switched the lights off and brought the car to a crawl as they approached the chain-link fence that surrounded the building. They'd turned off the quiet, derelict roads onto a gravel track twenty minutes after disposing of the bodies. As the car rolled to a stop, Sam scanned the facility. It was an abandoned textile factory, which had long been out of commission.

The brick work was crumbling, with many of the iron supporting beams visible through the cracks. The windows, once clear and bright, had been replaced with iron grates. All the exterior lights had been smashed, probably by a group of young vandals with keen throwing arms.

The place was derelict.

It was the perfect safehouse.

Sam was aware that a number of powerful organisations had dedicated facilities around the world for occasions such as this. He'd been in one once before, in a reinforced flat in an unremarkable block in the middle of Budapest. He'd been part of an extraction operation of a Persian drug lord who had fled to Hungary. After a violent shoot-out in a spa, they'd taken the man to the safe house where Wallace had organized for his transfer to the states.

All of these locations were off the books, as most things were. They were strictly *need to know* and Sam got the impression that only Sims knew of this location. Blackridge were heavily funded and had the right backing in the right places to operate where and how they wanted. It was how they'd been able to arrest him in the middle of Kiev airport or cause a mass panic at Berlin station and it all be reported as a 'false alarm'.

Somewhere in this building, was Marsden.

Sam was going to get him out.

The rain drummed against the window of the car like impatient fingers on a desk and Sam reached for the handle. As he did, Alex reached out and grabbed his arm. With a warm smile, he turned to her.

'You remember what I told you?'

'Just drive,' she said sternly.

'Just keep going,' Sam added. 'I promise you; I will help you get your family back.'

'If you go in there, you will die,' she said coldly, shaking her head, her dark hair swaying.

'If I don't, then Marsden will. And I can't walk away from that.' Sam pushed open the door of the car and stepped out gingerly into the cold rain. As he turned back to close the door, he ducked his head in, rain already dropping from his face. 'I'll see you soon.'

Sam closed the door and then reached up to the fence. His fingers clawed at the slippery wire and with a little discomfort, he scaled the perimeter. He dropped down, feeling a numbing pain in his thigh, before he hurried across the car park. A few rows of old cars were dotted around, along with a large delivery truck which had been used to transport the produce.

All relics from a bygone age.

Now, this building was a place of pain and death.

Sam was planning on towing the line.

With the pistol held downwards, he approached the door, surprised to find it unlocked. He whipped around quickly, scanning the parking lot over the sight of his pistol and once satisfied, slid inside.

The hallway was dark, the power out and Sam ensured he took the weight off each step. The likelihood was they were underground, protocol dictated they would have bagged Marsden and led him somewhere he couldn't return from should he escape.

Sam cleared each room that adorned the hallway, pushing open the door and fluidly entering the room, gun drawn.

Clear.

All the rooms were clear.

Something didn't feel right, and Sam stepped back out into the corridor, his finger caressing the trigger of his pistol. He pulled open a door, revealing the stairwell and he slowly descended into the dark, his eyes adjusted enough to make out the steps in front. Jagged fragments of memories began to circle in his mind from that fateful night where he was shot.

Project Hailstorm.

Marsden had told him the USB stick he'd entrusted to him had the truth of what happened that night on it. That everything Sam believed about their war on terror was a lie.

Marsden had wanted Sam to run free and spill the truth to the world. He would be furious that Sam had come back.

He would just have to deal with it.

As Sam reached the bottom step, a dim light crept through the exit door. Sam pressed his back to the wall and gently pushed the door open, sliding out gun first, his finger ready.

The corridor was empty.

Dim lights lined the entire ceiling, and another selection of doors awaited, leading to a large, metal door at the end. Sam ducked into the first few rooms, finding nothing but a few sofas and TVs. Most likely break out rooms for the crew.

The next room had a couple of unmade bunks.

No personal effects to be found.

The last room he checked before approaching the metal door was lined with empty lockers, one of them sporting a large dent from an angry fist. The table near the door was covered in playing cards, with one of the players taking the rest for everything they had judging by the chips. At the far end of the room, Sam recognized his sports bag, which was empty.

The whole place was empty.

Sam turned hesitantly and headed back to the metal door; his gun pointed to the floor as he walked. He shifted the large, metal handle and the door groaned loudly as it opened.

Sam saw the blood first.

The room was lit by a large, halogen tube which flickered every so often, its glow shining a spotlight down on the carnage below. To the side of the table, the prone, lifeless body of Sims was stretched out in a large pool of blood. The back of his head was missing, ripped apart by a well-placed bullet.

Sam felt nothing but contempt for the man.

Then he felt his legs buckle.

Marsden was on his back, a blood-soaked hand pressed to his stomach. The other clutching his chain, above another fresh bullet wound.

'No!' Sam exclaimed, splashing through the blood and dropping to his knees beside his mentor's body. 'Come on, sir. Stay with me.'

As Sam frantically scanned the injuries on Marsden's motionless body, Marsden slowly opened his eyes, wheezing as the air tried to find a way into his blood-filled lungs.

'Sam,' Marsden managed. 'I told you to go.'

'Not without you, sir.' Sam tried to smile, but his watery eyes betrayed his confidence. 'I came to get you out.'

'You need to…' Marsden coughed, a few speckles of blood spraying upwards like a horrific fountain. '…need to leave…'

'We don't leave men behind, sir. You know that.'

Marsden coughed again, more blood launching into the room. Sam felt his fists clenching, the pain of losing another person eating away at him. With a hard tug, Marsden snapped the chain on his tags and with his hand shaking, he handed them to Sam.

'Everything was always for these. Whatever they say, Sam, I was a soldier.'

'Yes, sir. You still are. Now let's try to get you up…'

'Sam… you're a good man. Remember that,' Marsden's struggled. 'A good man.'

Marsden's hand went limp.

'No, no, no, no,' Sam said panicked, leaning over his beloved mentor. 'Stay with me, stay with me.'

Sam gently rocked Marsden but within seconds knew it was futile. Sam rocked forward on his knees, letting a roar of anguish bellow into the room, his pain bouncing off every wall and down the corridor. Knee deep in Marsden's blood, Sam gripped the man's dog tags as tears fell down his face.

Marsden was dead.

Suddenly, the door swung open and before Sam could grasp his gun or a hold of the situation, three armed men swarmed in, their assault rifles locked onto Sam. He recognized one of them as Buck, while the other two were another bunch of faceless mercs, fresh off the Blackridge production line. As they fanned out slightly, sticking closely to the shadows on the outskirts of the room, Alex Stone was shoved into the room, her sorrow clearly etched across her face.

She had a large swelling over her right eye.

With a sad nod of her head, she offered Sam a useless apology.

Then, the heavy boots stomped towards the door and like an alpha wolf returning to its den, General Ervin Wallace stepped into the room, his fierce eyes locked on Sam, who was slowly getting to his feet.

Behind him, Marsden's motionless body lay in a pool of his own blood.

Murdered.

Sam could feel the reflexes in his body wanting desperately to reach for the gun and put a bullet between the man's eyes. But that would only leave him and most likely, Alex, riddled with bullets.

He fought the temptation and left the gun on the table.

Wallace glanced at Marsden's dead body and felt a flutter of guilt and regret pass through him.

He returned his gaze to Sam and smiled.

'Hello, Sam. I believe you have something that belongs to me.'

CHAPTER TWENTY-FOUR

There had been times in his life where Sam didn't believe in no-win situations. He remembered the conversation he'd had with Marsden, his mentor trying to explain to him that there would come a time that even a man with extraordinary gifts such as Sam, wouldn't be able to win.

That fighting wasn't going to get you out alive.

Sam had never believed it. Even when he was at his lowest, contemplating the horrors that had happened to his family, he knew he was taking the easy way out. By not confronting that pain or accepting the loss, it was easier to get by.

But he never thought he couldn't win.

Until now.

Sam held his hands up slowly, his pistol was on the table where he'd placed it when he raced to Marsden's aid. The three gunmen spread a little further out, keeping as big of a distance as possible.

There was no way out of this. If Sam went for the gun, he would be torn to shreds. If he went for one of the armed men, the other two would waste him in seconds.

'General,' Sam said coldly. 'You're looking horrible.'

Wallace smiled, stepping into the room and surveying the chaos he'd created.

'I'm doing better than Sims. I would say it was a shame…'

'But you'd be lying,' Sam finished, the two men nodding their appreciated disdain for the recently deceased.

'However, I'm truly hurt by the loss of our friend, Carl Marsden.' Wallace took a seat at the table, gesturing to Sam to follow. 'The man chose a path that unfortunately, had only one way out.'

'You killing him?' Sam spat angrily, taking his seat. One of the guards moved slowly towards the door, ensuring he had eyes on Alex. Sam shot her a look of reassurance, but knew it had little effect. Stood with her hands behind her back, she stared at the floor.

Both of them knew he was unlikely to leave the room. Her chances were slim but a little better.

'Like I told dear Carl, I'm in the unenviable position of having to do things I, and others, don't want to, to keep our country, hell, our world safe.' Wallace glanced past Sam at Marsden's dead body. 'I begged for him to choose another path and he made his decision.'

'Some men are willing to die for what they believe in.'

'Are you?' Wallace's face changed as he asked his thinly veiled threat. Gone was the well-practiced cadence and pally demeanor. Now, the man who led a series of bloodthirsty missions through war-torn states of Africa sat, his eyes locked on Sam like two sniper scopes.

'I fight for what I believe in,' Sam stated.

'And what is that, Sam? Really? Justice?' Wallace chuckled, shaking his head. 'Don't make me laugh. I've been following your little one-man crusade since you started it. The thing is, while some people will put you up on a pedestal and claim you're a hero, I know the truth.

217

You have always been a killer. One of the very best. God knows how many men, women, and children you eliminated for me over the years.'

'I never killed a child,' Sam said, his voice tinged with anger.

'You didn't pull the trigger. But how many people did you send to the afterlife, leaving them without a father? Eh? How many of them, after seeing their heroic dad murdered by the enemy, do you think joined the Taliban? Or ISIS?' Wallace gesticulated wildly as he ranted. 'They'll all join the cause and we will put them all in the ground. So, while you may not of flicked the switch, Sam, you strapped them to the electric chair.'

Sam felt his stomach knot. What truly made him sick, was on some level, he knew that Wallace was right. Sam had always followed his orders, eliminating whatever target was put in front of him. The missions were all for the liberation of the local people, but there would be those who didn't want to be saved.

There were those who would find salvation in fighting back.

Sam knew it, because he had found the same answer to deal with his own pain.

The room suddenly felt a little smaller, and the coppery smell and taste of blood lingered in the back of his throat. Sam had already noted the estimated steps between each of the guards and how quickly it would take for them to raise their weapons. But now, with his head slightly spinning, he couldn't trust those incremental details that could turn the situation in his favour.

'Sam,' Wallace called him back to the room. 'Have we lost you.'

Sam shook his head. Wallace grinned.

'Good. Now, like I said, Marsden died because he refused to see the bigger picture. Now, I'm not going to sit here and twist your testicles, Sam. This is a bad situation for you, and I want to help you. All you have to do, is give me the files.'

'What's on them?' Sam asked. 'Marsden said they had the names of the people who have destroyed this world. Are you on them?'

'*Saved* this world,' Wallace interjected, frustrated. 'There are things we have to do to keep the world safe. Things Carl and the masses wouldn't understand. Now, I implore you, hand over those files.'

'You know, Marsden always respected you,' Sam said, catching Wallace off guard. 'He didn't particularly like you, but he respected you. He said you were the exact person our country needed to fight the war on terror. Now you've killed him because he found out the truth. If he was willing to die for that truth to come out, then so am I.'

'What did you do?' Wallace said with venom hanging from his words.

'I don't have the USB stick.' Sam reached into his pocket, causing all three guards to raise their rifles. Sam held up a hand showing them he was removing a receipt.

It was from the international post office.

'What is this?' Wallace yelled, snatching the paper in his large grip. The bottom half of it was missing.

'I posted the files back to the UK, with a message saying if they haven't heard from me in the next two days, to publish them online and spread it across social media like a goddamn wildfire.'

Wallace angrily scanned the receipt then slammed it on the table. Sam had removed the tracking number and the address.

The stick was gone.

Sam leant forward.

'Do whatever the hell you want with me, sir. But this man didn't die for nothing.'

'Do you have any idea what you have done?' Wallace said shaking his head. 'You have risked the international security of the entire world.'

'The world needs the truth,' Sam responded. 'If the security is nothing but a lie, then it needs to be brought down brick by brick.'

'Where has this been sent to?' Wallace's asked impatiently.

'Like I said, do what you want to me.'

At that moment, the inside of Wallace's blazer shook, and he reached in, removing his phone. The screen flashed brightly, and Wallace smiled.

Whatever the message was, it was good news.

Sam shuffled uncomfortably on his chair and Wallace popped the phone back into the sweaty inside of his blazer and casually got to his feet.

'See, the thing is, Sam, I know people like you. You're not afraid of pain. Not afraid of death. You seemingly have no weaknesses.' Wallace pulled out Sam's own pistol from the back of his trousers. 'However, you're a man of honour. So, the fact that ballistics will show that this gun killed both Sims and Carl, along with our sworn testimony will mean you will rot in jail as the man who finally turned against those who helped him the most.'

Sam's jaw tightened with fury, but he remained seated, knowing Wallace was goading him. Yes, he was heading to prison, but lunging for the man would result in a justified execution. Wallace smirked, taking a few steps towards the door. Alex stepped to the side, not wanting any piece of the deplorable General. Wallace kept his eyes on Sam.

'I'll make sure you're buried in the deepest, darkest hole, where you will wish, every day, that I'd put a bullet in your head,' Wallace threatened. 'There will be no coming back, Sam. There are facilities where we put people that never see the light of day. That experience hell, every single day. But before you get there, you just sit where you are. I've arranged a little reunion for you.'

Sam frowned, confused by Wallace's words, who responded with a smug grin.

'Oh, trust me. He's been waiting to get his hands on you for a long time. Whatever he leaves of you, I'll toss into the pit and make sure every day, for the rest of your existence, is filled with more pain than your little boy felt when he was crushed by that car.'

Anger coursed through Sam like a cancer and he shook. It was a cheap shot from Wallace, but the mere mention of his son took him close to breaking point. It was the painful catalyst for everything, but Sam had always tried to deny that his son had felt any pain.

He knew that was a lie.

Wallace stood by the door, his evil glare landing on Alex who sheepishly pressed herself against the wall, her hands firmly behind her back. Sam noticed Wallace's intent and stood.

'Sir, please. You have me. Let her go.'

All the rifles were raised, and Sam heard the sound of feet shuffling into position. The bulb above hummed loudly, bathing the pooling blood on the floor in a glorious shimmer. Wallace lifted the gun and aimed it squarely at Alex's head. Her eyes widened with fear and she looked straight at Sam.

'Now, Sam, you might not give a fuck about what happens to yourself. But how does this rank on your *holier than thou* bullshit?'

'Sam?' Alex asked, her eyes wide with terror.

'It's going to be okay, Alex,' Sam offered helplessly. 'Sir, please put the gun down. You've done enough to her already.'

'I'll be honest, Sam, I don't deal much with the recruitment process,' Wallace said nonchalantly. 'However, as always, when it comes to saving the world, a few people have to die for the rest to survive. Now I'll ask you one last time. Where did you send the files?'

Sam took a deep breath and glanced at Marsden. The man had been a father figure to him, had brought him through the ranks of the military and been with him through every hardship. The man had dragged him from the dark, stone room where he was bleeding out. Had brought him back from the brink.

His dying wish was for the truth to come out.

But he, like Sam, was a good man.

And good men don't let the innocent die.

'Fine...' Sam began. Out of nowhere, Alex's voice filled the room.

'Sam,' she yelled, pulling her hands from behind her back. 'Don't look.'

In her hand, she grasped a flashbang grenade which she'd lifted from one of the guard's belts. In the other hand, she had the pin.

Before anyone could move, Sam covered his eyes and twisted downwards away from the blast. With a loud bang, the entire room was bathed in a blinding white light. Alex had tossed the grenade and as it exploded into the air, Wallace pulled the trigger.

A gunshot echoed through the abandoned factory.

CHAPTER TWENTY-FIVE

With a high pitch ringing in his ears, Sam looked up and immediately launched himself at the first guard, who had raised a hand to his eyes just a split second too late. As he tried to adjust, Sam reached forward, grabbed the rifle and lifted it upwards, the spray of bullets sending debris falling from the ceiling. The noise was close to deafening. Sam caught the man with a swift right into the stomach, doubling him over, before he rammed the man headfirst into the wall.

The man stumbled back, blood pouring from the top of his skull and Sam slapped both hands on either side of his head and snapped with all his might.

The neck broke instantly, and the man dropped limp to the bloody floor below. Sam reached for the rifle, hoisting it expertly to his shoulder and swivelling on his heel, aiming it at the door.

Wallace had fled.

As Sam realized he had left with the other soldier, he turned too late to see Buck charging at him, the brutish guard catching him with a vicious elbow to the side of the head that sent Sam sprawling across the metal table, off the other side, and crashing onto the unforgiving concrete. The pistol he'd left on the table also clattered into the scarlet puddle. With his hands covered in the blood of his friend, Sam looked up momentarily, noticing Alex laying by the door in considerable pain. As Sam shook the hard blow, trying to regather his thoughts, Buck loosened his shoulders, kicking the rifle to the side of the room.

'Oh, I'm going to fucking enjoy this,' Buck boasted, his hulking frame moving quickly around the table. As Sam tried to get to his feet, Buck clubbed down on him with vicious rights, which Sam managed to block with his forearm. Buck swung another, then followed it up with a swinging left that slammed into Sam's ribs like a sledgehammer. Sam hunched forward, only for Buck to thrust his knee upwards, catching Sam on the bridge of the nose.

The pain was instant, and his vision blurred with tears and Buck lunged forward, wrapping his arm around Sam's chest and heaving him across the metal table once more. Sam hit the metal hard, bounced and crumpled onto the floor below. Buck chuckled, cracking his neck as if he was just getting warmed up. Sam was beginning to regret embarrassing the man over the duration of their mission, as despite his short comings, Buck was Blackridge's best.

Which meant he was good.

Fatally good.

Sam tried to get to his feet, but a rib cracking boot collided with his side, flipping him over and across the room, the air driven from his body. Buck swung another boot, but Sam caught it, twisting it and dragging Buck to the floor. Both men scurried to their feet, the blue glow of the halogen bulb illuminating their final fight.

Both of them were battered, bruised, and covered in the blood of dead men.

Their eyes met across the table and they accepted that this was to the death.

As they approached each other, Buck weaved and swung a right, which Sam ducked, shooting two hard jabs into Buck's solid abdomen. Slightly rocked, Buck swung again. Sam dodged, let the arm move over his shoulder and he grabbed it. In one fell swoop, he launched Buck over his shoulder, the American's spine slamming off the edge of the table and he roared with pain.

Sam took a step back, his leg buckling under his damaged thigh and he pulled his fists up, ready to go again. Buck gingerly got to his feet; his eyes wide with murderous rage. As he planted his feet, he pulled a knife from his belt, the blade as sharp and serrated as the one Sam had used to disembowel Colin Mayer on a small boat on the British coast.

It had one purpose. To kill.

Buck lunged forward erratically, slashing wildly at Sam, who expertly dodged a few swings until one of them caught his forearm, ripping the flesh open and drawing blood. Sam grimaced, stepping back, while Buck smiled like a hungry shark. As he lunged again, Sam stepped to the side, clutched the knife wielding wrist and drove his other elbow into the forearm, snapping the bone. Buck howled in pain, relinquished his grip, but before Sam could move, Buck drove his forehead into Sam's cheek.

Sam stumbled back into the wall, the back of his head hitting the brick and both men collapsed to the floor.

Buck pushed himself to his feet, allowing his useless arm to flop loosely by the wayside and he bent down, his gloved hand sliding around the handle of the knife.

'You piece of shit,' he spat, gripping the blade which was now coated in the blood of dead men. As he took staggered, beaten steps towards him, Sam scanned the room.

Among the three dead men, he noticed Alex moving, her hand clasping at her leg. To the right of the table, next to the lifeless Marsden, was the handgun.

Buck launched forward, pinning Sam down with his superior body weight, with the knife firmly in his grip.

Sam got his forearm up, locking it under Buck's wrist and trapping it in mid plunge. The blade was a few inches from Sam's chest, and with his eyes filled with a maniacal pleasure, Buck pushed down with all his might.

The blade began to edge closer and closer to Sam's heart and despite his best efforts, Sam knew he wouldn't be able to hold on.

This was it.

The fight was over.

This time, there was no Marsden to pull him out from his dark, desolate crypt.

Buck pushed harder, the veins in his powerful neck straining. His face began to turn a dark shade of red and saliva dribbled from his mouth. The thrill of killing Sam had turned him into a rabid dog and Sam could feel his arm beginning to buckle.

This journey that had started with the death of his son, would end with him dying alone in a dark underground bunker. His body, likely to be paraded in a historic triumph by Wallace, who would position it in a way to gain more power.

The war would continue.

Sam would have altered nothing.

Just as he felt the last of his energy eb towards his forearm, he closed his eyes.

He thought of Jamie.

His beautiful son crouching by the flower beds of the garden that Lucy took such pride in. The glaring sun, shimmering off his thick, blonde hair. The young boy was curious, poking at a worm with a stick when suddenly, his head snapped to the side and he looked straight at Sam.

'*Not yet, Daddy.*'

With that, Sam felt a sudden jolt of adrenaline, his fight not yet done. A flicker of doubt filled Buck's eyes and Sam reached out with his other hand, latching onto Buck's shattered forearm and twisting as hard as he could. The pain was unbearable, and Buck sat up, screaming in anguish as he dropped the knife.

Sam caught it mid-air and drove it into Buck's side, the blade slicing through the skin like a birthday cake. Warm blood oozed out over Sam's hand as Buck fell back, Sam lifted his foot and drove it into the blade. With the blade cutting into his major organs, Buck scrambled towards the table, his life leaving him as quickly as the blood flow, and he reached up with a shaking hand towards the table, his other arm hanging loosely by his side.

As he pushed himself up, he hunched over. Sam, now to his feet, ran. As he approached Buck, he leapt over him, grabbing his broken arm and rolling across the table. The arm separated from the shoulder and Buck slammed into the hard metal and crumpled to the floor once more. Sam rolled off the other side, dropped to one knee, and swiftly picked up the gun.

Sam stood, arm outstretched, the gun aimed squarely at the dying Buck, whose mouth was now filled with his own blood. The knife was still embedded deeply into his side and his arm was loose bag of skin and assorted bone.

Buck spat blood at Sam.

Sam pulled the trigger.

The bullet ripped through the centre of Buck's forehead and he fell back, dead.

Sam's arm dropped and he took a deep breath, his head, body, and mind all aching with pain.

A groan from the corner attracted his attention and as

fast as his limp would carry him, he rushed towards Alex. Her bloodstained hands were clutching her thigh, where that rogue bullet had caught her. Sam dropped down to his knees and offered her a smile. The beating he had taken was clearly evident, judging by her reaction.

'You all right?' Sam asked, checking her leg.

'I've been better.' She joked, then regretted it immediately, wincing with pain. Sam checked the bullet wound.

'In and out. Good.' He flashed her a bloody grin. 'You'll be fine.'

'This fucking sucks,' she howled and Sam pulled off his jacket and ripped the sleeve from the seam. As tightly as he could, he knotted it around the wound, cutting off the blood flow and temporarily halting the bleeding. It was crude, but it would do.

Theo would certainly had done a better job, but he was just another good person who had met his end trying to help Sam.

Alex would not be another.

'We need to go,' Sam said softly, offering her his shoulder which she draped an arm over. Despite his own battered body, Sam pushed to his feet, hauling Alex up with him. The last time they'd been this close, they'd been making passionate love.

This was nowhere near as fun.

Sam glanced back towards Marsden one last time, offering him a final goodbye. It was unlikely that Wallace wouldn't cover his tracks, but Sam promised he wouldn't leave Marsden to rot in the dark. With Alex hobbling, they left the room.

As they'd slowly made their way back up the stairs, Alex told Sam how they'd been lying in wait for them and as she'd turned the car around, she'd been met by a barrage of gunfire and was forcibly taken from the car by Wallace's men. As the head of Blackridge, Wallace commanded their respect and fear, even more so after executing Sims, which he had taken great pride in. As they'd forced her back towards the building, they'd waited by the side entrance until Sam had gone underground, knowing there was no way of escape.

It was there that she'd found his weapons, and she'd managed to snatch a flash-bang grenade.

Sam would be eternally grateful.

As they reached the top of the stairs, Sam could hear the low, distant thud of a helicopter.

Wallace was still there. His ride was on its way, but Sam could still catch up with him. He turned back to Alex and judging from the expression on her face, she knew what he was thinking.

'Sam, just come with me. We can both go,' she pleaded.

'Do you remember the way back to the side entrance?'

'Sam, please?'

'Do you?' Sam regretfully raised his voice.

'Yes.'

'I need you to go back that way, get your car and drive.' Sam gently stroked her face. 'Thank you. You saved my life.'

Alex leant into Sam's touch and closed her eyes, fighting to hold back a tear. The darkness of the corridor enveloped them, and she leant forward and kissed him on the cheek. Then, with a significant amount of discomfort, she turned and began to hobble down the corridor. As she did, Sam watched her go, angry that another good person's life was in tatters because of him.

After a few steps, she stopped and turned back, locking eyes with him one more time.

'What about you?'

With the volume of the chopper growing, Sam looked

back towards the front door and the thunderous rain that awaited him.

'I'm going to finish this.'

With his pistol firmly in his hand, Sam shuffled towards the exit of the building, ready to confront Wallace for the final time.

CHAPTER TWENTY-SIX

After returning home to dry off, Singh had put on another white shirt and navy suit and made her way back to New Scotland Yard. The day had felt longer than usual, the horror they'd found at Etheridge's house was hanging heavy on her mind. She'd met the man before, in some of the preliminary follow-ups after Sam had taken out her Armed Response team on his landing.

The story checked out.

Sam had forced him at gun point to help him.

It was apparent now that it was a lie and as angry as Singh was that she'd been duped, it gave her an odd reassurance.

She wasn't the only one drawn to helping Sam.

As she sat her new desk, ostracized from her task force, she tried to figure out exactly what she was trying to do.

Did she want to help Sam because she no longer believed in the thin blue line she'd dedicated her life to?

Or did she want to help him by stopping him, by uncovering whatever dark truths she was on the verge of discovering and in turn, rendering his mission moot?

It was something she knew she had to figure out, as

there was nothing worse than making decisions without clarity. One of her biggest strengths had been her clear thinking, the ability to make a decision then stand by it. A lack of conviction was a trait she deemed unforgivable, and it was a reason why her love life had never ventured beyond a few nights of passion.

Men were just not capable of making decisions and Singh refused to allow a man's indecision to waste her own time.

The afternoon soon slipped seamlessly into the evening, the early sunsets of the bitter winter making tracking the time even more difficult. Singh was used to the long hours, her career had been built on the back of seeing jobs through to the end, no matter what impact it had on her life.

Another reason for her non-existent love life.

She looked at a picture of Sam and chuckled, finding herself thinking and talking about the man so much, she could probably introduce him to her parents as the man in her life.

As droll as that might be, the only life Sam was facing was in prison. Without parole.

The man had taken the law into his own hands, regardless of the targets he had taken down and the success he had achieved. And while her nagging doubts of her own conscience were fluttering around her head like fireflies, she knew that if Sam was to stand any chance, she needed to find out what happened at Project Hailstorm.

Something was being hidden.

As a high-ranking detective within the Metropolitan Police, having evidence withheld, and subsequently followed up with thinly veiled threats, did not sit well with her. For all she knew, Sam was part of something bigger and piecing it all together would help him.

Would bring an end to his mission and save him from prison or a fate much worse.

Singh knew she had to spend some time to struggle with her reasons and feelings for Sam, but now was not that moment. As Pearce had said, Ashton was pushing for her removal and her resources would soon be limited. After what happened to Etheridge, maybe even her safety was in short supply.

Staring at her computer screen, Singh hadn't even realized the shadow that had darkened her desk.

'Singh. A word.'

Singh looked up, into the stern face of Assistant Commissioner Ashton. Singh slowly pushed herself from her chair, locking her computer and sliding the USB stick she'd carefully hidden under a notepad, from the side of the computer. Ashton walked purposefully through the office, slamming her heels down to attract the attention of the rest of the task force.

She wanted all heads to turn, to see her marching Singh towards her office.

Singh had a bad feeling.

As she stepped into the office, Ashton asked her to close the door and take a seat.

'I'd prefer to stand, ma'am,' Singh said curtly, her hands behind her back, her shoulders straight.

'Not very good at taking orders, are you, Singh?' Ashton said spitefully, taking her own seat and propping her glasses onto her nose. With her short, greying hair tied back tight, she looked like a librarian. 'Very well. I'm afraid I have some unfortunate news.'

'Ma'am?'

'After a thorough investigation, DPS has collated sufficient evidence to flag you as a risk to our task force.'

'Excuse me?' Singh exclaimed, gripping the back of

the chair in frustration. The Depart of Professional Standards was Pearce's gig.

He had betrayed her.

'I'm afraid I had my suspicions and DI Pearce has provided me with enough evidence to not only open a case against you, but to have you removed from all duty immediately. You will be suspended without pay, effective immediately. Richards.'

On cue, PC Richards stepped into the doorway, a resigned look on his face. Singh scowled at him, before returning her gaze to her superior. Sat back in her plush, leather chair, Ashton antagonized her with a smile.

'This is bullshit.'

'If so, then you have nothing to worry about. But before you start pointing fingers, Singh. Perhaps you should look inwards. As you are not the only person this affects.'

'Oh really?' Singh snapped, her survival instincts kicking in.

'Yes.' Ashton responded coldly. 'Jake Manning, who works in IT, has been fired for essentially hacking sensitive military files.'

Singh felt sick. Jake was a nice guy who was doing her a favour.

'I asked him to.'

'Very noble of you, Singh.' Ashton responded. 'He already told us that. We were quite clear that Mr Manning would be spared a prison sentence if he told us the truth. General Wallace had made it clear that those files were off limits…'

'Wallace? I should have known.'

'Excuse me?' Ashton spat.

'Let me ask you, ma'am. Is Wallace's whole hand up this organisations arse, or just yours?'

Singh regretted the comment immediately and she saw

a flicker of rage in her superior's eyes. But, after a brief moment, Ashton recomposed. It was her job to be calm and assured and she knew she was good at it. Despite the truth of Singh's comment, she still felt in control of her organisation.

Didn't she?

Quickly shuffling the doubt from her mind, Ashton pulled her thin lips together in a grin.

'Due to the stress of the situation, I will ignore that comment. But please listen to me when I tell you this as a superior and someone who cares about your career. There are some people who you do not want the attention of. General Wallace is one of those men. Take this as a serious warning. Singh.' Ashton nodded curtly to underline her point. 'Now, please collect your things and follow Richards off the premises. Otherwise, I'll have you arrested.'

Singh held her tongue, feeling her fists clenching, but she knew the game. If she didn't comply, her chances of continuing her investigation would be over. They would book her into a cell, take her possessions, and confiscate the USB stick. With a deep sigh, she turned and headed to the door, not before Ashton threw one final dig.

'Oh, and don't worry, Singh. We'll continue your good work and bring Sam in.'

Singh stopped for a second but then marched out, pushing past Richards and striding back across the room towards her desk. The other detectives and police constables watched, but she ignored them all.

She needed to get out before she said something she regretted. She pulled her jacket from the back of her seat and gathered her phone and card holder, before tossing her badge and security pass onto the desk. Without a word to Richards, she headed to the door, making him follow like an obedient dog. As she stepped out into the hallway, an apologetic Pearce stood up from a chair.

'Singh, look I...'

'Fuck you, Adrian,' she barked at him, barging past him and heading straight to the stairs. Richards offered him a raised eyebrow and followed, leaving Pearce stood, hands on hips and his head bowed forward. It had been for her own good, he hoped she would soon realise that.

But as Singh marched all the way to the exit, she'd never felt so alone.

————

With the rain lashing against him, Sam stepped out from the abandoned facility and into the brightly lit car park. In the near distance, he could see the helicopter approaching.

A gunshot rang out.

A bullet whipped past Sam and hit the old bricks behind him, and he immediately dropped to his knee, lifting the handgun to his eyeline and allowing his training to kick in.

Throughout his illustrious career as a sniper, Sam had only ever been in a standoff twice, both times pegged down by an opposing sniper. The ability to place the shooter from sound, trajectory, and speed of impact allowed him to hone in on the shadows where the shooter was. His knowledge of wind resistance allowed him to line the shot up just right.

Sam sent a bullet back into the dark.

It hit the final guard between the eyes, sending a spray of blood into the rain and his dead body spinning to the ground.

He heard the body collide with the concrete, followed by the rifle.

'Wallace!' Sam shouted as he stood. The rain relentlessly crashed against him. 'It's over.'

Sam took a few steps forward, walking out into the

middle of the car park. It was the likely landing zone for Wallace's escape, and he was determined to block it. After a few more moments, Wallace eventually stepped out from the shadow, his hands up.

'What now, Sam?' Wallace yelled, roughly twenty feet from Sam. 'You're going to kill me?'

Sam lifted his gun, the barrel pointed straight at his former superior. Wallace took another step forward, his drenched suit clung to his hulking frame.

'I'm going to end this.'

'And how are you going to do that? By destroying the peace built up through years of hard work? Work that you yourself were a part of. Face it, Sam, you're just like me. A soldier.'

'I'm nothing like you,' Sam said, his finger itching to pull the trigger. The noise of the chopper thudded overhead, drowning out the torrential downpour.

'That's right. You're a criminal,' Wallace yelled provokingly.

'You're a terrorist.'

'I'm a necessity!' Wallace yelled; his arms outstretched. 'You, Sam, you're a soldier. One of the best I've ever seen. You're not going to shoot an unarmed man in cold blood. But just think, Sam. Think of what I could do for you. This war you're waging, I can help you take that to the next level. All the charges, they would go away. You would have unlimited resources. I could point you in the direction of the true criminals in this world and step out of your way.'

'I'm already dealing with the true criminals of the world!' Sam yelled, one eye closed, the other lining up the shot.

'Join me, Sam. Become one of my 'ghosts' and you can fight the real fight.'

'Get on your knees, General,' Sam ordered, his voice barely audible.

'Why are you doing this, Sam? You must know you're a marked man.' Wallace took a few more steps closer. 'What are you fighting for?'

Sam lowered his arm, letting the gun relax by his side. Now that Wallace was closer, he could see his emotionless face. Sam wanted nothing more than to put a bullet square between the eyes, but this was bigger. Killing Wallace wouldn't bring it down.

Pull one weed and another grows in its place.

It was why, after he took down the High Rise, he took down all those linked to it.

It was why after he had stopped the Kovalenkos in Tilbury, he had journeyed to Ukraine to take the head of the snake.

To truly kill something, to end it entirely, you had to remove the core.

Wallace contemplated Sam with a raised eyebrow, awaiting his answer. With the rain washing the blood from Sam's face and hands, he raised the gun up again.

'Someone has to fight back.'

A gunshot rang out.

The bullet hit Sam in the shoulder of his outstretched arm, ripping through his skin and bursting out his back. The impact spun him around, the immediate, burning pain caused him to drop his gun. Sam hit the wet concrete hard, gasping in agony as he pressed his hand to his shoulder. Wallace laughed loudly, before applauding. Grimacing in pain, Sam pushed himself to a seated position, staring out into the bright, rain-soaked car park.

Above them, the helicopter had approached, the propellers causing havoc with the rain, sending it flying in every direction. Beyond Wallace, who was holding his coat steady in the onslaught, Sam saw a figure emerge from the darkness that lined the car park.

The man was dressed entirely in black.

His face was covered with a balaclava and his long, black trench coat flapped in the wind.

In his hand was an assault rifle.

'I promised you a reunion,' Wallace yelled jovially, and he stepped back as the man lifted the rifle again.

Sam scrambled to his feet, and with his good arm, fired a shot in their general direction. He knew it was wide, but it brought him enough time to race towards the part of the car park untouched by the beaming spotlight.

The darkness would provide sanctuary for a few moments, and Sam hurried towards the abandoned vehicles.

As the chopper lowered itself to the concrete, the man in black walked past Wallace, his eyes firmly on his prey. Wallace reached out, gripping the man's broad shoulder with his hand.

'Get me that fucking USB stick. Then, he's all yours.'

Triumphantly, Wallace stepped onto the chopper as the man in black strode towards the darkness.

The hunt for Sam Pope was on.

CHAPTER TWENTY-SEVEN

It took a few moments for Sam's eyes to readjust to the dark, the glare of the floodlights blinding him temporarily as he had dashed into the darkness. After colliding with one car bonnet, he dropped down to a squat and kept himself as low as possible. Pressing himself against the body of the car, he shuffled further into the dark, using the vehicles as cover.

His shoulder was burning, the bullet passing clean through and he knew he needed to stem the bleeding as soon as possible. He'd abandoned the rest of his jacket in the facility, after administering a similar repair to Alex.

Sam cursed himself.

With the freezing rain clawing at his body, he ripped the blood-soaked sleeve of his shirt from the seam, and with gritted teeth, lifted it over his shoulder, tying it as tightly as he could. It wasn't much, but it was all he could do.

If he lost too much blood, he would collapse, leaving him prone for whoever it was that was hunting him.

Above, he saw the chopper ascend into the dark night,

knowing that Wallace was retreating most likely with a smug grin on his face.

The man would cover it all up, ensuring the deaths of Carl Marsden and Trevor Sims were pointed squarely at his door. Sam was already a wanted man, but for him to target the supposed 'good guys' would launch the man hunt for him into overdrive.

That was, of course, if he survived the current one.

With his body crying out in pain, Sam lowered himself to the wet pavement and peered under the cars towards the light.

Footsteps were approaching.

Sam had counted seven cars from the perimeter which meant he had a slight advantage. He could see the man approaching. The disadvantage was, the man was holding an M16 rifle and clearly knew how to use it. Rolling onto his bottom, Sam pressed himself against the abandoned car and slid the cartridge from his pistol.

One bullet left.

Fuck.

With the chopper still overhead, Sam's cover was quickly disappearing. He swung the gun up, smashing the driver side window above his head and allowing the shards of glass to fall around him. The noise had been masked by the departing helicopter which disappeared into the night sky.

Sam reached up into the car, popping the door handle and slowly, he slid in, keeping his head down. His memory flooded back to the time Etheridge had taught him how to hot-wire a car while under heavy fire.

A similar, high stakes situation had unfolded, and Sam needed those skills more than ever. With his feet hanging out of the door, he arched backwards across the driver's seat, grunted in pain as he raised his arms, and removed the panel under the steering wheel with a hard tug.

The exposed wires were old, the plastic hanging from the electrics like loose clothing.

Sam pulled a few of them out and then cautiously pressed them together.

Nothing.

The battery was dead.

A bullet shattered the passenger window.

Sam slid out from the car and kept low; his cover blown. He could hear the footsteps of his chaser, the man carefully moving around the car. From the gunshot, Sam approximated the man was four cars away.

To be able to see his movements from there, in these conditions, meant the man had a keen eye.

The eye of a sniper.

Sam kept low, shuffling to the rear of the car, before poking his head up to scan the area.

Two bullets sprayed across the boot.

Ducking down, Sam burst forward, hurriedly scampering between the next few cars and further into the dark. After a few moments, he took sanctuary behind another car. As he regrouped, he controlled his breathing, remembering the numerous times he had been under fire. The remote cliffs outside of Syria, where he had taken on an advancing team of ISIS, delivering a swift death to each of them with a well-placed bullet, as they unloaded in his direction.

The impossible shot of the gas cannister which saved the life of his comrade, whose convoy had been overturned.

Sam was built to survive.

He just had to stay calm.

From his position, he peered into the side mirror of the car, affording himself a view of the passage behind him.

Although the remnants of the floodlights and raindrops did their best to skew his vision, he could make out the mysterious figure slowly walking between the cars, his rifle at the ready.

He was sweeping each gap, professionally holding the rifle with the intent to blow Sam away.

The man was clearly trained.

One of Wallace's ghosts.

But a reunion?

Sam knew he didn't have time to ponder who was beneath the balaclava, but he couldn't help it. Over his career, he had certainly made a number of enemies. The issue was, all of them had been in the ground by his hand.

Whoever this man was, he clearly wanted Sam's blood.

With time being of the essence, Sam slid his hand under the door handle, trying his luck. For the first time in what felt like forever, his luck was in and the door silently came away on its hinge. With the darkness skewing the make and model of the car, Sam slid onto the seat again, the interior in better condition than the previous one.

Sam had hope.

Quickly, he hauled the panel open and grabbed the first wire.

A bullet shattered the passenger window.

He'd been spotted.

As he took the second wire, the window to the driver's side door shattered, the bullet whipping by just above him. As the glass shattered and sprinkled him like the first snow fall of the year, he pressed the wires together.

The car roared into life.

A spray of bullets rattled the car, thudding across the bonnet in a well-timed spray.

Sam's attacker was trying to sabotage his exit.

Sam pushed himself up, swiveled across the side of the car and slammed his good arm onto the roof of the car.

His hand was wrapped around the gun.

His finger was on the trigger.

The final bullet left the gun with a pinpoint, murderous accuracy and slammed into the centre of the mystery man's chest, sending him arching backwards into the car behind. The rifle fell to the floor. Despite his curiosity, Sam slid into the car, his shoulder aching, his leg begging him to stop and slipped the car into reverse. He slammed backwards into the car parked behind him, his foot on the accelerator as he tried to force his way through the car graveyard. He shifted to first, pulling forward as far as he could, before ramming the car full on once again.

The abandoned car spun out of the way, colliding with another in an almighty crash.

Sam felt the impact, his shoulder taking the most impact and he wearily reached for the gear stick.

A bullet pierced through the windscreen, burying itself in the passenger seat beside him.

Sam looked up to see the masked man stumbling to his feet, his bullet driving the air from his lungs at it slammed into the bulletproof vest. As the attacker tried to regain his composure, Sam floored it, the wheel spinning in the torrential rain and he spun the car through the gap, another few bullets rattling against the boot of the car. Seamlessly, he slipped the gear into first and shot forward, climbing through the gears as he raced towards the metal gate.

Sam braced himself, and the front of his car slammed into the metal barrier, the gates bursting open and he had to wrestle control back of the wheel as he spun onto the gravel path.

Sam straightened the car, the headlights showed nothing but the dirt path, rain, and darkness ahead.

Sam floored it.

He'd escaped. Barely.

———

On a separate, dark and desolate road, Alex Stone was hurtling as fast as she could away from Rome.

The entire mission had gone to hell.

Sims, the man who had forced her into the crew, was dead. The man they were trying to capture was dead.

And she was pretty certain, despite his apparent gift for survival, that the man who she'd grown to trust, Sam, was also going to suffer a similar fate.

She'd managed to put about twenty miles between herself and the facility, reluctantly heeding Sam's advice to leave. Alex had hated the thought of leaving Sam, but he was dealing with some of the most dangerous people she'd ever known, and she knew, despite his vulnerable state, that he didn't want to put her in harm's way. There was no future between them, they both knew that, but that special night they'd shared had forged a bond between them.

Now she had to leave, head to the nearest place where she could lie low, disappear, and then try to figure out how she could make her way back to the States. She was headed north, seeing signs for Bologna telling her she was over three hundred kilometres away. She checked her petrol levels. The tank was almost full, and she was confident enough of making the three-hour journey.

Then she could figure out her next steps.

She didn't even want to comprehend how she was going to get her siblings back.

Sims had used them as leverage, threatening their futures if she didn't play ball. After suffering throughout her youth, Alex couldn't bear the thought of her younger brother and sister going through the same.

Joel and Nattie were innocent.

Alex angrily slammed her fists against the wheel.

She'd agreed to the job for them, and now, with everything ruined, Blackridge could just as easily click their fingers and plunge her brother and sister into the darkness that she suffered through. Their mum was unreliable, incapable of resisting the escape of her next pill. She couldn't let them be taken into care.

Selfishly, she knew she needed Sam.

If she had any hope of being reunited with her family, she needed the only person she knew who could take down Blackridge.

She thumped the wheel in frustration again.

She should never have left him. He was a lamb to the slaughter, and she knew he had only done it to give her enough time to get away.

It was the right thing to do.

That's what Sam had said.

As she flew down the motorway, tears streamed down her cheeks, a mixture of her regret, her fear, and her pain. Her leg was aching, and Alex knew she needed to get it patched up as soon as possible. But she didn't know anyone out here, she was as lost as she'd ever been, driving aimlessly into the night, heading for a destination she could only hope would offer some solace.

She thought of Sam, telling her to leave before he turned and walked towards the door, ready to confront his demons head on.

She was running away.

Alex had witnessed Sam risk his freedom and his life to try to save a man who he had cared for. He'd willingly run into a firefight, outnumbered and outgunned, to try to save his friend.

Sam had tragically been too late.

But at least he had fought.

Had tried.

An angry tear slid down Alex's cheek and she swatted it away like an inconvenient fly.

At least Sam had tried to save someone he cared about.

As she sped past the next sign, she took a deep breath

and as the junction approached, she pulled hard on the steering wheel, her car veering off the motorway at top speed, before heading off into the dark, unfamiliar streets ahead.

She was tired of running.

It was time to start trying.

CHAPTER TWENTY-EIGHT

It hadn't taken long for Wallace's helicopter to make it back to the airport, the chopper slicing through the torrential rain at breakneck speed. As it landed, he had checked his phone, agitated that he was yet to receive an update from his assassin.

He'd gift wrapped Sam to him and now he expected his end of the bargain to be delivered.

Stepping off the helicopter, he was met by one of the faceless suits who ran the logistical side of Blackridge, none of whom were important enough to remember by name. One of them held a large black umbrella over him, sheltering him as they marched across the tarmac towards the private jet which was waiting his arrival and delaying all commuter flights from leaving the country. It was less than a few weeks until Christmas, and people were making plans to spend the festive period with loved ones or on holidays.

Wallace didn't care.

While Pope may have had enough help to sneak guns through airports, he had the ability to ground all flights whenever the hell he wanted.

The power he wielded was vast.

But it was under threat, by the very soldier he had helped to create.

As he strode across the tarmac, another suit handed him a dossier, filled with paperwork he had no interest in reading. There were no fine details he needed to know. The only fact he needed confirming was that Sam Pope had been neutralized and the location of the files had been recovered. As he approached the steps to the jet, the rain began to lighten up, the gods offering up a small mercy after the relentless downpour. Wallace boarded the plane, not even offering so much as a courteous nod to his chaperones.

Once inside, he marched through to the plush seating area, walking past the leather chairs to the bar and poured himself a Scotch.

He swallowed it in one gulp.

Another large one followed and with the glass in his hand, Wallace collapsed into one of the chairs. He felt tired, his years of being out in the field, hunting down targets were long behind him and it infuriated him that what should have been a simple extraction had turned into a cluster fuck.

There would be inquisitions from the Ukrainian, German, and Italian governments, all of them wanting to know why blood was shed and guns were fired in their back yards. It would be easy to sweep under the rug, but Wallace could do without the inconvenience.

What angered him most was the death of his old friend.

Carl Marsden had been a good man and a damn fine soldier. The world was a worse place without him, and Wallace felt sick that it was at his hand that the man had died. But like any true soldier, Marsden would understand that sacrifices needed to be made for the greater good.

Somewhere along the way, the man had lost sight of that, instead wanting to derail years of hard, blood-soaked work that Wallace had carefully put together.

All for the supposed notion of what is right.

Wallace silently toasted his friend's memory and took a sip of the expensive Scotch, allowing the liquid to burn at the back of his throat before swallowing.

The pilot's voice piped through the overhead speakers, assuring Wallace of a safe journey back to the UK. Wallace ignored it, staring out of the window as the plane slowly moved towards the runway. He downed his drink and gripped the arms of his chair, his knuckles whitening as the plane shot through the airport and up into the thick, dark clouds that were hiding the moon.

As the plane gradually straightened out after climbing thousands of feet into the air, Wallace pulled out his phone.

Still no update.

He cursed, unlocking the phone and selecting Ashton's number from his contacts. He knew that when his name embellished someone's screen, the answer was immediate and always laced with a little concern.

It was the power he held.

It made him smile.

'General Wallace. What a lovely surprise.' Ashton's voice was calm and collected. The consummate professional.

'Ruth, I told you, please call me Ervin.' He gestured to the on-flight attendant that he wanted another drink, rudely shaking his glass at her. She obliged him with no fuss.

'Of course, sorry, Ervin.' She sounded like a teenager on the phone with her crush. 'I trust everything went well?'

'Never better.' Wallace snatched the glass and took a

sip. 'I just wanted to check in regarding my request. I trust all is in hand.'

'You will be happy to know, that as of this evening, Amara Singh is no longer a factor. I won't bore you with the details, but I have suspen—'

'Good,' Wallace rudely interrupted, finishing his drink in another long swig.

'And, if it's not too rude of me to ask, how are we getting on with my end of the bargain?'

Wallace grinned. He didn't have any strong feelings towards the woman, but he found her craving of power and authority attractive. It reminded him of himself and his mind was already racing for when he would be able to have his way with her.

'All in good time, Ruth. All in good time.'

Wallace cancelled the call, checked again for an update on Sam, and then tossed the phone onto the table before him. He stared out of the window, the bright lights of civilization below him and he looked down on them all with disdain. They had no idea what he did to keep this world safe. The decisions and sacrifices he had to make. One of them had been that evening, when he had shot and killed a good man who had stepped beyond his boundaries.

Up here, he was a god to them.

But behind it all, he felt an irritating nervousness creeping in. He needed his man to take care of Sam and find those files. The only problem was, he knew Sam better than most.

The man was built to survive.

————

The Renault Clio handled surprisingly well, especially as Sam had no idea how long it had sat idle at the facility. The rain had let up, with just the odd splattering crashing onto his windscreen which the wipers took care of immediately.

Sam had not taken his foot off the accelerator, partly due to the need to get back to civilization. Partly due to the pain emanating from his leg.

His shoulder had begun to numb, making even the slightest turn of the wheel a painful task.

He'd followed the gravel path back the way he and Alex had come in, before turning in the opposite direction and heading back towards the bright lights of Rome. He'd been driving for over twenty minutes, averaging a speed of ninety miles per hours.

In the distance, he could see the city skyline.

Like a moth drawn towards the light, he thundered on, knowing that once he got to Rome, he would be able to pull himself together. Appropriating cash wouldn't be a problem, and although he didn't like stealing, mugging a drug dealer didn't rank too highly on the list of awful things he had done.

When he had the money, he would find a doctor who would patch him up for a few hundred euros. Maybe even let him use their phone. He needed make contact with Etheridge.

He needed to get out of Italy and back to the UK.

Sam needed to finish it, once and for all.

As he approached the city, a few more cars littered the motorway, most likely taxis, shepherding the night life to their next hot spot. It was the festive season and Sam was sure there were more than enough parties happening throughout the Italian capital to keep the bar tabs piling up and taxi drivers in work.

Weaving in and out of the traffic, Sam noticed a pair of headlights fast approaching. Checking his speed dial, he was clocking over ninety, but the headlights behind him were slowly, but surely gaining on him.

As they approached closer, he could make out the outline of the large truck, not dissimilar to the one in the facility car park.

The man in black.

'Shit,' Sam uttered, turning sharply, cutting across the middle lane of traffic and receiving a barrage of horns from the angry drivers. The truck followed suit, dangerously sliding in between two cars and following Sam as he raced to the slow lane. With excruciating discomfort, Sam turned the wheel as hard as he could, taking the exit at ninety miles an hour, the back of the car sliding out slightly on the wet tarmac. It clipped the stone barrier, shaking the car and Sam, yelling in agony, wrestled back control of the car.

His makeshift tourniquet had fallen, and blood slowly began to seep down his chest.

The bright lights of the truck followed, taking the corner slightly slower, before rapidly racing down the off ramp towards the city. Sam took the next corner as quickly as he could, hauling up the handbrake and skidding around the car which had slammed on the breaks.

The Clio skimmed its bumper, but Sam slammed down the handbrake, and burst forward up the street, the wide streets of Rome welcoming him with open arms.

Behind him, the truck ploughed through the parked car, sending it spinning into a nearby phone box and causing a horrifying crash.

The man in black did not stop.

With a potential death left behind, he slammed his foot down, eager to catch Sam at all costs.

Their dangerous arrival in the city had been reported and somewhere in the city, Sam could hear the wailing of sirens.

The last thing Sam needed was to be taken in by the Polizia. They would hand him over, gift wrapped to

Wallace who would make sure Sam never saw the light of day again.

The truck gained speed and as it roared forward, it collided with the back of Sam's car. The entire vehicle shunted forward and Sam once again had to steady the car, straining his torn shoulder.

The truck sped forward again, but this time Sam turned the wheel, engaged the hand brake once more and slid off down a narrow side street, clipping two parked Vespas which he sent colliding into the wall of the nearby club. The patrons, huddled under the smoking gazebo screamed in terror and Sam whizzed past them, doing his best to maintain control of the car.

He flicked a glance to the rear-view mirror.

The truck was gone.

His hunter had missed the turning.

Relief poured over Sam like a hot shower and he slowed the car down considerably, wanting to blend in with the other night-time drivers. As he turned onto the next road, he could see the entrance towards the Vatican lit up, the stunning, religious epicentre was magnificent to behold. Despite the time and the horrific weather, a number of tourists and locals were still gathered near it, drawn to the residence of the Pope and storied history of the famous structure.

Sam could see the large pillars that circled the fore-court, along with the towers behind the walls, all awash with the glow of thousands of lights.

The display was majestic, and Sam continued down the street, knowing if he could get beyond the tourist hot spot, he could slide into a side street, abandon the car, and disappear into the shadows of Rome.

He was nearly home.

The truck slammed into the side of Sam's car, launching from a side road and colliding with Sam at full speed. The impact rocked Sam in his seat, pulling his hands from the wheel and whipping his neck back violently into the head rest. The car spun out of control, careening wildly to the left among a downpour of glass and horrified screams.

The collision with the lamppost brought the car to an abrupt stop, shooting Sam forward, and his head collided with the leather steering wheel, splitting his eyebrow open.

He slumped back into his chair, the horn of the car constantly blasting into the air.

The truck killed its engine and the door opened.

CHAPTER TWENTY-NINE

Sam had clambered from the wreckage of his car, pain wrapped around him like a straightjacket. As he had crawled through the shattered glass, he could feel the shards slicing at his hands. Blood gushed from the gash above his right eye, scuppering his vision. His right arm was completely numb, the bullet wound sustained to the shoulder needed treating.

Sam had been to war.

This time, it didn't look like he was coming back.

As he stumbled down the road, he tried earnestly to tell the terrified public to run, the danger in the truck behind was something they could never fathom.

Whoever was behind the wheel, they'd made it their personal mission to end Sam.

Wallace had said it was a reunion, but Sam had racked his brain the entire drive back to Rome, trying to decipher who was under the balaclava. Now, his brain was still rattling from the head on collision with the steering wheel.

The rain had begun to fall again, the icy water once again washing the blood from Sam's face.

From his hands.

Sam had killed again, his war with Blackridge had claimed a few lives, most regrettably, the man he had tried to save. Carl Marsden had been his mentor, but more importantly, his friend, and as Sam trudged slowly through the middle of the street, he felt a sense of failure.

Marsden was dead.

Sam couldn't save him.

Just like he couldn't save Jamie.

Beyond the festively decorated buildings that lined the streets, Sam could hear the wailing of sirens, the calling card of the law. The threat of jail didn't worry him now.

He wouldn't be handed over to Wallace.

A gunshot echoed on the street, causing the final few watchers to scurry in a blind panic.

The burning sensation was immediate as the bullet entered through Sam's lower back, channelling through his insides and burst out of his abdomen in a glorious spray. Sam fell to his knees, the pain finally overwhelming him to the point of finality.

There was no going on.

With holes in his shoulder and stomach, Sam slumped back on his heels, taking a moment to feel the rain against his face, allowing it to wash over him with a calming clarity.

He was about to die.

To be with Jamie.

That was okay.

As the footsteps behind him grew louder, he tried to take a deep breath and straighten up, but the searing pain in his spine stopped him. His body was broken, he was losing blood and the fight had all but left him.

Sam had lived his entire life as a soldier, fighting for the freedom of others, and for what was right. He accepted death as a risk of the profession, but never had he wanted to go out on his knees.

He would not beg.

Whoever the man was, whoever he had wronged in such a way that it required his execution as payment, he would never know.

The footsteps behind him stopped. Sam could feel the presence of the man behind him, knowing the final shot was being lined up. Sam let the images of his son and ex-wife flow through his mind, jumping from wonderful memory to wonderful memory. Flickers of those he cared about filtered through, like a projector slideshow, and Sam finally rested on an image of his son, looking up at him from a book, with a smile across his innocent face.

He wanted to reach out and run his fingers through his hair.

Hold his boy just one, last time.

Sam's executioner disengaged the safety and Sam visualized him lifting the gun, aiming the barrel at the back of Sam's skull.

'I've been waiting a long time for this.'

The Manchurian accent hit Sam's ears and his eyebrows lifted in shock. The voice, it belonged to a distant memory, one that still manifested as nightmares on a regular basis.

It couldn't be?

Before Sam could turn and confront his suspicion, both of them were cast in a sudden, bright glow. A car sped up, switching the lights on at the last second before swerving towards them. Behind the wheel, Alex Stone tried desperately to only hit one of them.

As she collided with the man in black, his finger squeezed the trigger. The split second between the impact and the trigger had shifted the bullet just slightly, the bullet whizzing past Sam's ear and into the ground in front. The loud explosion perforated Sam's ear drum and he dropped to the side, clutching at his ear with his working hand.

It was a small price to pay to survive.

The man in black took the impact of the skidding car in the side of the legs, rolling up the back window before momentum carried him back down and he collapsed on the concrete, motionless.

Alex threw open the passenger door, staring out with disbelief at the state Sam was in. His face was covered in cuts, his right eye swollen and scarred. His right arm and his lower abdomen were pumping blood. The trail of blood trickling from his ears seemed the least of his problems.

'Get in,' she yelled. At the end of the street, she saw the flashing lights of the police cars, the cavalry on its way. Just ahead of her, she saw the wreck of the car that Sam had escaped from.

The man had been through hell.

Sam slumped forward, crawling with one arm to the car and reaching up onto the seat.

'Hurry the fuck up,' Alex yelled, leaning over and wrapping both hands around Sam's arm. She hauled with all her might, causing Sam to cry out in agony as she lifted him over the frame of the door and into the car. He was bleeding heavily, and he slumped towards her, losing consciousness.

The police were closing in quickly.

With Sam's dead weight against her, she pushed forward and with strained fingers, managed to claw the door closed. Fluidly, she slipped the car into first and pulled away, gathering speed at a rapid rate as she raced away from the collision. A few police cars stopped at the decimated vehicle. A few of them continued to follow her.

She was okay with that, as it would only take her a few minutes to give them the slip. While she wasn't a soldier, put behind the wheel of a car, and she was deadly.

As she spun the car expertly around the corner, Sam

collided gently with the window, bringing him back from his black out.

'I told you to leave,' he murmured, still concerned for others.

'Yeah, well, lucky for you, I have a listening problem.'

Alex spun the wheel again, slipping into a side street and cutting back through towards the main road. The cars sped past, missing their turning and she shot down the alleyway, the car slicing through the rain. As she turned onto the main street, she saw the signs leading her back towards the motorway.

Away from the city.

Anywhere but there.

'Why did you come back?' Sam asked feebly, before closing his eyes and resting his head against the window. She looked at him, knowing full well he needed medical assistance and quickly.

'It was the right thing to do.'

She smiled as she spoke, knowing full well they were in a bad situation but as she turned off onto the motorway, she pressed her foot down, a renewed purpose coursing through her.

Sam would be okay.

Sam Pope was built to survive.

———

The car crash and shooting was headline news the following morning, with many press offices authorizing a second print run to get the scoop. A number of the locals who had been in the vicinity came forward, with varying levels of accuracy on what happened. After giving their statements to the Polizia, they were all too happy to speak to the press.

Social media was rife with it, with the story trending on

Twitter and a number of the witnesses quickly gathering followers on Instagram. Some of them used their new-found exposure wisely, drip feeding photos of the incident to their new-found enthusiasts.

It was these pictures that caused the Polizia the most trouble and was already sparking cries of a government conspiracy online.

The main culprit was a picture taken by a foreign exchange student, who was watching the events unfold from the window of her flat from the street above. With a bird's-eye view of the goings on, she'd taken a clear photo of a man, decked in black, holding a gun to another man's head.

The reports also claimed there were two men, one of whom was shot by the other and was only saved at the death by a speeding car, which subsequently drove the man to safety.

While the Polizia had to report that they did indeed chase the vehicle and subsequently lost it, the embarrassment didn't matter. What mattered was the biggest mystery.

Not what had driven these two men to speed into the city, or why one of them tried to execute the other.

The mystery was, where was the man in black.

While the stories corroborated that he was indeed at the scene and was clipped by the car, there were no sightings of the man by any of the police officers.

As they'd swarmed the area and others had raced past, not one officer had seen him.

The man in black had disappeared.

Like a ghost.

CHAPTER THIRTY

Assistant Commissioner Ruth Ashton sheepishly stared into her lukewarm tea. The thought of drinking it turned her stomach and she placed it onto her desk. After a few more moments, she looked up, offering a meek smile.

General Ervin Wallace returned a harrowing glare.

It had been nearly a week since he had returned from Italy and ever since then, he had been stepping into her office on a daily basis, demanding updates on the Sam Pope task force and berating her in front of her subordinates.

It was a power play, reducing her authority in front of her team to show them the gravity of the situation.

It didn't feel great, but she couldn't help but admire the man for it.

Wallace sat back in his chair, one leg crossed over the other and he rested his fingers together.

'So what?' he asked sharply. 'Nothing.'

'I'm afraid not,' Ashton responded. 'However, we are hoping to make a breakthrough soon. Apparently, we are tracing another safe house of Pope's somewhere in the Kensal Green area.'

'Whoopie-fucking-do.' Wallace rolled his eyes. 'Another locker with a bag of weapons in it. You can throw it in the cupboard with the rest of them.'

He pushed himself out of the chair and began to pace the office slowly. Wallace peered out through the plastic slats that hung on Ashton's window, his eyes scanning the task force as they tirelessly worked.

All of them were useless in his eyes.

While Sims was an arse-kissing creep, the man at least had the gumption to get things done. That being said, planting a bullet in the man's head had given Wallace a deep sense of satisfaction. But that quickly eroded as the issue of Sam Pope had returned. Pope was missing and without him, Wallace didn't know the location of the USB stick.

He'd asked the task force to check in with Etheridge, although the man was still in hospital after being subjected to a brutal torture and beating.

Wallace wanted them to search the house, but without a warrant, any infringement on Etheridge's property was off limits. And a man with his resources, he could very feasibly take the Met to court.

Ever since the marathon bombing and the subsequent revelation of corrupt officers, the public had been a baying mob, waiting with sharpened pitch forks for the Met to slip up.

They would have to wait for Etheridge to make a speedy recovery and hope he cooperated.

Wallace stepped towards the wall opposite the desk, a number of framed plaques were neatly lined across it. All of them were certifications, affirmations that Ashton was qualified for the high-ranking role she sat. Wallace appreci-ated the display, nothing said *respect me* better than proof of success.

But they were not succeeding.

Casually, he took one of Ashton's commendations from its place and held the cheap frame in his hands. Ashton stood, slightly unnerved.

'Please, Ervin. Be careful with that.'

'You can address me as General Wallace,' he said with a firm grin. 'I think that's more appropriate.'

'Oh.' Ashton startled. 'I thought we were…'

'Working together? So, did I, Assistant Commissioner, but it seems like this task force you have nailed your name to couldn't find a fucking priest in a pre-school.'

'Sir, I assure you, we are doing everything we can to find Sam. It's our number one priority.'

Ashton stepped forward, enamored with the hulking general who gently placed the frame back on its hook. Wallace had no intention of breaking off their arrangement. In fact, he enjoyed Ashton's company and was planning on making an advance within the coming week.

She would be a fine distraction from the failed mission.

But he wanted her to know he was in charge, to tremble before him. Pope had defied him, undermined the power and control he had worked so hard and shed so much blood for.

His future hung in the balance and Pope was the one holding the scales.

With a tired frustration, Wallace squeezed the bridge of his nose.

'Everything? You've tried everything?'

'Yes, we are chasing all leads and we haven't heard a thing from Singh since she began her suspension.'

The mention of Singh's name caused Wallace to look up. A figurative light bulb burst into light above his head.

'That will be all. I'll see you tomorrow. Ruth.'

Ashton smiled as Wallace charmingly waved to her, striding through the door and among the officers, all of them stepping respectfully to the side. Asserting his dominance over the task force had felt good and it was a much-needed exercise in power and control.

But it was on thin ice and Wallace knew he needed to track down Sam.

Singh was the way to him. Detective Pearce, too.

Wallace grinned deviously as he headed to the exit, his mind tempting him to think of just how difficult he was about to make things for them.

———

Amara lifted herself up to a seated position, fingers interlocked behind her head and she breathed out. Her abdominal muscles were burning due to the circuit session she was bringing to an end and as she sat up into another crunch, she called out 'one hundred' and then dropped back onto the mat.

Her daily circuit had become a real highlight of her day, especially since all her access had been revoked.

Suspended for over a week with the likelihood of a return as bleak as the weather outside.

The British weather was doing its damndest to flush out the Christmas spirit, with the big day less than a week away and the only snow the UK had enjoyed was on *Game of Thrones*.

Singh took a few deep breaths and then pushed herself up, reaching for her towel and dabbing the sweat that was running down the back of her neck. She checked her phone.

No messages.

Her parents had been surprisingly understanding of her suspension, telling her to take the two weeks to look after herself and spend some time on her. It only took a day before her mother began suggesting she join a few dating apps and try to find a nice man.

That wasn't going to fill the void.

The only man she was trying to find was Sam Pope.

She'd got word from a colleague she'd met for a drink that Sam had been in Italy and was in fact the man from the shooting near the Vatican. All photos of the incident had been removed from social media, but it was something. Singh wasn't going to fly out to Italy and try to hunt the man herself, but his location coincided with Wallace's trip to Rome.

The General was clearly trying to keep something covered and her persistence had rattled his cage.

Even an idiot knows you don't provoke a cornered animal and Wallace struck her as a man who, although wielded a dangerous amount of power, always maintained that cornered mentality.

It meant he could lash out at any second.

She was under no illusion that he had given the directive to Ashton to remove her by any means necessary. She just couldn't believe who had pulled the trigger.

Despite a rocky start, she'd grown increasingly fond of DI Pearce, considering him more than just a colleague wrapped up in the same mess as she was. He'd become a friend and through all the slander, he had backed her. They were cut from the same cloth and although his assistance to Sam had been more blatant, they were both skirting with the idea that he was only trying to do the right thing.

For him to hand her over to Ashton was unforgivable.

He'd left her a few messages, telling her he had done it for her own safety after what had happened to Etheridge, but she'd deleted them straight away.

Amara Singh didn't need rescuing.

She needed the truth.

And she thought Adrian Pearce was one of the few people she could depend on to help her get there.

With her workout complete, Singh left the gym promptly, preferring to shower in the privacy of her own flat. It was a short jog back through the rain to her flat and she used it as an opportunity to warm down and clear her thoughts. She entered through the front door, nodded to the concierge and boarded the lift. She thought she heard the receptionist call for her, but with her wireless ear phones drowning the world out with drum and bass, she decided to ignore her. The lift shot up, granting her a view of the incredible city of London. Singh had been proud to serve it and felt a twinge of sadness for the road her career had taken her down. With a deep sigh she looked out over the city, shrouded with dark clouds and wondered if that was a metaphor for what was ahead.

Whatever awaited her, she would face.

Only this time, alone.

Singh stepped out onto her floor and saw a few of her neighbours stood in the hallway, the panic palpable. It only took her a few steps to realise they were looking to her apartment, the door hanging from the broken frame.

A firm boot had caved in the side of the panel and whoever had entered had kept the same level of care.

She could see her large TV on the floor, the glass screen covering the floor like a sadistic rug. Every photo from her mantlepiece had been broken. Her furniture was overturned, knife marks in each cushion. The back of the sofa had been ripped open.

Every drawer had been yanked from its case and overturned.

Singh stopped in the doorway, feeling her hand shaking in a mixture of fear and fury.

Wallace.

Whatever she had downloaded, whatever locked files she had in her possession, were clearly a cause for concern.

The furniture and the possessions didn't matter. They could be replaced.

But pinned to her front door, with a knife shunted straight through her photo, was a copy of her police badge.

The message was clear.

Singh was in deep trouble.

And this time, she didn't have anyone to pull her out of it.

———

'Easy does it, fella.'

Pearce held out his hand for Etheridge, who gingerly took it. Slowly, he eased himself out of the passenger seat of Pearce's car and gently placed the weight down on his cast. After the surgery to his knee, the hospital had wrapped the leg in a cast which Etheridge would need for the following month.

His hand also bore the thick, white, solid plaster after the brutal attack of the man in black.

Pearce offered him a warm smile as Etheridge eased himself to his feet, grimacing as the cold rain hit him. Pearce reached into the backseat of the car and pulled out Etheridge's crutches. Etheridge accepted them with a grunt and then slid them under his arms, before clawing his way towards his front door.

Pearce walked slowly behind him, watching the poor man struggle with his current situation. It was unlikely he would ever walk unaided again, but with a solid rehab program, he should at least retain an acceptable amount of mobility.

Acceptable.

None of it was acceptable.

The man had been brutally tortured and the chances

of them even identifying the man responsible were less than zero.

Etheridge knew it, but whenever Pearce breached the subject of what happened, Etheridge calmly told him he didn't want to discuss it. Pearce understood. A lot of people don't want to recount a traumatic experience, the fear and pain it could conjure up was too big of a risk.

But something about Etheridge's tone said something else. The man had withdrawn slightly, more than Pearce would have expected and now seemed determined to return home.

Etheridge seemed to have had a renewed purpose and Pearce felt a little uneasy at what it could be.

With a slight struggle, Etheridge pulled the keys from his jeans pocket and pushed open the door. The frame was still busted from where his intruder had slammed his boot into it. His mind retraced back to that night, the vomit inducing pain of having his fingers snapped.

Etheridge shuddered and stepped into the house.

'Thank you, detective,' he said, reaching for the door.

'Paul, wait…'

Etheridge closed the door, and Pearce rested his hand on the door, dropping his head in defeat. The bonds that had been forged by their faith in Sam had been broken and now the support network that Sam might one day return to was no more. Pearce knew Etheridge was an innocent man caught in the crossfire, but to lock himself away and hide was disappointing.

With his hands stuffed in his pockets and the weight of the situation hanging from him like a lead chain, Pearce marched back to his car.

.   .   .

Inside the house, Etheridge struggled to the kitchen and pulled open the fridge. He pulled a cold beer from the top shelf, twisted the lid and downed half of it one go.

The icy alcohol tickled his taste buds and the refreshing feeling washed through him.

With considerable difficulty, he lowered himself onto one of the chairs that surrounded the oak dining table and he took another sip.

He thought he would breakdown the moment he got home. As if returning to the scene of his torture would be too much. But all it had done was reinforce his decision.

He would take the rest of the evening, probably to get hammered, and then the next day, he would call the meeting.

It was time for a change.

As he sipped his beer, he turned his attention to the pile of mail that was neatly stacked on the table. Cecilia cleaned the house three times a week and had kindly collected his post for him.

The weeks' worth of mail was mainly junk, a combination of off-brand pizza menus and letters addressed 'To the Home Owner'. As Etheridge was about to mark the pile as trash, a final envelope felt different.

There was something solid inside and as he inspected the envelope, he noticed the Italian postage stamp.

With a curious frenzy, he ripped open the envelope, only for a USB stick to fall onto his table.

———

Sam slowly opened his eyes and winced at the brightness. The sun was shining wherever he was, and the rays had infiltrated his room, cutting across his pillow. He tried to push himself up, but the searing pain in his abdomen sent him crashing back against the lumpy mattress.

He groaned in pain and inspected his stomach.

The bullet wound that had almost killed him had been sewn shut, a bloodstained bandage taped against his solid stomach. The surrounding area was a bright red and Sam knew the operation had to have been recent.

Likewise, with his shoulder, with a similar, bloody bandage hiding the recent stitching.

By the feeling coursing through his body, he had received little anaesthetic, the loss of blood keeping him unconscious for the duration of the procedure. But now, with his eyes open, the agony was almost unbearable.

'You're awake.'

Alex stepped into the room with a smile on her face. She looked tired, and her usually vibrant eyes were dark and encompassed by dark circles. Her hair was frizzy and in need of a good wash.

Sam tried to speak, but his throat croaked like a bull frog. Alex stepped forward and lifted his glass of water, tipping it to his lips and letting him slowly drink. The refreshing water felt amazing and Sam cleared his throat.

'Where am I?' he eventually asked, trying his hardest to open his right eye.

'I don't know. Somewhere near Genoa.' Alex said vaguely. 'I just drove, like you said. But you needed some help and I found a veterinarian student who spoke English and…'

'A vet?' Sam chuckled. 'You took me to a vet?'

'It was the best I could do.' Alex shrugged, reciprocating Sam's grin. 'Then I just drove until we ran out of gas and I found this place. Paid for four nights and just prayed you wouldn't die.'

'Thank you,' Sam spoke sincerely. 'You saved my life.'

'Well, someone has to keep you out of trouble.' Alex reached out and gently ran the back of her fingers against Sam's stubble covered cheek. He appreciated the gesture and she stood up and moved to the window, picking up the mug of coffee she'd left on the sill.

Two streets away, the coastline calmly lapped at the beach, the serenity of the ocean crashing against the rocks filled her with as much warmth as the coffee did. The weather was still appalling, but growing up in New York City, she didn't get to see the beach an awful lot.

It was beautiful.

'How's the view?' Sam asked, staring up at the ceiling.

'Beautiful,' Alex replied, taking a final sip of her coffee before placing it back down. She turned to Sam, her face as serious as he had ever seen it. 'What's the plan?'

Sam stretched his arm, gritting his teeth at the shooting pain that shot up from his shoulder.

He was in a bad way.

But he had survived.

Sam turned to Alex, returning her stare and his words were colder than the freezing rain that clattered their window.

'I'm going to get better, then, it's time to fight back.'

EPILOGUE

The television was white noise in the background, the language barrier a mere hindrance as the man in black watched the news cycle on repeat. The TV itself had to be over twenty years old, a cumbersome box with a curved screen that flickered with every heavy movement.

The man in black didn't care.

He wasn't one for materialistic living. As long as it showed what he needed to see, he couldn't care about the aesthetics.

The news reel was running on repeat, images and videos of the night he almost executed Sam Pope.

Half an inch.

That was what had saved Sam's life.

The man in black had managed to slither into the shadows as the unknown vehicle made its getaway with Sam in tow, and he watched from the alleyway as a few police cars darted past in a fruitless attempt to apprehend them. As the Polizia began to turn the street into a crime scene, the man had turned and stumbled down the alley-way, the collision with the car had severely bruised his leg and twisted his knee. Beyond that and a few scrapes, the collision with the vehicle itself hadn't done too much damage. It was colliding with the asphalt that had cracked three ribs and separated his shoulder.

After putting enough distance between himself and the crime scene, the man in black assessed his arm, which was hanging loosely from its socket. Practically thinking, he pressed it up against the wall, twisted his body and with a sharp grunt of pain, he snapped it back into place.

He was used to pain.

He could handle it.

Eventually, he had made his way towards the more poverty-stricken part of Rome, finding a hostel where the owner, after taking one look at his disfigured face, allowed him the private room for a minimal price.

Now, he had removed his shirt and was looking at the bruising that was forming on the right-hand side of his toned chest. The cracked ribs were aching and the internal bleeding while not serious, would cause severe discomfort.

He would allow Wallace to send him to a medical facility when he made contact. For now, the protocol was to lie low for a week and remain completely off the radar.

As he inspected his injuries in the mirror, his eyes landed on the left-hand side of his body. While his face was hard to keep out of sight, he rarely studied the severity of his scars.

His entire left arm, shoulder, and pectoral was charred, covered in rough scar tissue from the severe burns he had received when the missile had collided with the mountain face.

The deep, thick scars that ran across his back were the result of the torturous Taliban squadron that had found his dying body. They'd nursed him back to health, a cruelty that would turn out to be a fate worse than death.

They used him as a statement of intent to their

younger recruits, beating him in public. Lashing him with razor wire.

Burning him with cattle prods.

His fingertips were sliced off. Seven teeth were pulled from the gums. All his finger and toenails were removed with bamboo.

For five years he was at their mercy. Beaten daily. Raped monthly.

He'd begged for death but was eventually found by General Wallace, who had not only freed him from his prison but had captured the four leaders of that particular unit and left them in a room with him.

He'd slowly disembowelled them all, ensuring their deaths were slow, painful, and horrifying.

Just like his life had been. But since then, Wallace had given him all the treatment and medical help he had needed in return for his loyalty. As he continued to train, he soon became one of Wallace's ghosts, eliminating high profile targets and doing the man's bidding.

All in the name of loyalty.

The man in black walked away from the mirror towards the small dressing table beside his single mattress bed. On it, lay his phone and his wallet.

And a metal chain.

He chuckled at the notion of loyalty. That was what Sam Pope had spoken about during their time in the barracks together. Or when they were out on missions together.

Loyalty.

How they never left a man behind.

As he glared into the mirror at the mutilated figure that stared back, he slammed his charred fist into the centre of the glass, cracking it into several pieces.

The jagged reflection was much better. It suited him more.

He was a monster.

Because of Sam Pope.

Slowly, with the pain barely an afterthought, he opened his fist to look at the dog tags attached to the metal chain.

On one side, it read 'Matthew McLaughlin.'

On the other, it read 'Mac'.

GET EXCLUSIVE ROBERT ENRIGHT MATERIAL

Hey there,

I really hope you enjoyed the book and hopefully, you will want to continue following Sam Pope's war on crime. If so, then why not sign up to my reader group? I send out regular updates, polls and special offers as well as some cool free stuff. Sound good?

Well, if you do sign up to the mailing list, I'll send you an **EXCLUSIVE** copy of the Sam Pope prequel novella, **THE RIGHT REASON**, absolutely free. (This book is not available anywhere else!)

You can get your FREE copy by signing up at www.robertenright.co.uk

SAM POPE NOVELS

For more information about the Sam Pope series, please visit:

www.robertenright.co.uk

ABOUT THE AUTHOR

Robert lives in Buckinghamshire with his family, writing books and dreaming of getting a dog.

For more information:
www.robertenright.co.uk
robert@robertenright.co.uk

You can also connect with Robert on Social Media:

 facebook.com/robenrightauthor

twitter.com/REnright_Author

 instagram.com/robenrightauthor

COPYRIGHT © ROBERT ENRIGHT,
2019

All rights reserved. No part of this publication may be reproduced, stored in a retrieval system, or transmitted in any form or by any means, electronic, photocopying, mechanical, recording, or otherwise, without the prior permission of the copyright owner.

All characters in this book are fictitious and any resemblance to actual persons living or dead is purely coincidental.

Cover by Phillip Griffiths

Edited by Emma Mitchell

Milton Keynes UK
Ingram Content Group UK Ltd.
UKHW021556140924
1642UKWH00004B/91

9 781838 074029